D.M. GI

FROZEN MOON

A Jenny-Dog and the Son of Light Novel

outskirtspress

DENVER, COLORADO

FROZEN MOON
A Jenny-Dog and the Son of Light Novel
All Rights Reserved.
Copyright © 2013 D.M. Greenwald
v3.0

Cover Photo © 2013 JupiterImages Corporation. All rights reserved - used with permission.

We gratefully acknowledge the use of p.6 first two sentences + 3 words from 'February: Good Oak' from A Sand County ALMANAC and sketches Here and There by Aldo Leopold (1949) by permission of Oxford University Press, Inc.

Outskirts Press, Inc.
http://www.outskirtspress.com

Paperback ISBN: 978-1-4787-0911-4
Hardback ISBN: 978-1-4787-0905-3

Outskirts Press and the "OP" logo are trademarks belonging to Outskirts Press, Inc.

PRINTED IN THE UNITED STATES OF AMERICA

February

Good Oak
There are two spiritual dangers in not owning a farm. One is the danger of supposing that breakfast comes from the grocery, and the other that heat comes from the furnace.

> *Aldo Leopold*
> *A Sand County ALMANAC and Sketches Here and There*

Prologue

Jay Peak, Vermont
Sunday, February 7, 1978
4:36 A.M.

It was the worst damn winter storm the sheriff had ever seen. Probably the worst damn storm in fifty, maybe a hundred years. The ski lifts stood silent and unused along the eastern slopes. They had been that way for two-and-a-half days and three nights. Breaking clouds revealed bright stars and a quarter moon. But a bank of white, low on the western horizon, was already moving in. That had him worried.

Sam Hanson stood alone outside on the timbered porch of the chalet. The snow reached the top step. The temperature was still below zero. And there wasn't any wind. No wind for the first time in three days was what had awakened the sheriff from the armchair inside. Now, the air outside felt fairly tolerable. A hell of a lot better than it had been.

Hanson was out there alone and quiet, thinking about what had happened. Not looking forward to what would have to follow.

On a small farm outside Merrill, Wisconsin Jonathan VanStavern lies awake in his bed, next to his wife of thirty years. He hasn't been able to sleep since returning home from the Blazer Pub, well past midnight. They showed the championship game film from 1955. Again. He damns himself for what he has done, thinking, hell, what other choice was there?

In San Francisco, on the balcony of a stylish Mansard townhouse, Kristian Fisk-Travis looks out at the empty lights of the city and the bay.

She puts out another cigarette in a small china ashtray and wonders... She turns and goes inside, takes another pill, and hopes that this time she will be able to sleep.

High on the Tusayan Plateau, in the ancient Shongopovi pueblo, an old Indian medicine-woman is having trouble breathing through her Vision. She must awaken soon or she will die.

Chapter One

S am Hanson took the call from the ski lodge at Jay Peak. The weather had been piss poor since around eleven, and he knew that soon more calls would start coming in. Cars would slide into ditches; power lines would come down; people would have heart attacks trying to dig out. And who the hell knew what else? The call from the ski resort was the last damn thing he needed.

"Nobody's seen her for over an hour, Sam," Nancy Grady explained. "They're up here from Virginia, and her folks wanted to get in one last run before the lifts shut down. They left her with me, and I left her with Sharon and another kid, building a snowman by the side of the lodge. I had to answer a phone call from a guy I was waiting for, but I was just gone for a moment or two. When I got back outside, my daughter and the other kid were still working on their snowman, and Kelly – that's her name, Kelly Martin – was gone."

"What time was that?" Hanson asked.

"A little before noon. About quarter to, I think... At first, nobody was too upset. We all thought that the little girl had just gone inside and would turn up soon enough. But by the time her parents had finished their run the weather was really turning nasty. We've been looking and asking and making paging announcements for a good forty-five minutes now, and we're starting to get panicky. God, Sam, the weather's turning awful out here..." The recreation director was starting to lose it.

"Now take it easy, honey. What did the kids say?"

Nancy tried to get a grip. "Sharon and the Nickelson kid said they were building their snowman with Kelly when she decided that she didn't want to play anymore. And that's the last anybody's seen of her. My God, Sam, if she's still outside...."

"Easy now, Nancy. How old did you say she is?"

"About six, I think. Just a little older than Sharon."

"You got the ski patrol still looking around outside?"

"Of course. And since the slopes are shutting down they have plenty of people helping out."

"Good. Was she seen talking to anybody before she disappeared? Any adults?"

"I don't think so. Not that I know of. The kids didn't mention anything. Why?"

"Oh nothing, just trying to get a handle on things." Hanson didn't want to alarm her. He failed.

"Oh my God, Sam! You don't think...." The woman was in tears.

"Now take it easy," Hanson told her. "She's probably playing hide'n-go-seek and will turn up any time now. I'll tell you what now, you folks keep on looking and I'll send a couple of the boys up to help out. And if she hasn't been found by the time they get there, we'll get the State Police to send over a couple of dogs."

Nancy thanked him and he hung up. He asked Sarah to check who was in the area and who didn't have an emergency on.

"Send them on over. Have them check in when they get there."

Hanson hated to send anyone out on a goose hunt, especially with the calls starting to come in. On the other hand, if that little girl was outside, she was going to need lots of help and plenty quick. There was another possibility too. The one that had alarmed Nancy.

Hanson decided not to wait for the deputies to check in. He called the State Police at 1:09 PM.

"She's been missing for over an hour, Sergeant. We need to find her now."

"We'll do what we can, Sheriff. I'll contact Lieutenant Leah and see what he says about dogs. I'll see who else we can spare, but we're getting pretty busy right now."

"Look, Sergeant, we got a six-year-old kid lost in a snowstorm. I'd say that's about as busy as it gets."

"We'll do what we can, Sheriff."

Hanson slammed down the phone.

At 1:20 PM, Andy Johnson called in. He was the first and only deputy to make it to the Jay Peak ski lodge.

"It don't look good, Sam. I talked to some people up here and poked around a bit myself. It sure don't look like the kid's inside."

"You checked all the out-buildings, Andy, under the porches and all the nooks and crannies?"

"Not personally, Sam, but they've been checked. Leastwise, the people up here say they been checked. Weather's getting mean. Pressure and temperature dropping, snow and wind picking up."

"Check as many of those places as you can yourself, Andy, and anyplace else you can think of." Hanson hesitated. "Is anyone else on the line or listening?"

"No, Sam? What's up?"

"Any chance of foul play?"

"Jesus, Sam, I hadn't thought of that. Nobody up here has mentioned that as a possibility."

"Don't say anything just yet. I'm just trying to make sure I cover all the bases. Keep looking for her, but for Christ's sake keep those people linked up out there. I don't want to have anyone else getting lost up there. I'll be up as soon as I can."

The sheriff was just starting to button his wool shirt when Sarah told him that Leah was on the line. Lieutenant Ted Leah was the state's main dog handler, but Hanson grimaced. He never did like Ted much. Leah was the kind of man who liked dogs better than people. And the only people he liked less than those who didn't know much about dogs were the ones who thought they knew as much about them as he did. Hanson hoped Leah was up at the lodge already and maybe had some good news.

"I really don't think we'd be much help, Sheriff. Even *my* dogs can't be expected to pick up an airborne scent with all the wind and snow blowing around out there. Any ground scent is long covered, especially with all those people you've got running around up there."

"What if the kid's inside?" Hanson asked. "Could your damn dogs find her then?" *Easy, Sam, he thought. Don't piss him off while you still need him. Just get him up to the lodge. Maybe the dogs will turn up something despite him.*

"They might. But what's the point? If the kid is inside then she's probably all right, and she'll turn up sooner or later."

"What if she's tied up in somebody's closet, or stashed in someone's footlocker?"

"You think she's been abducted? C'mon Hanson, get real. This is Jay, Vermont we're talking about. People come up here to ski, not to steal children. What the hell you smoking in that pipe of yours?"

Hanson was getting angry. He caught himself.

"Anything's possible, Ted. You know that. I just want to find the little girl."

"All right, we'll do what we can. Just don't expect much. These are just dogs we're dealing with, not machines. Besides, Sheriff, you know as well as I do that if the kid's been outside all this time, she's probably history."

Hanson knew lots of cops like Leah. Leah should have retired years ago, but he had found a niche and couldn't afford to let go. Now, he was burned out and bitter.

"Just do what you can. That's all I'm asking. Who knows, maybe you'll get lucky." Hanson put the phone down. *That son of a bitch.* He had had to put Leah on the spot with that abduction theory just to get him into gear. He considered calling Captain Herman, Leah's commanding officer. Herman might light a fire under Leah, but Hanson knew that would just ruffle feathers all around.

Sheriff Hanson checked up at the lodge again. The situation was the same; no sign of Kelly Martin, weather getting worse. He figured he had one more option, but it was a long shot. One helluva long shot. He had started flipping it over in his mind while he was talking to Leah, maybe even before. It was the kind of move that wouldn't give him much glory even if it succeeded, but it would sure make him a goat if it didn't, especially after talking to Leah. On top of it all, it was an election year. *What the hell, I never figured on being sheriff of this county the rest of my life anyway.*

It was 1:29 P.M. EST when Sam Hanson called the sheriff of Lincoln County, Wisconsin.

Chapter Two

"Hello, Jonathan? This is Sam Hanson calling, from Newport, Vermont."

"Sam! How the heck are you, buddy? What can I do for you?"

"Listen up, Jon, and tell me if you can help or if I got my head up my ass. I got a lost kid and one hell of a winter storm building out here. The kid may be dead already, but if she's not she's sure gonna be if we don't find her pretty damn fast. I'm trying to get some dogs looking for her now, but the damn handler out here says they probably can't do much in the storm conditions. I don't know if that's right or not, but I thought about that neighbor of yours who you introduced me to after he spoke at that convention in Madison last year. After meeting the guy and hearing your stories about him, I thought he might be able to help out. What do you think?"

"Well, I can't rightly say, Sam. Doesn't seem like there's much time. But I'll tell you this much, buddy, if there's a ghost of a chance of finding that kid alive, Joshua's the one to do it. Hang on, Sheriff, and I'll try to hunt him up for you."

Sam Hanson waited forever while the sheriff in Lincoln County, Wisconsin tried to locate a man Hanson had met only once before in his life. *I must be crazy*, he thought.

At 12:36, Central Standard Time, the horn on the four-by-four started going off. Joshua Travis knew he had a call on the emergency band. He and his crew were out on a job over on state highway 64, just a few miles east of Merrill. Things were going so well, they were working through lunch. The day was cold and clear, from a nice high-pressure zone that had worked down from Canada, and they had just hooked onto the main joists. They were about ready to bring the barn down when the call came in from Emily at the office.

"Joshua, I've got Jonathan on the line, dear. Emergency."

"Patch him through, Em."

The seventy-three-year-old Gal Friday positioned the speaker-phone and flicked the switch.

"Josh, I got a buddy of mine on the line, out in Vermont. He's got one helluva snowstorm out there and a little girl lost. Wants to know if dogs will help. Hang on a second and we'll set up a three-way. Name is Sam Hanson." Van Stavern pressed the buttons on his phone and prayed he wouldn't lose anybody. By some miracle, it worked.

"How long has she been out there?" Travis asked.

"She's been lost about an hour or so, but she's been outside longer'n that."

"What's the wind chill?"

"Between 0 and 20 below and going down."

"Any shelter nearby?"

"The resort has several out-buildings nearby but they've all been searched. There are a lot of woods around, and they'd give her some shelter if she made it to them. But I don't know that it'd be enough, and they're not a real good place to be right now either, what with the wind and all."

Travis knew *that* was right. "Are there dogs up there now?"

"There aren't any there yet, but they should be there within the hour. Their handler wasn't very optimistic, but he always likes to cover his ass."

Joshua Travis thought about the situation for a moment.

"How long will it take to get me in, Jon?"

"We'll have to get out the Guard. How long will it take you to get your team set?"

"We can be ready for a chopper in thirty-five minutes."

"If the weather don't get no worse, we can still fly you into Burlington, and I can have someone from a local four-wheeler club pick you up and bring you up to The Peak. Those boys can make a run like that in, oh, maybe an hour and change if the weather don't get worse and the cops look the other way. What do you figure air time?"

"Jon?"

"It all depends on what we can work out logistically. My guess is an hour-and-a-half, maybe two hours if there are no delays and we get a jet and the pilot is a hot-dog. But that's from Mitchell Field or Truax. We still got to get you there"

"Let's see,"Travis calculated, "that means we're looking at at least three to four hours, and she's been out there over an hour already with no telling how long it will take to find her, assuming we can find her at all.... That's a helluva long time for a kid to be out in a sub-zero storm. The chances of finding her alive aren't very good."

"I just thought it might be worth a try. Jonathan talks about you and your dogs like you're some kind of magician, so I just thought I'd ask. Besides, I needed to know if the state boys here were shootin' straight or just jerkin' me around."

"They're not exactly jerking you around. Everything the handler told you is probably true. I can tell you this much, though: If the handler doesn't expect to find the kid, he probably won't. You got any private rescue clubs nearby? Bloodhounds? Bernese mountain dogs and the like?"

"Not that I'm aware of. I can put out a request for help over the radio and TV stations. Anything else?"

Joshua Travis knew that he should let this one go. Instead, he asked, "Do you want me to come out?"

That was what Hanson had been waiting for. "I'd be obliged."

Travis knew that if he gave it much thought he'd find plenty of reasons for not getting involved, so he didn't think anymore. "I'll tell you what, Jon, you and Sheriff Hanson get on the Guard and the other arrangements. We'll be ready to go in half an hour at my place. Sheriff Hanson, make sure they have a quart thermos of hot chocolate waiting for me at the ski place, and make sure it's made with real whole milk. I want another one filled with Gatorade and heated up. And tell them not to touch anything of the kid's or anything in the kid's room other than what the dog handlers need. Sheriff, kids don't usually wander off that far. Usually an eighth to a quarter of a mile tops. You might want to have your searchers work expanding concentric circles out to that distance if you can."

"We'll do it, Mr. Travis."

"Jon, keep a line open. I'll call you when I get home. I can't promise anything, but we'll give it a shot"

Sam Hanson wasn't sure whether he felt better or not. It was 1:39 P.M. EST.

Joshua Travis told the crew to finish pulling the barn with the wrecker and the flatbed. He left Matthew in charge. They were a good bunch. Joshua could leave them alone, knowing the job would get done. He climbed into the Jeep pickup, flipped on the gumball that the state had given him so he wouldn't get stopped, and headed for home.

More than two feet of snow covered the ground, but the roads were well plowed and sanded. Travis moved right along. On the way, he called the office and asked Emily to call his neighbors and have their kids take care of the dogs and horses and the rest of the menagerie he kept at the house. He knew Jon VanStavern and his sons would see to it, but they lived several sections away, and Joshua did not want to burden them if he could help it. Lord only knew there'd had been times enough when it couldn't be helped.

Travis pressed to get home. He needed to check everything and get on the trail as soon as possible, but he had a bad feeling in his gut. Four or five hours in a sub-zero storm *was* a helluva long time. *Who the hell are you kidding?* And, even though it was entirely different, Cody, Wyoming kept coming to mind. Joshua Travis did not want another trip like that one.

At the house, Travis went straight in and read down the checklist he had pinned to the winter pack. He checked the fuel bottles for the little stove and stuffed in five one pound summer sausages he had made from venison, pork and beef. He packed a bag of Milkbones, a carton of instant oatmeal, a jar of homemade granola, some raisin/nut trail mix he had on hand, and a box of Hershey Bars. He made certain he had two homemade tin-can candles and plenty of waterproofed matches and fire starters. He decided to go with the geodesic-dome tent. The pup would be easier to set, but he wanted a free standing shelter, and one that would be big enough to get the dogs into if need be. It would also be stronger. He stuffed his down parka, mitts, hat, sweater, goggles, and a towel into a duffel, and he guessed that modified bear paws would be the best snowshoes to go with. He rigged them onto the back of the pack. Then he changed his clothes and grabbed something to eat. It was time to start pacing himself.

Joshua Travis forced himself to slow down.

Chapter Three

At six foot three, Jonathan VanStavern was almost as tall as Joshua. Despite thin, graying hair and bifocals, the fifty-year-old sheriff maintained a calm diligence and a strong competence that earned him universal respect. As soon as he finished talking with Travis and Hanson, VanStavern called Wausau Paper. He would not ask them to fly into a storm, just to get Joshua and his dogs to the closest air force base ASAP. He then dialed the personal number of Brigadier General John Henry Harrison, commanding officer of the 128th Air Refueling Group, based at Bill Mitchell Field in Milwaukee. He got Harrison's civilian secretary.

"This is Colonel VanStavern. I need to speak with General Harrison right away. It's an emergency."

Harrison's secretary knew who VanStavern was. She switched him right through. Harrison and VanStavern went way back together, even before Korea. They had trained together, flown together, and Harrison had commanded some of the flyers that VanStavern had plucked to safety with a daring night landing of an old C-47 on the frozen plateau near Pyongyang. It had been Harrison who had worked previously with VanStavern, arranging transportation for Joshua Travis and his dogs. He knew that if Jon VanStavern said there was an emergency, he wasn't blowing smoke.

"Jonathan, what's up?"

"General, there's a little girl lost in a blizzard out in Vermont. We need transport for Josh Travis and his dogs, pronto."

"Vermont..., that's a long way off. Just a moment, Colonel, let me check the duty roster."

There was one refueling wing, up for two weeks from Arkansas, logging in winter flying time. Harrison did not recognize any of the names.

"Jon, we've got one group here from Arkansas. I don't know any of the men personally. Let me check records and their C.O. I'll put something together for you."

"General, I know this is a tall order on short notice, but we need a real hot-dog crew. Volunteers only. The weather out east is piss poor, and whoever you get better know how to fly snow and land icy."

"Can you get Travis and his dogs here?"

"I can get the State Police to ferry them down to Wausau. Wausau Paper has offered its corporate jet for the ride to Mitchell. I couldn't ask them to risk an adverse weather landing, and they didn't offer. Can't really blame them."

"Anything else he needs, Jon?"

"Yeah, Hank, he needs a miracle."

"We'll see what we can do."

Brigadier General Harrison and his aide went through the crew records the secretary had brought in. It would have been easier if this was just a milk run. Most of the crews only flew one or two weekends a month, mostly to get away from their wives. Colonel Billings poured over one file that was thicker than the others.

"General Harrison, take a look at this one, Sir."

Harrison flipped through the file and dialed up the commanding officer of the 189th Air Refueling Group, Arkansas Air National Guard, Colonel Robert Hayes.

"Colonel Hayes, this is General Harrison, what can you tell me about Lieutenant Colonel Reuger?"

"What has he done now, Sir?" Colonel Hayes responded.

Lieutenant Colonel David Reuger and his crew relaxed in their barracks. They had just come in from lunch. Most of the company was there, the men stretched out on their cots, flipping cards, reading, or just shooting the shit. Only one crew was scheduled for flying time that afternoon. The rest had either classes to attend or down time. The whole barracks jumped when Colonel Hayes and General Harrison walked in. Harrison put them at ease.

"Gentlemen," Harrison began, "I need a crew for a transport to Vermont: KC-135E. It's a mercy mission. The weather is bad and it might be rough going. Volunteers only."

Some of the flyers asked for specifics. Others looked at their boots. As soon as Reuger's crew heard the words *rough going and volunteers* they started gathering up their gear.

"I'll go." Reuger answered. Where he went, they went.

Travis gave VanStavern a call.

"I'm ready, Jon. Where do we stand?"

"The kid is still lost, Josh. State has a chopper on the way. Wausau Paper has a jet prepped and waiting to ferry you to Mitchell Field, and the Air Guard just *happens* to have a KC-135 with a crew that needed some winter flying time on hand." Every once in a while VanStavern's being a full bird colonel in the Air Force Reserve, *and* a Korean War hero, came in real handy.

They were set to get Travis and his team to Burlington, so long as the weather there held. The sheriff in Vermont was working on the ride from Burlington to the lodge.

"Be sure they have the hot chocolate and Gatorade ready, Jon." He also reminded him about the kid's things.

"Sheriff Hanson has put out a call for rescue dogs over the airways. He got one possible from a kennel near Lake George. Said they'd do what they could, if they can get through."

That would be good, Travis thought, if the dogs and handlers knew what they were doing. Otherwise it would just add to the confusion. It probably didn't matter anyway. He caught himself. *Damn, but I know better than to think like that.*

Joshua carried the pack and duffel out to the porch and went over to the tack room. He already knew which dogs he was going to take. He had decided to go with Buck and Jenny-Dog almost as soon as he had agreed to go to Vermont.

Buck was relatively new. He had had him less than two years, but he was proving to be a natural. More than that, he chose Buck because Buck was born for a winter storm. A wild mixture of malamute and mountain dog with some shepherd blood stirring in him somewhere, Buck was close to his wolf ancestors. VanStavern had named him for the Jack London character. He was one hundred-and-thirty pounds of tooth and fur and muscle, with thick, fur filled pads and just enough fat marbled in to withstand sub-zero weather like most dogs would take to a balmy spring day.

No one knew for sure exactly where Buck had come from. He just showed up at VanStavern's one night and Jon had brought him over to Joshua. Jon had thought about keeping him for himself, especially for those long lonely night patrols during hunting season, but he decided that Joshua might have more use for the dog than he did. Jon VanStavern figured the least he could do was give Josh Travis first crack at any dog that might show potential. He owed him that much, and VanStavern didn't need a dog to assert his authority in Lincoln County. Still, if the dog had not worked out for Joshua, Jon would have taken him back in a New York minute.

Jenny-Dog was another story. Joshua had picked her up more than ten years ago, back in the sixties, while he was on the road working construction. He used to like to take long evening walks through the Oregon potato country to relax, and Jenny used to tag along. She was a long glumpy mix of black lab and red-bone, with a little blue-tick hound and some black-and-tan tossed in for good measure. There were probably other breeds mixed in too, but only God knew what *they* were.

The potato farmer who fed her told Joshua he was going to shoot her because the damn bitch kept on getting knocked up and havin' puppies. But when Josh offered to take her, well that was another matter, don't you know, and anyone could see what a fine huntin' dog she would be with just a little work. Joshua gave the man fifteen dollars for the dog and then shelled out another twenty-five to have her spayed. He never regretted a penny of it. From then on they belonged to each other.

Now Jenny-Dog was pushing thirteen and Travis was reluctant to take her out to what looked to be extreme conditions. He chose her anyway. He knew he had to. If there was one thing in this world that could find a lost kid, it was Jenny-Dog. Joshua Travis also knew that Jenny would never understand being left behind.

He picked out tracking harnesses that would fit each dog and one polyester guide rope. He called Jenny-Dog and Buck out of the yard. They waited on the porch for the helicopter that was coming up.

They didn't have to wait long. Joshua was glad. The other dogs were making a racket because they were being left, and Joshua was still tight about the whole business to begin with. He wanted to be on the trail.

The helicopter came in from the south, loud and windy, and hovered inches over the widest part of the plowed drive. The rotors swirled the lightly packed snow into frigid whirlwinds and drove it stinging into the faces of the man and his dogs as they approached.

The snow hit like frozen sand and caught in Joshua's winter beard. Travis knew they were getting a taste of things to come. He watched the dogs to see how they would react. Jenny-Dog knew the drill. She made her way to the clattering chopper and jumped right into the open hatch. Buck wasn't so sure. He charged out, teeth bared and barking, to ward off the intruders. Travis told him to cool it, and the big dog settled down and followed along. Joshua told him *kennel* once and the Buck jumped in. The snow and wind hadn't been a factor for either. That was a good sign.

"How long to Wausau?" Travis asked as they lifted off into the sun.

"Less than fifteen minutes, sir," replied the co-pilot.

The chopper was cold, even with the hatch closed. That was good. The bright sun and the snow glare hurt his eyes, despite dark glasses, but he didn't complain. He knew the folks out in Vermont would give their eyeteeth for some sun and glare.

Twenty miles by helicopter doesn't take long, Travis thought, just go up and come down. Joshua liked clear, cold February days. Under other circumstances he would have enjoyed the ride over the winter Wisconsin countryside. Instead, he concentrated on the task at hand.

"Thank you, gentlemen," Travis told the crew as he gathered his gear and scrambled out. He didn't take time to shake their hands. The dogs waited for his call.

At Wausau Airport, the Gulfstream jet was waiting. Joshua and the dogs bounded up the hatch stairs and were greeted by typical corporate comfort and luxury.

"Don't get used to the carpet, guys," he told the dogs. During the thirty minute flight to Milwaukee Joshua checked his pack one more time.

The KC-135E at Mitchell Field was primed and ready to go. Travis and his team ran from the small jet and banged up the steps to the open forward hatch.

"You'd best hang onto your dogs, sir. Make yourself at home," he was told by Captain Davis. The last part was a bad joke. The cargo hold was cold and empty and dark, save a few yellow lights. There were metal benches with seat belts parallel to the padded walls. Everything was olive green and black. He could smell jet fuel from the empty refueling tanks below. Joshua sat near the front and belted himself in. He put the dogs at *sit* and held onto their collars. It looked to be one long fucking ride.

Up in the cockpit, Lt. Colonel Reuger checked with the tower. They had been holding an emergency priority clearance. In a matter of minutes the big empty plane would be airborne. It was 1:29 P.M. Central Time, 2:29 in the East.

Chapter Four

In northern Arizona the air is cool and heavy. The sky is gray. The old Indian woman looks into the dark sky enclosing the mesa and shivers. She knows another trial is coming.

The woman was born near the end of the last century. Blue birth spots appeared on her lower back, typical among Hopi children. As the child matured into womanhood, the spots remained. Atypical, everyone knew.

"Abuse," diagnosed the white doctors in their ignorance and their arrogance.

"Touched by the gods," affirmed the tribal elders. They called her Blue Corn Woman.

The old woman returns to her house. She is met by her son's daughter, who nods recognition, and is helped to her bed. Before passing into her Vision, the medicine-woman utters one word.

"Nuva" – Snow

In San Francisco, the attractive architect looks over her drawings and peers out the window of her office into the cold California rain. She has not yet heard that her estranged husband has been called to another rescue – another dangerous rescue.

In central Vermont, Deputy Andy Johnson keeps people linked up outside. He tells the Martins to go inside to warm up. They refuse.

Sheriff Hanson arranged for Bill Peterson to pick up Joshua Travis and his dogs.

"I hear Burlington is shutting down, Sheriff."

"Do me a favor, Bill, and be there anyway. Just in case. Hell, if he can't get into Burlington, and we don't find the kid soon, we might just as well call off the whole damn shootin' match."

"You got it, Sam. I'm on my way."

Peterson was young and wild, but he was the best damn mechanic in northern Vermont, and he had a four-by-four that could go anywhere. Hanson knew that nobody else was crazy enough to get Travis from the airfield to the ski lodge as fast as Bill Peterson would.

Hanson also knew he should stay at headquarters to handle the other emergencies that were coming in, but he was too involved in finding the lost child. He left Roy Mackleroy nominally in charge, with Sarah at the switchboard. In reality it was sixty-three-year-old Sarah Biggs who held the office together and ran everything, from the switchboard to Hanson's campaign.

The storm was intensifying. Waves of snow were falling and blowing. Hanson had played tackle for the local team some thirty years ago even though most people would have thought him too short. Now, he rolled his shoulders and pushed through the wind as if he were hitting a blocking sled. It was a bitch just getting the windshields of the patrol car clear enough to see through. Keeping them clear was another matter. With the heater and defrosters going full blast, the wipers kept icing up. Sheriff Hanson spun his wheels as he tried to pull out. He got nowhere. He rocked the heavy squad car back and forth a half dozen times before he finally caught enough traction to drive, and that was with a full set of chains. He flicked on the light-bar and the siren and hoped that nothing got in his way. Hanson knew it was good he was leaving when he was. Any later he would never have made it, chains or no chains.

Ted Leah, from the State Police, was also on his way. He had his two favorite dogs, Gretchen and Heidi, loaded in the K-9 Suburban the state assigned to him. Both dogs were purebred German shepherds. All Vermont State Police dogs underwent *schutzhund* training in Albany, a combination of obedience, tracking, and attack training brought over from Germany. Leah also entered his dogs in sanctioned tracking matches during the spring and summer to keep them sharp.

Leah cursed the weather and the roads and the lazy state and county workers for not doing a better job keeping things clear. He also cursed Sam Hanson for calling him out on a day like this. What the hell did Hanson expect? If the girl was outside, his dogs might locate her body, but even that was doubtful given the weather and the conditions at the lodge. If the damn kid was inside, she would turn up sooner or later. So what the hell did Hanson need him for? That business about the kid maybe being snatched was a bunch of bull, Leah knew. Still, he couldn't take any chances. How would it look if the kid had been kidnapped and he had refused to help? He wondered if Hanson had called the FBI. Probably not. He drove at a judicious rate. The storm was getting worse. *Sonofabitch...*

"What's the situation, Andy?" Sheriff Hanson asked as soon as he arrived at the resort.

"About the same as before, Sheriff, except the weather's gotten worse. Everyone's inside now, including most of the ski patrol and the little girl's father. The only good news is that we haven't lost nobody else. The parents are in pretty bad shape. Doc Whitman is treating Mr. Martin for frostbite on his ears and face. The mom was hysterical and had to be sedated. She was damn near in shock."

They seemed like nice enough folks. Hanson couldn't help but feel sorry for them. Helluva thing to lose a kid. When the last of the ski patrol came in both parents went to pieces.

The sheriff put his arm around his deputy's shoulder.

"Is the kid's room secured?" he asked, confidentially.

"Not exactly, Sheriff," Johnson replied. "People been checkin' every now and again on the off chance the little girl wandered back and curled up somewhere."

The sheriff frowned. "Okay, secure it now. Nobody goes in or out, including the parents, without my say so. Understand?"

"Yes, sir." Johnson was an easy going, baby faced Vietnam vet who had had difficulty finding himself and supporting his wife and kid until Sam Hanson put him on. He idolized the sheriff.

"George," the sheriff called to the resort owner, "will you have your kitchen put up a couple of Thermoses please? One of hot chocolate and the other with heated up Gatorade. Make it near boiling and make the hot chocolate with real, whole milk, okay?"

"Sure thing, Sam," the owner replied. "Anything else?"

"Come see me when that's taken care of, will you?"

"I'll be right there."

Sheriff Hanson walked over to the Martins who were on the couch near the fireplace. Nancy Grady joined them. Nancy was an attractive single mom. Blond shoulder length hair, deep searching blue eyes, she was always fighting the battle of the last five pounds that men didn't care whether she won or not. On this day Nancy Grady looked horrible. Sam Hanson put his arm around her.

"How're you doin', honey?" he asked. Nancy never minded Sam calling her "honey," but she just looked at him wanly.

"Mr. and Mrs. Martin," she began, "this is Sheriff Hanson. He's organizing the search for Kelly."

They looked up at him, expectantly. All he could do was nod.

"How are you folks holdin' up?"

Diane Martin looked down and started to sob. Dark hair, big dark eyes, beautiful smooth white skin, she was probably pretty when she was happy, the sheriff noted. Mr. Martin threw off the blanket around his shoulders and started to get up.

"We've got to get back out there, Sheriff. There's still plenty of places we haven't checked."

Sheriff Hanson looked over to Jim Beard, the ski patrol team leader. Beard shook his head quickly.

"Try to stay calm, Mr. Martin. We'll do everything we possibly can. I've got a call out to some tracking-dog units and they should be on their way right now. In the meantime, I need you folks right here, and I need you to hold it together, okay?"

Mr. Martin nodded reluctantly.

"Okay, now I need you folks to think of some things we might be able to use to give the tracking-dogs a scent: dirty laundry, shoes, boots, blankets, toys and the like. Okay?"

Both parents looked up and nodded. Diane Martin's big dark eyes were ringed wet and puffy. Her crimson cheeks were tear-soaked.

"Now I don't want you to go to your room just yet. Understand? I just want you to think of what we can use. We'll let the dog handlers tell us what they want. Okay?"

"Sheriff, my little girl's outside! We've got to get back out there and find her!"

"I know, Mr. Martin. I'm just tryin' to get this situation organized and systematic. We won't do your little girl any good losin' someone else outside, yourself included."

Hanson guessed it was Mr. Martin who had pushed for one last run down the slope, even with the storm coming up. He was pleasant and athletic looking, but he also looked like the kind of person who would want to make certain he got his money's worth out of a lift ticket. Hanson could understand him wanting to be outside looking for his lost daughter. It must have been hell for him sitting inside next to his wife, even if the recriminations hadn't started yet.

"Nancy, I want you to show me exactly where the little girl was last seen. And I want to talk to your daughter and that other kid.

"Mr. and Mrs. Martin, I'll be right back. Get that list of articles together if you can."

Nancy Grady led the sheriff to the large picture window on the south side of the lodge. The wind was gusting and swirling with the brunt of the storm pushing down from the north, putting that particular window on the leeward side of the building. When the wind gusts eased momentarily, it was still possible to make out the remnants of a snowman.

"Right over there is where they were playing, Sam."

"Which way did she take off?"

"It's hard to say. The kids are scared and say whatever they think you want to hear."

"Let me talk to them, will you?"

Nancy left to fetch the children. George Hoffman walked up to Sheriff Hanson.

"The hot-chocolate and hot Gatorade are all taken care of. What else do you need, Sheriff?"

"Can you check and tell me how many people checked out between oh, say, ten A.M. and noon?"

"Sure thing, Sam. That shouldn't be too hard. Check-out is at 11:00 so sometimes we get a rush around ten, but this being Thursday, most folks are checking in, not out."

"Just get me the list, will you George?"

Nancy returned with the two children, her daughter, Sharon, and Patti Nickelson. Hanson squatted in front of the two children.

"Hi guys," he began. "You know who I am?"

Both children nodded.

"Well now Nancy here tells me you guys were out playing with Kelly Martin just before she disappeared. Is that right?"

Again, both little girls nodded.

"Can you tell me which way she went off when she left you?"

This time both children looked at the floor.

"Did she go off towards those woods over there?" Hanson asked, "or did she head more towards the parking lot?"

"Towards the woods." Sharon Grady was the first to respond.

"Are you sure?" Hanson challenged gently.

The little girls looked at each other like they were taking a test in school, unsure of the correct answer.

"Which way is the parking lot?" Patti Nickelson asked.

"It's over that way, around the front of the building."

"She could have gone that way," Patti volunteered, trying to get it right.

"But which way do you *really* think she went?"

Again, both girls looked at each other. Then they seemed to silently agree.

"She went that way," Sharon told him, pointing past the deteriorating snowman towards the dark, obscured woods.

"Did you notice Kelly talking to anyone, any grownup, or were any grownups talking to her?"

Both girls shook their heads, no.

George Hoffman returned with the checkout list. "Here you are Sam, only three departures. What are you looking for?"

"Any single men on the list?"

George looked down the printout.

"No, they're all couples or families."

"Any couples that don't have children?"

George looked again.

"Just one. Dr. and Mrs. Erlichman. Why? ...You don't think...?"

"I'm just trying to cover all bases. Do you know these people?"

"They've been coming here for years. He's a plastic surgeon at Mass. General. She used to be a nurse, now she's his wife. About twenty years younger than he is. Believe me, Sam, a six-year-old kid is the last thing they want. They're into the 'good life' if you get my meaning."

Hanson did, but he felt he had to check. Now Mr. Martin came over to him.

"Sheriff, I'm going back outside. My wife can help you pick out things for the dogs."

"I can't let you do that, Mr. Martin. Now please, just settle down and I'll get the ski-patrol and my man to organize another search."

"I'm going out there, Sheriff!"

"Please, Mr. Martin. Don't make me have to restrain you. I know it's rough, but please let me do my job. Don't make it any harder than it is," Hanson reasoned. *Where the hell is Leah and those damn dogs,* he cursed to himself. It was a prescient thought. The desk clerk called over to him.

"Sheriff Hanson, there's a call for you."

Hanson's pulse increased as he walked over to take the call. He knew any call to him would not be good news.

"Sam, it's Will Herman over at Morrisville."

Captain Herman was the State Police commander for the northern part of the state.

"What's up, Will?"

"Leah's vehicle went off the road and into a ditch. Henderson's there with him now. Leah and the dogs are okay, but he's fit to be tied. He wants to know if you still need him up there."

Hanson thought for a moment. He didn't really have a choice.

"Hell yes I want them. How far out are they?"

"They're down by Westfield. In this storm, barring any more problems, we're looking at at least twenty-five minutes to a half-hour, if we're lucky."

Damn! "Will, we need all the help we can get up here. If there's one chance in a million those dogs might turn up something, I want them here. Henderson too."

"Okay, Sam. I'll pass it on. Leah's not going to be a very happy camper."

"Tough shit, Will. Get his ass up here. He would have been here by now if he knew how to drive. Don't you boys still do that snow course you have?"

"I'll get him there, Sam. The rest is up to you. Just be prepared to kiss his ass a little once he gets there."

"I'll kiss his dogs' asses if it will find the little girl."

"Good luck."

Damn, Hanson thought, now what do I do? It was 2:36 P.M. Kelly Martin had been lost for more than two hours, outside for more than three.

The large military transport at Billy Mitchell Field in Milwaukee, Wisconsin lifted off.

Chapter Five

"Mr. Travis, sir, Colonel Reuger wants to know if you would like to come into the cockpit. It's a bit warmer and a helluva lot quieter."

Joshua was glad for the opportunity to get out of the main hold. He didn't mind the cool temperature, but the dark, hollow fuselage, with its all too exposed infrastructure and ringing metallic echoes, was not a good place for him to be alone with his thoughts. His heart was racing and his stomach was queasy. Cody was still on his mind.

"Is there room for my dogs?"

"Why sure thing, sir," the flight engineer replied with his Arkansas smile. "Hell, the more the merrier."

Joshua and the dogs moved up. He took his place in a fifth seat in the cockpit, fitted specially for flight evaluators. He nodded to the crew but for the most part kept quiet except to ask, "How long do you figure to touchdown?"

Except for Lt. Colonel Reuger the crew looked to Lieutenant Gilliam, the navigator. It was Reuger, however, who spoke.

"We're fixin' on givin' you one helluva ride, Mr. Travis. With this buggy empty and the tail wind we're a ridin', we're lookin' at pushin' 600 knots across the ground. We're gonna push her up to 37,000 feet wide open, and from then on we're gonna point her nose down and let gravity help us right on into Burlington. We'll have you on the ground inside an hour and twenty minutes. There's just one thing..."

Travis looked at him. "What's that, Colonel?"

"I can't rightly say how many pieces we'll all be in when we hit the damn ground." Reuger didn't smile.

Lt. Colonel David Reuger was of average height and above average condition. He had closely cropped blond hair, chiseled features, and twinkling, mischievous eyes. Reuger had flown jets in 'Nam and the polar arc for SAC. He was flying hurricane chasers for the National Weather Service when he met Genevieve Ciotto. He never saw it coming and he never knew what hit him, but he fell harder than a night jump over red clay and at her behest settled into the mundane routine of an airline pilot for United. His share of the bargain was the understanding that he would remain in the Guard, and whenever duty called all bets were off. It always amazed Genevieve how often duty called. His crew was fucking astounded.

The big jet bowed smoothly and cleanly up to 37,000 feet and east towards Vermont. The sun was to the right and slightly behind, causing the right wing to glow hot orange. Only the navigator and the flight engineer didn't wear sunglasses. As the plane arced over Ontario and began its gradual descent, the men in the cockpit could look ahead and see the giant storm in the distance. Davis gave a long, low whistle. "I sure as hell hope they still have radar and a beacon working when we get there."

As the words were spoken, a message came over the radio from Toronto.

"Lifeguard-532, contact Toronto Center now on 132.75."

"Lifeguard-532 to Toronto Center. Good day." Reuger replied. The new frequency was set in the radio. "Lifeguard-532 flight level 370."

"Roger, Lifeguard-532. You have pilot's discretion to 11,000 feet, altimeter 29.85."

"Roger, Center, PD 11,000, altimeter 29.85. Any word on

conditions at Burlington? Over."

"Burlington reports weather ceiling 100 feet indefinite, visibility less than ¼ mile heavy blowing snow, winds 310 degrees 25 knots gusting to 40. Drifting snow on all runways, braking action poor. Burlington airport is closed until further notice. What are your intentions?"

Reuger thought for a second and looked at his crew. Then he responded.

"Thank you, Toronto Center. Will consider and advise." Then to his navigator, "Gilly, what's our alternate destination?"

"Griffis at Rome. Or, we could try Plattsburg but they're probably shut down too."

"What do they mean for our passengers?"

The crew was looking at the navigator. He shook his head. "Plattsburg will mean at least two more hours, assuming he can get around Lake Champlain at all."

"Maybe they can run him across with some sort of half-track," Davis suggested.

"What do you think, Mr. Travis?" from the pilot.

The navigator showed Travis a map. "Maybe they can run you north, around South Grand Isle. Make up some of the time."

"My pickup is in Burlington. We'd have to arrange some sort of rendezvous somewhere else."

"Ground communications are liable to be piss poor," informed the flight engineer.

"Hell, if we're gonna land blind, we might just as well aim for Burlington as for Plattsburg. What about Rome?"

Reuger looked at Gilly. Gilly shook his head. Rome was too far out. They might as well turn back.

"What do you think?" Reuger asked his crew.

"What are our chances, Gilly?" Davis asked the navigator.

"If Burlington's ILS stays on and our ILS is working properly, we might make it with a downwind landing, assuming we had some-one who could fly this plane right. You'd best fly a dot below the glidescope."

Reuger smiled. "What do you say, Mr. Travis?"

Joshua knew the little girl was most likely dead. Risking the lives of four men beside himself made little sense. Neither did putting down in Rome, or even Plattsburg.

"If we can't get to Burlington, we might as well go home."

"My feelings exactly," from Colonel Reuger.

"Just remember, Colonel, we don't do anybody any good dead. You all have families and I'll have other rescues." Travis hated saying that.

"Nobody's plannin' on windin' up dead, Mr. Travis. What do you say, boys, are we up for playin' in the snow?" Reuger asked.

They weren't joking around now. They looked from one to an-other and then back to Reuger.

"In for a penny, in for a pound."

"It's your call, Colonel." They knew that this was what they had signed on for.

You really have to love these guys, Joshua thought. *Here they are, weekend warriors, with wives and kids and regular jobs at home, risking it all to save me a three hours ride in a truck... and maybe, just maybe, a little girl's life.*

"Center, this is Lifeguard-532. Tell Burlington to keep their bea-cons and their lights on. And ask them to make a couple of extra passes on the runway with the plow."

The Indian woman soars through her Vision, high above the earth.

"Where are you going, Gogyeng Sowuhti?" spotted eagle inquires.

"To the land of the morning sun. Taknokwunu is angry," the woman replies.

"What will you find there?" gray hawk asks.

"I do not know."

"You will be cold, Grandmother," red hawk tells her.

"It does not matter," answers the woman.

Through her exhilaration she feels a dangerous trepidation. Beneath her is only light and darkness – tokpella – space without form or order. Her heart races. She knows that she must return to earth. If she comes down at the wrong place she will die.

Chapter Six

"Andy, I want you and George to get everybody here to check their cars. Make sure they look inside carefully, and underneath too. They'll have to clear out some drifted snow to look underneath, but I want it done.

"Jim, as soon as you and your patrol are up to it I want you to check outside again. Take volunteers from the guests but only expert skiers. Team up the guests with your patrol people and don't get anyone lost. Work a systematic grid from the south side out to the woods, and then along the woods perimeter. Use the rods," Hanson told the leader of the ski patrol, and then confidentially, "Do the best you can but come back in if it gets too rough out there."

He didn't really think the girl would be found in the parking lot, but he wanted to keep people busy, and he figured you never know. He wasn't hopeful that the ski patrol would turn up anything either, but he had to do something.

The guests and ski patrol bundled up again and went outside. Eight inches of snow had fallen since the storm had begun. It was much deeper where it had drifted. The temperature was still dropping and the wind chill was minus 37 degrees. No one was very happy, but no one refused. Neither search turned up anything. The ski patrol was still out when Ted Leah and Fred Henderson arrived. It was 3:00 P.M.

"Where the hell's all the FBI, Hanson?"

"Give it a rest, Ted. Let's just get down to business. What do you need?"

"What do I need? I need halfway decent weather and a fresh track. Hell, we've had eight or ten inches of new snow and it's still coming down. The goddamn wind is comin' out of every direction, and you've covered any trail that might have been out there with a hundred people traipsing around. And you ask me what I need?"

"Look Leah, all I'm asking is that you give it a shot, all right? Just get your dogs out there and see if they can come up with something. We've turned this place upside down and haven't come up with diddly. Maybe you can do better, at least I hope so. So what do you say?"

"Yeah, yeah, all right, we'll give it a shot. You sure the kid wasn't kidnapped now, Hanson?"

Sheriff Hanson wasn't sure at all, but he had to go with his best hunch. Everything pointed to the child being lost, plain and simple. He held his tongue.

"Where are the parents?"

Hanson took Leah over to the Martins. They looked up expectantly at the short, craggy state trooper. Leah handed them a plastic bag.

"Get me some of your daughter's dirty underwear, okay? Pick it up with these ice tongs and put it in this bag. Don't touch any of it with your hands, understand?"

The Martins nodded and rushed to their room to get what the dog handler asked for.

"I noticed some bodies moving around out there as we came in. You still got people out there looking, Hanson?"

"The ski patrol and some volunteers are still out there."

"Well get them the hell in here! I don't need anymore goddamn fresh scents out there to confuse things even more."

"I'll go," Andy Johnson offered.

"No, Andy, I'll do it." Sam Hanson had to get out of there. He had had it with Leah and was about ready to lay him out, the arrogant little sonofabitch. "See that Leah and Henderson get whatever they need. Have George fix them up with skis or snowshoes if they want."

"I can't run dogs and screw around with goddamn skis or snowshoes." Leah told them. He was wearing pac boots. They would be okay around the lodge, and perhaps on the road, but the new snow was covering a six foot base, at least two of it powder. Hanson wondered what Leah would do if the dogs led him cross country.

The sheriff went outside to round up the volunteers. The cold was penetrating. The wind had picked up and conditions were near white-out. He worried about how long the power lines and the phone lines would hold.

The Martins came down with the laundry articles.

"Is this okay?" Mr. Martin asked tentatively. He wanted to do everything just right for the man who would probably be his daughter's last hope.

"I suppose," Leah responded. "Where was the kid last seen?"

Nancy Grady showed him the snowman. Leah took the sac and the tongs and was led by his overheated and exuberant dogs towards the door. He looked over his shoulder.

"Fred, you take Gretchen. Just watch us and do what I do. We'll do our damnedest. Just don't expect too much," he tells the Martins as he zipped up his parka and went out the door.

Leah heeled his dog, Heidi, over to the snowman. The wind cut through his hood like a cold shiv. The swirling snowfall nearly blinded him. Damn, he thought, it's colder than a witch's tit out here. Henderson followed Leah. He was a large, quiet man who didn't much like Leah regardless of what his dogs might be able to do.

Heidi crouched as she moved, staying low to the ground. Gretchen thought it was a big game. Even on lead, she jumped and snapped at the wind.

At the snowman, Leah carefully used the ice tongs to remove the articles of clothing from the plastic bag. Heidi sniffed the articles thoroughly and was ready to work. She checked the air then began sniffing the ground, casting from side to side. Gretchen still wanted to play. She grabbed the little girl's T-shirt and shook it out of Leah's hand, ripping it in the process. She bounded up and down, shaking the shirt clasped in her jaws in victory.

"Here, damnit," Leah told Henderson. "Hold on to Heidi for a minute."

Ted Leah and Henderson exchanged leashes. Then Leah sharply and soundly jerked the large German shepherd to the ground! Both hands on the leash jerked her straight up, her front paws in the air, her hind feet struggling to keep contact with the ground...Slam! The dog's head came back down to the snow. Leah's boot found her rear end.

"Now get to work, goddamnit! We're not out here to play." He put another article of clothing to the dog. This time she sniffed it without grabbing it. Gretchen was ready to work.

Leah had to remove his gloves to switch the leads from the choke-chain collars to the tracking harness "D" rings. "Goddamnit," he cursed as his fingers nearly stuck to the metal.

"Go Find!" he commanded. "C'mon girls," he urged, "find the goddamn kid."

The dogs began to work, scampering around, their heads to the ground. In the ski lodge, the Martins, the sheriff and his deputy, Nancy Grady and Jim Beard and as many others as could fit crowded around the large picture window and tried to see what was happening. It was difficult to make out much of anything at all, but occasionally they could catch a glimpse of the dogs followed by the men on the other end of their leashes. Once in a while the dogs and men got tangled.

Gretchen wasn't sure what she was looking for. She kept return-ing to the plastic bag with the clothing articles until Leah finally picked up the sac and tucked it inside his coat. Heidi kept searching but it was hard. Every time she put her nose to the wind her impulse was to return inside. She did not think that was right, so she went back to looking for a ground trail. There was something about the snowman that was connected to what she was hunting for, and she kept returning to it, checking its base, but that wasn't right either.

"C'mon girls, Go Find! Find the trail! Find the trail!" Leah ordered. Henderson mimicked Leah but his tone was more encour-aging than commanding.

Find the trail. Find the trail, Heidi knew as she scurried around the snowman, her nose to the ground. *Find the trail. Find the trail.* She checked the drifted area between the snowman's base and its decapitated head. *Scent, Image. There's something there.* She started digging. *Scent. Image stronger. There's something there.* She started barking. Gretchen strained to get over by Heidi. Both dogs were barking. *There's something there!*

Leah couldn't believe it. How could it be? He rolled the snow-man's head a few feet with his foot. The dogs didn't move. They continued to bark and scratch at the snow near the base of the snowman.

"Tell Hanson to get some men and some digging tools," he or-dered Henderson. "Keep the parents inside."

I'll be a sonofabitch, Leah thought silently. I'll bet those damn kids were playing a goddamn game and this one got buried. They probably panicked when she didn't get up and concocted that cock-'n-bull story about the kid wandering off. We're going to dig up the kid right here at the base of this snowman. And won't that be one helluva kick in the crotch.

Jim Beard and Andy Johnson came out from the chalet. They had some ice choppers that had been on the lodge porch. Fred Henderson and Sam Hanson went to their squad cars to get the picks and shovels they carried in the trunks. When they were all assembled, Leah told them, "There's something down there. I'll stake my reputation on it. Looks like you were right after all, Hanson. Looks like my team came up with something even in all this shit, don't it?"

Sheriff Hanson knew that Leah was doing more than bragging about himself and his dogs. He knew the dog handler was reminding him that he had told him they would find the girl dead if she was outside. Hanson swallowed his bile and carefully began to scrape away snow from the area the dogs were indicating.

Despite the advice of Officer Henderson and the pleading of Nancy Grady, Mr. and Mrs. Martin threw on their ski jackets and rushed outdoors. Panic stricken, they did not even bother with hats or gloves. They fought the cold and the wind to get to the snowman. Snow spilled down their necks.

"What is it?" Mr. Martin yelled. It was hard to be heard above the wind and the dogs.

"We don't know yet, Mr. Martin. The dogs have found something. It's best if you wait inside." Leah advised.

"The hell I will," Martin said angrily. He grabbed one of the ice scrapers and began furiously attacking the frozen snow. Sam Hanson stopped him.

"Stop it Mr. Martin! You're going to freeze out here like that. You and your wife both. Is that what you want? Now take your wife inside and wait there. We'll let you know as soon as we find anything. Andy, help Mr. and Mrs. Martin back inside."

The deputy took the arm of each parent and guided them back towards the lodge.

"What is it, John? What's happening? What's going on? Where's my little girl?" The tears were freezing to her cheeks.

It was Fred Henderson who first made contact and felt more than saw what the dogs had discovered. The men carefully dug and scraped the snow away from the buried object. It was pink and it was frozen.

Chapter Seven

The Martins pushed to the front of the group standing by the picture window. They refused the offers of hot mulled cider and the misguided suggestions they take some brandy. They were desperate to know what was going on. It was difficult to see what was happening outside. The possibility that their little girl was buried out there, in an area that had been walked over a hundred times and was just yards from the lodge, was incomprehensible. Fred Henderson and Jim Beard were walking towards the lodge. Henderson was carrying something.

The crowd of guests moved towards the door, opening a way for John and Diane Martin. They were afraid to approach the opening door. When the two men walked in, Mrs. Martin fell apart. Jim Henderson was holding a pink, knitted scarf.

"Do you recognize this scarf?" Henderson asked the Martins.

John Martin was sick. "It belongs to Kelly," he choked. "Her *Yia Yah*...," he hesitated, "her grandmother knitted it for her for Christmas." He could barely speak.

"We found it outside, by the snowman, under about a foot of snow. Any ideas how it might have gotten there?"

Diane Martin was hysterical. John Martin was ashen. It was all they could do to shake their heads, no.

"Where are the kids who were playing with her?" Henderson asked. "I want to talk to them."

Sheriff Hanson was still outside with Ted Leah and the dogs.

"C'mon, Ted. Just work your dogs a little while longer. Hell, they found something, didn't they? Maybe they'll come up with something else."

"Give it up, Hanson. It's over. They've shot their wad. Believe me, I know. Besides, you know as well as I do that the kid is a goner, so what's the point? Hell, she's been out in this crap for what now.. three, four hours? You know there's no way for her to make it. Shit, I'm almost half frozen myself, and I've only been out here twenty goddamn minutes. It's over. Give it up. It's almost too bad she wasn't kidnapped. At least then she might have had a chance. Give me a call in the spring, and I'll help you locate the body."

Hanson knew Leah was probably right, but he couldn't let it go.

"Look, how about working them in concentric circles around the snowman, only a little farther out. See if they can pick up a trail or find anything else. Let's finish this thing tonight."

Leah thought for a moment. He was cold. The tip of his nose was starting to freeze. His dogs were whining.

"We'll give you fifteen more minutes, Hanson. That's it. Then we're calling it a day. You got that? Now go send Henderson back out."

"Just do the best you can, Ted. That's all I ask." Hanson turned and fought his way back to the chalet.

Sam Hanson walked over to Officer Henderson, who had just finished interviewing the children.

"Leah wants you outside. What's the deal with the scarf?"

"It belongs to the lost girl. The kids say she gave it to them to use on the snowman. It must have blown off and gotten buried by the snow."

"Any reason to doubt them?"

"I don't think so. They seem like good kids, and they seem really worried about their friend. I don't think there's anything dark going on. That's just Leah."

"Okay, Fred. You better go on out and give Leah a hand. Maybe you'll turn up something else. Keep him out there as long as you can." He glanced towards the Martins. "These people need some answers."

Twenty minutes later Ted Leah and his dogs were back inside, warming up.

"They're not finding anything new. They just keep going back to the place where we dug up the scarf. Don't say I didn't tell you, Hanson. Anyway, we're out of here while we still can. Give me a call when the weather clears, if you want." Then, almost as an afterthought, he turned to the Martins and said, "Sorry folks," as he left.

The Martins went to pieces. Nancy Grady was crying also. Sam Hanson looked at the door for a moment. How do you reason with an asshole like that, he wondered. He decided you couldn't, so he walked over to Nancy and the Martins instead.

"Now, don't go giving up just yet. We're trying to get another dog team in here, one that's done some pretty amazing things in the past. In the meantime, Jim and Andy and I are going to go back out and see if we can't check out the woods some. Don't give up hope. We haven't. Right, Jim?"

"Heck no," Beard chimed in. "There's lots of possibilities. The Martins brightened just a little. Nancy Grady wondered if both men were lying.

As the two men moved towards the door, the sheriff was approached by Barry Steiner, a reporter with the Burlington Free Press. Steiner was at the lodge for a week of skiing. He had helped look for the little girl along with everybody else. Still, he knew a story when he heard one.

"Sheriff, did I hear you say you have another dog team coming in?"

"Who are you?"

"Barry Steiner. I'm with the Free Press."

Hanson hesitated a moment, then he figured what the hell.

"That's right, Mr. Steiner. If they can get here."

"Do you mind if I call that in to my paper? You know they're interested in this story."

"Go ahead, Mr. Steiner, it won't make any difference here."

"Who are they? Where are they coming from?"

"One is coming in from Lake George, the other from Wisconsin. His name is..."

"Do you really think there's still a chance of finding the little girl alive?" the reporter asked.

Hanson had to give that one some thought. If he didn't, then why was he having a man from Wisconsin and a National Guard air crew risking their necks? "Until you find a body, there's always a chance."

Once again, Hanson and the ski patrol volunteers prepared to push out into the raging blizzard that was nearing full force. The reporter rushed to the nearest telephone and hoped it was still working. The KC-135 began the steep descent for its final approach into Burlington. It was beginning to feel the effects of the storm.

Chapter Eight

"Everyone strapped in?" Reuger asked. The flight was getting bumpy.

"Mr. Travis, you'd best hang on to your dogs."

Joshua had both dogs sitting in front of him. He had been scratching their throats. He slipped his hands between the dogs' fur and their collars and securely gripped the chains.

Whomp! As the plane entered the front. It dropped fifty feet without warning.

"Lifeguard-532, contact Boston Center now on 128.5"

"We copy, Toronto, thank you."

"Get Boston Center," Reuger told his co-pilot. "Tell them we're going to Burlington. We'll need all the help we can get." Then to the navigator, "Gilly, what's Burlington's altitude?"

"327."

The plane bucked and jerked.

"Boston Center, Lifeguard-532, 15,000."

"Lifeguard-532, Burlington is shut down. Suggest you put down at Rome or Syracuse."

"No good, Boston. We got a special delivery package. Has to go to Burlington."

"Are you declaring an emergency, Lifeguard-532?"

"Affirmative, Center."

"You'll have to make a downwind approach and landing. Descend and maintain 11,000 feet. Contact Burlington Approach in 20 miles on 118.3."

"118.3 MHz. Check, Center." The bucking and dipping worsened.

"You're cleared down to 11,000 feet. We'll hand you off to Burlington Approach just past Massena. Good luck, Lifeguard."

"Roger, Boston, Lifeguard-532 out of 15 for 11,000, and thanks." Reuger didn't look around. "Here we go. Ride 'em cowboy." And then to Gilliam, "How far to Massena?"

The navigator looked at his maps and his instruments. The plane was in the clouds and beginning to buck hard. "Probably around here somewhere."

Reuger looked around quickly. The crew nodded.

"Close enough. Here we go." It was snowing outside. Snowing hard.

The big plane shuddered and rumbled. The hollowness of the fuselage amplified every noise. Buck whined. "Steady, boy," Joshua comforted. Jenny-Dog was calm. She had unquestioning confidence in the man she was with. Confidence probably misplaced, Travis thought as he looked into the windshield. All he could see were reflections and snow. Snow coming at them at the speed of light.

"John, see if you can raise Burlington Approach. Keep an eye on the altimeter and glidescope. Gilly, you watch the course guidance and glidescope too." Reuger increased the throttle to compensate for the wind. They hadn't put it behind them yet.

"Davie we're dipping too much to the left!" Davis told him. Without visual references it was impossible to know how much the plane was banking except by the instruments. Too much bank and they wouldn't be able to bring it back. They would go into an uncontrollable spin. In this wind, it wouldn't take much.

Reuger brought the left wing up, until the silhouette wings on the instrument lined up with the horizontal line on the gauge. It wasn't easy. Everyone and everything was bouncing hard.

"Rock 'n Roll!"

Whomp, whomp!

"What the fuck was that!?"

No one said anything. Davis looked out his window.

"Have we still got our wings?" Reuger asked.

"It's hard to tell."

"Lifeguard 532, this is Burlington. Radar contact. Altimeter 28.35 Ceiling 50 feet indefinite, visibility 1/10 mile heavy blowing snow, wind 310 degrees 30 knots gusting to 45. Drifting snow on all runways. Burlington Airport is closed. Strongly suggest you put down at alternate destination."

"Roger, Burlington. Altimeter 28.35. We're coming in. Request radar vectors to final approach."

"Turn right, heading 155 degrees and hold it steady."

"Roger," Reuger replied, and then under his breath, "what the hell do they think I'm trying to do. How're we doin', Gilly?"

"We're thirty miles out. 9000 feet."

"Lifeguard-532, descend and maintain 6000 feet."

"Lifeguard-532 out of 11 for 6,000. Burlington, request you make a couple of more passes on the runway with the plows and clear us for landing."

"Will do, Lifeguard-532. Turn left, heading 146. Descend and maintain 2,500 until established on the localizer. You are cleared for the ILS runway 15 approach. Burlington altimeter 28.25. Burlington Tower clears you to land."

"Roger, Burlington. Lifeguard-532 out of 6 for 2,500. Altimeter 28.25. We're coming in. Keep your heads down."

Reuger looked at Travis. Joshua nodded.

"Go for it," Reuger told his navigator as the plane banked and dove for the ground. It was everything Reuger could do to hold the nose to an acceptable angle of attack. The white snow rushed by in the black air, exaggerating the feeling of speed. The rest of the universe was gray. Travis knew that for the little girl time was rushing faster than they were.

The plane shuddered and banged and wobbled. When they banked to the correct heading, it felt as if the wind would flip the giant aircraft like a paper plane thrown out a high school window. Travis said a silent prayer. Well, not exactly a prayer. More like cutting a deal with God.

"Twenty miles. Are you putting down gear or are we going in on our belly?"

"Hell yes, I'm putting down gear. You think I want to answer to a board of inquiry for scratching the Air Force's nice plane?"

Davis smiled.

"Landing gear down."

The landing gear clunked, hesitated, and whirred into position with another clunk.

"Landing gear down," Davis confirmed. It didn't make the plane any easier to handle.

"Hold her steady… Bring her nose up a tad… Ease off on the throttle –don't let her stall."

Whomp. The plane dropped unexpectedly.

"Bring her up! Bring her up! That's better. Okay, now easy.... easy.... Gilly, how we doin'?"

"Hold her steady...., steady."

"Colonel, we should be almost there. You see anything?"

It was a complete white-out. Zero ceiling, zero visibility.

"Flaps 10 degrees," Reuger ordered.

"Flaps 10 degrees," Davis confirmed.

"I show nine hundred feet on the radar altimeter. You see anything?"

"Negative."

"Eight hundred feet. Seven hundred and fifty feet...."

"Six hundred feet. Watch for lights," Reuger told the crew. Then to himself, "Hold her... Hold her steady... Throttle back...nose up. That's it. Hold her steady."

The wind hit and jerked the plane and pushed it towards oblivion. The thin metallic skin rang and popped like an old sheet metal barn roof about to come off in a twister.

"Four hundred feet... three-fifty... three hundred...two-fifty."

Each member of the crew had his own thoughts.

"Colonel, I don't see any lights. Better pull up!"

One hundred and fifty feet... one-thirty... one hundred... ninety... eighty... seventy... sixty... fifty... Whomp! The plane bounced!

"Power off! Full flaps!" Reuger forced the nose down.

Thump!... Thud! The giant plane skidded and plowed through the snow.

"Thrust reversers!"

A fury of white erupted around them. The murderous tail wind made it difficult to stop. They were down. Somehow, with the help of God or the devil, they were down. And finally, finally, they stopped. Somewhere.

"Burlington, we are down. Over"

"Welcome to Vermont, Lifeguard-532."

"We read you five-by-five, but we haven't got a clue where we are or where you are. Over"

"Well we know where we are, and we've got a pretty good idea where you are. Sit tight Lifeguard-532 and we'll send a 'follow-me' to fetch you."

"Much obliged, Burlington. Our passenger is in a bit of a hurry. Over"

"Just sit tight, Lifeguard-532."

Joshua looked at his watch. It read 3:32, 4:32 in Vermont. He gathered his gear and got the dogs set to deplane. Five minutes later the large jet was jolted with a thud.

"What the fuck was that?" demanded Reuger. Nobody could tell him. He got back on the radio.

"Burlington, this is Lifeguard-532. We've just been hit by something. Have the follow-me truck check it out when he gets here, will you?"

"Ah...Lifeguard-532, we're sorry about that, but that *was* the follow-me that hit you. He lost track of you in the storm. Can you still follow him?"

"I don't think so, Burlington. We can't see him any more than he can see us. "

"What do you want to do, Lifeguard?"

Reuger looked at Travis and his dogs.

"You can ride in the follow-me. They can come back for the rest of us later. All we got to do is get you on the ground. You can use the emergency hatch, down there." Reuger indicated the grate on the left side of the cockpit floor.

"That'll work," Joshua agreed.

Reuger opened the hatch. The cold and snow swept into the cockpit like an icy hand. Reuger yelled out to the embarrassed follow-me driver, checking out the landing gear, hoping it wasn't damaged.

"Back off a couple of yards and wait for some passengers!"

The driver was happy to return to his vehicle before he got too cold... and before he got chewed out.

Joshua looked at the crew as he stood bracing himself by the hatch.

"You guys sure are something," he told them, shaking his head.

"Just get the hell outta my plane and find that goddamn kid, tracker!" Then, the cock-sure pilot added gravely, "Good luck, Mr. Travis."

Chapter Nine

I n San Francisco, at offices of Wheaton, Princeton and South, the senior draftsmen and associate architects finally break for lunch.

Sarah Lane-Toffler knocked on the office door of Kristian Fisk-Travis and peeked in. The architect was pouring over some plans on her drawing table.

"Hey Kris, a bunch of us are going over to Cronin's for lunch. Care to join us?"

Kristian Fisk-Travis was a full partner. She had a brilliant mind, dancing green eyes, and a ready smile that put people at ease. She headed the lucrative residential/vacation home division of the firm. It was a small division, but a highly profitable one. On top of that, Kristian possessed a rare classic beauty, coupled with an exquisite figure that made men ache. Whenever she walked by, heads involuntarily turned, eyes shifted. Kristian was well liked and admired by most of the firm except for the few men who resented her intelligence or were intimidated by her beauty.

Kristian liked Cronin's. It reminded her of the Blazer Pub, back in Wisconsin. She gave Sarah's offer serious consideration. Then she decided.

"No thanks, Sarah. I'm just putting the finishing touches on the Bennington place."

She still had no idea that her husband was in Vermont.

Joshua tossed his packs into the snow. He lowered himself

through the emergency hatch. "Okay, Jenny, Come!"

The crew helped the older dog through the opening. Buck was another story. The crewmen were wisely reluctant to put their hands on him.

"It's okay. He won't hurt you," Travis reassured them. "Come on, Buck."

Buck jumped on his own.

The local sheriff had not exaggerated the strength of the storm. The four hundred yard distance between the plane and the terminal was a regular trek. The driver was especially careful not to hit anything unexpected. As soon as they got inside, Joshua and the dogs were met by a kid who could have been the All-American Boy except for a thin beard and mustache. The young man wore a black "Cat-Diesel Powered" hat and a snowmobile suit. Travis noticed that instead of snowmobile boots the man had on heavy, cleated logging corks that you could kick the tar out of a mule with, if you had a mind to.

"Mr. Travis? Your limousine awaits. I'm Bill Peterson."

"Glad to see you, Bill. I was a little worried you might not make it, or that they might have sent you to Plattsburg."

"Sheriff Hanson said if you couldn't get in at Burlington, you might just as well not get in at all. And as to makin' it, I can make it anywhere, anytime." Joshua thought the young man was a bit ruffled, but then Peterson added, "And with anyone I goddamn please," and he grinned.

Out in front of the terminal, parked in the no parking zone, was what had to be the biggest four-by-four Travis had ever seen. "How do you get that thing up so high?"

"Six-inch suspension lift, three-inch body lift."

"Damn." Travis whistled, impressed, as they got set to load the dogs. "Where'd those wheels and chains come from, a front-end loader?"

Peterson just smiled. The '72 Chevy was clear-coated cherry red. There was a Colt cap over the bed. That would be good for the dogs. Joshua hoped he had plenty of weight in the back, but he didn't say anything. He didn't want to miff the boy again.

When Peterson opened the back, Travis saw that the whole bed was filled with sandbags. A two-piece plywood shelf covered them. It was just what the doctor had ordered. He told the dogs to hop up. Buck had no problem, but Joshua gave Jenny-Dog a hand. The truck bed was awfully high, and Jenny was pushing thirteen.

They threw his gear in after the dogs, closed up the back, cleared off the windshield, and were on their way. It felt good to get into the truck. Joshua was still dressed lightly for this kind of weather, but he knew they would have to keep the heater and defroster going full blast to keep the windshield clear.

"What's under the hood?" Joshua asked as they roared out the airport access road.

"Four-fifty-four, two Holly four-barrels."

"How far to the ski area?"

"About seventy-five, eighty miles."

"How long?" Travis added.

Peterson looked at him for a moment. "How are your balls?" he asked.

He was already driving faster than Joshua would have under those conditions.

"Intact," Travis decided. Peterson popped in a tape and let her rip.

The over-built truck skidded as Bill Peterson lay on the juice. A plume of white shot out from his wheels. It wasn't yet five o'clock but there was no light except from the truck's headlights and reflected snow. The snow rushing towards them, reflecting the lights, reminded Joshua of the special effect used in Star Trek when the Enterprise jumped to Warp speed. He wondered how Peterson would be able to know where to turn or how he was even able to stay on the road. *It would be a bitch to make it all this way just to get stuck in a snow bank.*

Peterson read his mind. "Got a Warn 12,000lb. winch."

The truck churned and swerved through the blizzard at an incredible forty miles per hour. On the interstate, behind a plow truck, Peterson cranked it past sixty. Absolute insanity, Travis thought. But he was glad.

Joshua looked through the rear window, trying to make out Buck and Jenny-Dog. He could barely make out their forms tensely crouching on the shelf, trying to hold their balance and grip the plywood with their claws. Joshua knew the dogs were getting knocked around pretty good. He hoped they were all right. He also hoped the local wildlife had the good sense to keep to cover. Especially the big ones.

"How do you carry enough gas to make a run like this?"

"Two twenty gallon tanks. I filled 'em at the airport, compliments of Hertz. You really think you can find that kid alive?"

"I don't know."

"Seems like it's gonna take a miracle for her to survive in this crap."

"Maybe," was all Joshua replied. He had seen miracles happen before. He had also seen people die.

Sheriff Hanson was outside with Jim Beard, Andy Johnson, Nancy Grady and two other members of the ski patrol, one man and one woman. They stayed in pairs, under strict orders not to lose sight of the lodge. Snow was coming down hard and fast, more than two inches per hour, and the murderous winds rushed in from the northwest and swirled with rage as they venturied between the mountains and through the trees. The cold pierced their hi-tech gear, and Hanson admitted to himself that they wouldn't be able to remain out for long.

The volunteer search team re-checked beneath the lodge porches and inside all the sheds and out-buildings in the vicinity of the chalet. Beard and Hanson checked the lift-houses and booths, a risky operation since the lodge was barely visible from the advanced slope lift-house. Only by returning to the intermediate slope were the two men able to once again see the glow from the chalet windows.

Hanson wanted to check along the perimeter of the woods, but he knew that was dangerous. The forest began on the far side of the bunny slope, some fifty to one hundred yards away, and gradually swept back from a rolling open area of meadow and pasture. From fifty yards out the resort lodge was just a glow. From one hundred yards out it was a memory.

"Jim, how about we split up? You take Andy and Nancy and follow the edge of the woods to the right. I'll go with Barb and Paul to the left. Don't go more than ten minutes out. If you don't find nothin', come on back to the slope and head on in."

"Will do, Sam. You know, there are some cross-country ski trails through these woods. Maybe we should check them."

Hanson was cold. He knew the others must be also. He could feel the frostbite trying to take hold on his exposed cheeks. His fingers and toes were numb.

"We could stay out here all night checking all the possibilities. We've already been out too long. Just check the perimeter unless you find signs the kid passed that way. Then get back here and get in."

"Okay, Sam. Good luck."

Yeah, Hanson thought. *Good fuckin' luck.* They hadn't had any luck since it had started to snow. Even now, these experienced winter sportspeople were using cross-country skis instead of snowshoes. They sank down eight to twelve inches as they trudged through the newly fallen snow, especially the point man who was breaking the trail. *Yeah, good fuckin' luck. This little girl was going to need a hell of a lot more than good fuckin' luck.*

Twenty-five minutes later, Jim Beard and his team got back to the lodge. Five minutes afterwards, Sheriff Hanson and the last of the patrol walked in. Kelly Martin's parents looked up hopefully and then fell apart. Sam Hanson couldn't remember ever feeling lower. Not only was the little girl still missing, but in his desperation he and the searchers had probably obscured any trail the little girl might have left. Even if that damn tracker from Wisconsin and his dogs did manage to get in, there was no way Sheriff Hanson could ask him to go out, given the brutal conditions. Hanson tried to reconcile himself to the fact that it was over and that that sonofabitch Leah had been right all along. He sunk down into a sofa and tried to figure out what to do next, or at least what to say. The waiting was pure hell.

"Uh, Sam, we just got a call from an Erin Harper." George Hoffman began.

"Don't tell me... She and her dogs aren't going to make it."

"She said they tried, but couldn't even get to the state line. She sounded real apologetic."

"A lot of good that'll do."

What next? Hanson wondered.

Steiner was on the phone again to his editor. Things didn't look good, he reported.

"This place is like a wake," Andy Johnson commented to Beard as they helped themselves to hot cider and sandwiches that George Hoffman had had set out. Beard nodded silently. Nancy Grady overheard him and was struck to the quick. It was a wake, and it had been all her fault. She started to cry.

Beard put his arm around Nancy. He wasn't sure what to say.

"Don't blame yourself, Nancy. It wasn't your fault." It was the wrong thing. Nancy knew differently as she looked over at the people who had entrusted their daughter to her.

"Where's my daughter? I want my little girl," Diane Martin

cried inconsolably in her husband's arms. All John Martin could do was hold his wife tightly and cry also. The other people at the resort looked on embarrassedly and tried to look away. Couples held each other. Families hugged their kids. It was 4:56.

The "Mr. Coffee" in Kristian's office was empty, so she went to the coffee room down the hall. She needed to stretch anyway. In the coffee room were Laura Hawley and Frank Means, two young associates. Kris smiled and nodded. "How was Cronin's?"

"Crowded," Laura replied, "but fun."

Kris knew what she meant. Cronin's always had a warm, cozy feel to it, especially on rainy days. It was the kind of place where people went on a rainy winter Friday for lunch and stayed until eight o'clock.

"How about that weather they're having back East?" Frank put in politely.

Kristian had had no reason to keep abreast of the weather three thousand miles away. "What weather is that?"

"They're having one hell of a snowstorm throughout New England and New York. The TV report at Cronin's said they had already gotten a foot and were getting new snow at a rate of one to three inches per hour. You should have seen it. With the winds they've got, the drifts are already covering cars in some places."

"And what about that poor little girl?" Laura remarked.

"What little girl?" Kristian queried further, becoming uncomfortable now.

"Some poor kid up at a ski resort in Vermont is missing in that mess. They said they didn't expect to find her alive, possibly not before spring."

It was ridiculous, Kristian knew. How would he get in even if he was called? But she could not help it. Red flags went up. Her stomach tightened.

Chapter Ten

It had taken the KC-135 less than an hour and a half to travel more than eight hundred miles from Wisconsin to Vermont. Now, even driving like maniacs, it took nearly two hours to cover the seventy-seven winding miles from Burlington to the ski lodge.

"There it is!" shouted Peterson.

Travis could just make out the glow coming from the chalet. "Nice going, son. You're one helluva driver."

Peterson grinned.

Travis was surprised that they had made it at all, and they had made it in one piece to boot. But it was almost seven o'clock.

"Look! What's that?" shouted one of the guests looking out the glass on the west side.

A bouncing glow could be seen in the distance, dimming and intensifying with the wind. Hanson and Johnson joined the crowd trying to discern the phenomena. The unexplained luminescence created an eerie anticipation among the guests as it definitely intensified with each moment.

"Maybe it's Bill Peterson," Johnson suggested.

Could it be? Hanson thought. Does he have the team with him? With all he had been doing, the sheriff had not thought to call Burlington to see if Joshua Travis had actually arrived. Stupid oversight.

Now there was no doubt in Hanson's mind. The increasing glow had resolved into distinct bright lights moving like furies in the night. They had to be the plow lights on Bill's pickup. Sam Hanson hoped that nothing living had gotten in the way of the crazy mechanic because Bill Peterson was hauling ass, and the visibility was piss poor.

Peterson plowed full speed through the parking lot and skidded to a stop in front of the main steps. The steps were only half exposed because of the snow. A charge of curiosity and anticipation swept through the chalet. Even Diane Martin looked up. The tension inside the lodge grew thick. People became oblivious to their surroundings. Their only focus was this new development.

Sam Hanson didn't know why, but for some damn reason he felt better as soon as he saw the man from Wisconsin get out of the truck. He decided that he would wait for Mr. Travis to tell him that he and his mutts couldn't go out.

Joshua Travis had a calm, deliberate manner about him, even out in that damn storm. He walked to the back of the pickup, let his dogs loose, and gathered his gear. Sheriff Hanson had forgotten how big Travis was. Even wearing soft moosehide mukluks to go with snowshoes, Joshua appeared very big and very strong, but his beard, streaked with gray, and all his wool clothing gave him a softer, almost mellow look.

But Joshua Paul Travis was anything but mellow as he and his free ranging dogs walked into the lodge. Everyone could tell he was all business. He wasted neither word nor movement as he set his gear down near the door and took charge.

Joshua Travis entered the ski lodge. The warm smell of wood smoke and red cedar struck him hard. Cody flashed through his mind once again. People looked at him like they weren't quite sure whether he was a messiah or a madman, and when the first thing he did was take off his woolen shirt, some people decided. But the temperature in the lodge was near seventy degrees, and the last thing Joshua needed was to get overheated. Sheriff Hanson greeted him. Barry Steiner tried to snap pictures with his pocket Minolta.

"You made it, Mr. Travis! I didn't think you'd be able to get in."

Travis shook his hand briefly. "I had lots of help. Are the Thermoses ready?"

"We've got them all set."

"Put them over by the packs, please," Joshua directed.

Sheriff Hanson pointed to the Martins. "Those are the little girl's parents."

It was an unnecessary gesture. Hell, Travis thought, a blind man could have picked them out. The two men walked over to the couple, followed by the dogs.

"Mr. and Mrs. Martin, my name is Joshua Travis. I know this is difficult but I need you to take me to your room, please." George Hoffman was there, and Barry Steiner was trying to crowd in so he could hear. The manager of the resort suggested that they take the elevator, but to Travis the staircase looked faster so they headed that way.

People were starting to crowd around. Joshua always got a kick out of the way grown men and women would try to cop pats off the dogs like fifteen-year-old boys around fourteen-year-old girls. Jenny-Dog ate up all the attention, grinning in that way that she has, her tail going like a rumba dancer. Buck was more aloof around people, a mark of his shepherd/malamute ancestry. His great size and the way that he carried himself generally kept people from pressing.

The Martins started up the stairs while Joshua had a word with the sheriff. He caught up, taking the stairs two by two. The dogs raced ahead, stopping on the landing to make certain Joshua was following.

"Keep the guests back and out of the way," Hanson told Andy Johnson, posting him at the foot of the stairs, "including that dang reporter."

Interest was high. Johnson had his hands full.

Joshua couldn't help but notice his surroundings as he surveyed the situation. The chalet wasn't very contemporary, but there was an elegant use of tongue-n-groove soft woods and an abundance of glass that gave the resort a special feel. The Martins had a nice room with a large picture window overlooking the slopes, and their own gas log fireplace. The carpet was thick pile and there was a separate area for reading or writing letters that made it almost, but not quite, a suite. Away from the windows, between the fireplace and the ample bathroom, were a king size bed and a cot. Both were made up.

"Does the little girl really sleep in the cot, or does she crawl in bed with you folks?" Travis asked the Martins. He knew young children well enough to know that sleeping arrangements aren't always what you might expect, especially on vacation.

The Martins immediately picked up on the soft-spoken man's use of the present tense. They responded immediately.

"She always goes to bed in the cot. Sometimes, early in the morning, she crawls into bed with us."

"Has the linen been changed since the little girl was last in the cot?"

George Hoffman provided the answer to that. "Our establishment makes it a policy to change all sheets and pillow-cases every single day. It gives...."

"Damn," Travis muttered to himself. "How about the mattress cover?"

"Well, there is a limit to what we can..."

Travis didn't wait for him to finish. He ripped the cot apart, throwing the blankets and sheets on the floor. He hoped that enough of Kelly Martin had gotten into the mattress cover and mattress to give the dogs a scent.

"Do you have any of Kelly's laundry?"

Sam Hanson still had the bag of articles that Ted Leah had used.

"Here are the things that the State Police dog handler used. Can you still use them?" Travis peered into the bag.

"Sure. Dump all that stuff on the cot."

"Leah's dogs found this scarf also, outside in the snow. It belongs to Kelly, but it may have been handled by some other kids."

"Let's pass on that one," Travis advised. He noticed the parents were breaking down again and going for something over by the dresser.

"Don't touch that!" he shouted louder than he had intended and startling Mrs. Martin into tears. He went over to the Martins and picked up the teddy bear and blue PJ's on the floor. George Hoffman looked embarrassed and ready to give some chambermaid hell for being so careless, but Joshua would have kissed her. He added them to the pile already on the cot.

"Uppa!" Travis commanded. Both dogs immediately jumped on the cot.

"Get the scent, guys, get it. Come-on Buck, come-on Jenny girl, get the scent! That's Kelly we're looking for, now get the scent and get to the trail!"

The dogs nuzzled the articles enthusiastically, including the mattress, imprinting scents and images, vibrations and patterns in their brains. They didn't waste any time. Travis stuffed some of the girl's things into a clean garbage bag, and that was it. They went back downstairs. Now the test would come. Sheriff Hanson noticed that this man didn't use ice tongs. He wondered if that was good or bad.

Joshua packed the Thermoses in the top of his pack and put on his Pendleton shirt.

"Can someone show me exactly where the little girl was last seen?"

"I can," volunteered Nancy. "You can see it from inside."

She led him to the large wall of windows on the south side of the chalet. Through the windows, with a spotlight on, you could just make out the remnants of the snowman: two large humps on the ground, the smaller head completely buried.

"Out there is where Kelly was playing before she went off. My daughter and another little girl were the last ones to see her." Nancy started to cry again.

"It's also where we found the scarf," added the sheriff. "The kids used it on the snowman. Be careful out there. We didn't fill in the hole."

"Do you have a topographical map of the area?" Travis asked.

The manager hurried over. "No, but we do have these maps of the trails in the vicinity."

"That'll do. Any shelters along any of these trails?"

"Not until one to three miles out, depending on which trail you take."

Joshua doubted the little girl would have made it that far. He put on his sweater, hooded sweatshirt, and ski mask. Then he opened the doors. It was blowing to beat the band and everybody else moved back, but he was starting to get warm. The dogs were whining and barking, anxious to get out, but they waited for the man from Wisconsin. He pulled on some black Gore-tex over-pants and his red Gore-tex/down parka. He pulled down his ski mask, put on goggles and woolen gloves, and adjusted his hoods. Joshua Travis jammed large, gauntlet cuffed, fleece lined leather mitts into his jacket pockets. Then he saw that Sheriff Hanson was getting ready to go outside too.

"You'll just be in the way, Sheriff, and I don't have enough gear for two men," Travis told him, knowing what he was thinking.

"I can't ask you to go out there by yourself."

"We'll do better by ourselves."

"What if you need some help out there?"

"We'll be okay."

"You sure?"

"I'm sure," Joshua told him.

"At least take this walkie-talkie," Jim Beard offered. "We'll keep someone manning the receiver."

"Okay. Thanks." Travis agreed. He didn't have much confidence in the hand held radio transceiver. He had used them before and found them to be unreliable under adverse conditions, especially where there were a lot of hills. He evaluated the added weight to his pack against the possible usefulness of the device but decided to take it anyway. If it worked, it might come in handy.

Travis picked up the tracking gear and the bag of laundry in one hand and his pack in the other and took the dogs outside. At the halfway point of the steps, where they met the drifting snow, he put on his snowshoes and got into his pack. He called for his dogs, and the team marched around to the side of the chalet that had the light on the snowman. It wasn't easy going on any of them, especially the dogs. Joshua worried about Jenny.

He put the laundry and the teddy bear to the dogs again and set them to finding the trail, but it was a monstrous night. Joshua Travis knew that any trail there might have been was long covered and well trampled by all the previous searchers. The wind was pure murder. With his outdoors savvy and dressed as he was he could handle the cold. But if the wind blew him over he would be in trouble. He stood with his back to it the best he could and watched his dogs.

"Go Find!" he told them when he first sent them out, but after that he didn't say anything because he didn't need to and because he was afraid that they would. It was going to take a miracle to find

Kelly Martin alive that night, and that night did not seem like a night for miracles.

People in the lodge crowded over to the picture window on the side where Joshua and the dogs were working and tried to watch what was going on. It was hard to see much of anything. The whirling, wind driven snow obscured almost everything, and the window was fogging up.

"This guy Travis is a little different from Leah, eh?" Deputy Johnson observed.

"You can say that again," replied Hanson.

"He sure don't handle his dogs like Leah. And for that matter, his dogs just look like big mutts. One thing you got to give Leah, his dogs are top of the line."

Hanson didn't say anything. He was trying hard to see what was going on. It was difficult, but what he could see was the damnedest thing he ever had seen. Andy was right. This Mr. Travis sure didn't work like any other dog handler Hanson had ever watched. Travis had both dogs running around loose in the night, and after he gave them the scent from the laundry he just stood still, his back to the wind. He didn't even appear to be encouraging the dogs.

Nancy was staring out the window, watching intently. The tension and the guilt were catching up to her. She was sobbing.

"What the hell's he doing?" Bill Peterson piped out.

The Sheriff still didn't say anything. If it had been Leah, he'd have thought the man was slacking, just going through the motions without any intentions of following through. After being out there himself, he wouldn't rightly blame him. But with this fellow he didn't know, so he kept his mouth shut. And by God those damn dogs at least sure looked like they were looking for something. You had to give them that much.

The dogs were hustling every which way, casting for the scent. They stuck their noses deep into the snow and up into the cold wind. Then they gave up on the wind and kept their heads down, moving all over and popping their faces in and out of the snow. Buck marked everywhere they went.

The dogs scrambled for quite a few minutes, and Sheriff Hanson knew Josh Travis had to be getting cold. He wasn't sure but he thought maybe Travis was watching the black female more than that monster wolf-like dog, so he tried to watch her too. She worked much like the other one at first, but then Hanson noticed she was starting to dig holes. Dig a hole and pop out; move a little, dig another hole and pop out again. She was getting an irregular series of holes, and some were deep enough for her to stick half of her long body into. Then she dug one last hole and it happened...

Jenny-Dog scrambled back out and started going crazy. She was barking like mad and spinning around, diving back into the hole for a few seconds and then going crazy again. The other dog raced over to where she was and he dove into the same hole and he started going crazy too. Both of them spinning and barking like all get out!

No one inside was sure of what they were seeing. They all held their breath. Then they watched the man from Wisconsin walk over to where his dogs were, calm as could be, and squat down beside them. He patted both but he held onto the big shepherd dog. The black one disappeared out of the light. Travis still had the big one and was doing something to him. Putting on the tracking harness was what Hanson and Johnson guessed. Then, with that big dog still barking, he stood up, attached the guide line to his utility belt, and put on his overmitts. Holding onto a guide rope attached to that giant dog, Joshua Travis left the lighted area and disappeared. Hanson was ashamed of what he had thought. He was damned glad he had at least had the sense to keep his yap shut.

Chapter Eleven

Kristian couldn't take it anymore. She had not been able to concentrate since hearing about the child lost in the blizzard. She found herself making careless mistakes, and Kristian Fisk-Travis would not tolerate mistakes in her work.

"This is crazy," she said, mostly to herself and then, "I'm taking lunch now," she announced to David, one of her associates. She threw on the European trench coat she had purchased in Florence, grabbed an umbrella from the stand, and made her way through the mist and the rain to Cronin's.

Cronin's was old and smelled of cigarette smoke and stale beer. The woodwork was oak and walnut stained dark. The bar rails and trim were brass. The windows were dirty. Kristian loved it.

The lunch crowd was gone. The bartenders and waitresses were casually taking care of business in preparation for the after work regulars.

"Well hello there, Miss Krissy. I missed you at lunch. What'll it be?"

Shamus Cronin was a large, rotund Irishman. With thick hardworking arms and thin gray hair, he was the only person in the world permitted to call her Krissy.

"Is it too late to get a roast beef sandwich, Shamus?"

"Not for you, my pretty colleen. Will you be wantin' fries with that sandwich?"

"No. Thank you. Just a beer." She hesitated and then added, "and maybe a shot. C.C. up." The bartender looked at her.

Shamus Cronin served up the drinks. When he brought out the sandwich, he quietly asked, "Is everything all right, Kristian?"

The woman tried to smile. "Sure. Say, I hear they're having quite a snowstorm out east."

"That they are, miss."

"Laura and Frank were saying that a little girl is lost in that storm somewhere."

"Aye, up in Vermont, the poor kid. And think of the wee child's poor mother and father." Shamus shook his head.

Half-way through her sandwich, Kristian could eat no more.

"Jim, how about seeing if there's anything more on the news about the storm out east."

"Sure Kris." The second bartender cordially switched the channel from the game highlights to the news. The reporter was talking about Afghanistan and the Olympics. The next story dealt with the economy: The Federal Reserve was trying to bring inflation under control by restricting the money supply. It didn't seem to be working. At long last there was a report on the blizzard. Kristian watched impatiently as the television showed endless pictures of snarled traffic in Boston and hardy sojourners emptying grocery store shelves in Albany. Finally the report she was anxious about came.

"And finally this update on the fate of little Kelly Martin, the six-year-old girl missing from the Jay Peak ski resort in Vermont. The Associated Press is reporting that a second tracking-dog team has joined the search in the blizzard conditions. Earlier we reported that a Vermont State Police K-9 team had been unsuccessful in its attempt to locate the missing child, although it did locate a scarf belonging to the little girl. Privately authorities are saying that unless Kelly Martin somehow found shelter, her chances for survival are almost non-existent."

Kristian was pale. Cronin wondered what was wrong. He poured her another drink.

The architect returned to her office distracted but not distraught. She closed the door to her office. There's no sense in going nuts, she told herself. Hell, it might not even be him. She tried calling the resort.

Damn, a busy signal, again and again. *Maybe the lines are down. Perhaps the Vermont State Police.*

"Yes, I was wondering if you could give me any information about the second dog team involved in the search for the little girl lost at the ski resort?"

Damn, placed on hold.

"This is Captain Herman. May I help you?"

"Captain, I was wondering if you could give me any information about the second dog team involved in the search for the little girl at the ski resort?"

"What second dog team?"

"The news said a second tracking-dog team had been called in."

"I'm sorry, but I don't know anything about a second tracking-dog team. You'll have to contact whoever originated that story."

Damn. Jon VanStavern would know, or Emily at the office, but Kristian could not bring herself to call them.

Kristian did not know where the story had originated or how to contact the national news station that had aired it without getting caught up in an endless game of telephone tag, but she did have a local contact who might be able to help.

Maureen Anderson was a freelance writer who had been a reporter and journalist for the San Francisco Examiner. Like Kristian, she had worked hard to become successful in a highly competitive, male dominated field. Five years ago, when Kristian had first returned to the San Francisco area, Maureen had done an article on her fledgling practice. The article led to several important commissions for Kristian and ultimately helped to secure the partnership offer from Wheaton, Princeton and South.

Maureen and Kristian had become quite friendly, especially during the period that Anderson coordinated the *Home /Living* section of the paper. Kristian occasionally pointed out things of architectural interest or importance to her, and she returned the favor by featuring articles on several of Wheaton's projects. They had drifted apart when Maureen moved on to an editorial position in the newsroom and then finally to freelance, but they still called each other now and again and got together for drinks.

Kristian worked her way through her Rolodex to find Maureen's number. It wasn't where it should have been. She found it; dialed...

"Anderson...," the writer answered.

"Hi, Maureen, it's Kristian, Kristian Fisk-Travis."

"Well hello Kristian Fisk-Travis. It's been a while. How are you?"

"I'm fine. How are you doing?"

"Can't complain. What's up?"

"Maureen, I have a favor to ask."

"What's up? Just remember, I'm not in the *Home* section of the Examiner anymore."

"I know." Kristian hesitated.

"What's up, Kris?"

"Do you know anything about the little girl that's lost in the blizzard in Vermont?"

Maureen Anderson was puzzled. The question had caught her completely off guard. "Just what I've seen on TV and in the paper. Kid wandered off and got lost. They've been looking for her, but it doesn't sound like they expect to find her alive. Why?"

"I know some people out there. I just wondered if they were involved." Kristian didn't like lying to Maureen. "I heard on the news that a second tracking-dog team had been called in. Do you know anything about that?"

"Not at all. You want me to do some checking?"

"Could you?"

"Sure. Let me put you on hold while I make some calls."

"Thanks." Kristian was on hold. Three minutes later, the writer returned.

"Kris? All they have at the paper is that a dog handler from Wisconsin was called in. They don't know if he made it or not. Hey, aren't you from Wisconsin? Any connection? Kris?... Kristian, are you there?..."

There was a long pause. Finally Kristian replied, "Thanks, Maureen, I owe you one," and hung up.

Chapter Twelve

"*Taknokwunu! Why do you rage so?*"

"*The Pahanas in this land have lost the old ways, Gogyeng Sowuhti. They have become selfish and greedy. They have forgotten how to work together. They have forgotten how to share. They no longer value community. The Pahanas must be taught a lesson.*"

"*Taknokwunu, you harm the good as well as the bad. You punish the innocent as you punish the guilty.*"

"*There are no innocents, Gogyeng Sowuhti.*"

"*There are the children.*"

Taknokwunu pauses for a moment and considers the words of the old woman. Then he replies.

"*It cannot be helped.*"

The medicine-woman shivers and shakes. Goose-flesh shows on her arms and neck. Her son's wife places another blanket over her. Build up the fire she tells the granddaughters. Build up the fire.

It was Jenny-Dog who first picked up the trail. Travis knew that in itself was a miracle. He went over to the dogs, knelt down and praised them both. Buck was trying to make up for being second by his eagerness, but Joshua held him back as he sent Jenny off. *Tough luck old Buckaroo, he smiled to himself, but you've just been beaten out by a twelve-year-old bitch.*

Buck was excited as Travis harnessed him up. That was good

because Joshua didn't want Jenny getting too far ahead. Travis put on his leather mitts, picked up the guide rope, secured it to his utility belt and headed out into the night. He didn't know what time it was, probably about seven-thirty, but it was dark as hell. Travis gave Buck ten feet of lead. Into the beating snow, he could not always see the dog at the end of the rope. Often he could only feel him jumping and pulling. He carried two battery operated lanterns, a small one pinned to his parka and a larger one, hung from his waist. He did not bother with the lights so long as they were in the open. There was a constant roar from the wind. It changed pitch when it changed direction, but for the most part the wind stayed behind them. That was good for now, but Travis wondered if Buck would hear Jenny-Dog. It also meant that they would have to face it going back. Joshua steadied Buck down and leaned back. He used the big dog for balance as they followed Jenny's trail.

The snow was packed hard except for the several inches of fresh powder and the places where it was drifting, but Joshua knew that probably would not last. The previous searchers had packed down the area near the lodge. The trails used for cross-country skiing were groomed daily with a Cat. He hoped Kelly Martin had stayed on a cross-country trail and found shelter somewhere along the way. Joshua knew that if she strayed far from the path she would be dead. He skimmed through the snow at a nice even pace. He didn't want Buck catching up to Jenny or crossing the track she was following. And he did not want any unexpected surprises, like holes in the snow or blown tree branches, that could trip him up. His heart sank as Buck led him off the cross-country trail and across an open area towards the woods.

The storm was as brutal as before and getting worse. Joshua tried not to think about it. He concentrated on his balance and his pace and on watching for the woods. Two hard and fast rules he had learned from his Poppa were ringing clear in his head. The first one was: KEEP CALM; and the other, IF YOU SWEAT YOU DIE!

Slowly they progress, farther and farther away from the warmth and the light of the lodge. Two dogs and a man from Merrill, Wisconsin out in a winter storm that no one should be out in, a storm that is completely ruthless, in search of a little girl who has been out in that same storm for at least seven hours. It's utter madness! But the man does not think about the madness, even though he knows of it, as he concentrates on each step and the task at hand. And the giant Bernese mountain-German shepherd mixed dog does not think of the madness as he fights and struggles to prove that he is just as good a dog as the twelve-year-old bitch that has beaten him to the trail. And the twelve-year-old bitch does not think of the madness as she does what she believes she has been born to do: search for human beings, the finding of which brings great pleasure to the Human Being that she loves above all other things in the universe.

It is hard on her at first. The snow is deep and packed hard and there are all those other human scents to sort through. She has to keep digging deep holes to make certain, and there is nothing in the air at all. An image flashes in her mind, a pattern begins to form. Gradually, as she works her way from the big house, it begins to get easier for her. The image flashes more frequently. The pattern is more definite. She doesn't have to check as frequently to be sure. The snow isn't packed quite so hard when she digs. And, best of all, there aren't so many other human trails to cross and confuse her. The traveling gets harder as the snow gets deeper, but the trail gets stronger so she fights on, and on. Then she enters the woods.

Jenny-Dog enters the woods, wary of the movement and the cracking of the frozen trees. The trail makes an abrupt turn and she has to pick her way carefully through the undergrowth. Soon she is in ecstasy. The snow is not quite as deep, and the trail is twice as strong. Only a part of the wind follows her in, and there are bonuses like broken twigs and brushed bark, and what is this? Even droppings from a parallel trail she thought she had been aware of! She spins and barks in excitement and knows it will be easy from here on. She will have this one in no time now and then

*He will come and He will be happy. And Jenny pushes forward with re-
newed enthusiasm. Following the trail is easy for her now, and she moves
along quickly and smoothly until suddenly, in the dark and blowing snow,
she hits her head on something hard, and the trail abruptly ends.*

Travis wanted to hold up for a minute but he didn't. He wanted
to scan the area for any sign that Jenny-Dog had passed that way,
but he knew that every second counted. He wondered why Buck
had decided to leave the hard-pack, and he hoped the young dog
knew what he was doing. He hoped Buck was following a ground
trail and not some sound or airborne scent that could have blown in
from anywhere. Buck had always been an ace in training, occasionally even beating Jenny to the target, but this was only his fourth
actual rescue and Travis was worried. If Buck made a mistake, they
could easily become lost. Travis might have to make camp without
finding the child or Jenny-Dog or anything. And that was one of the
better scenarios.

*Jenny-Dog sneezes and is puzzled. What was that? Where did the
trail go to? Though she can see nothing, she knows there is a large mass in
front of her. She knows where the trail ended, but where did it go from
there? She hunts quickly on each side of the mass, digging and sniffing,
sniffing and digging. The scent is strong but she finds nothing. Then it
suddenly strikes her that the human being she is looking for is inside that
unknown, formless mass she has struck her head against. Jenny does not
understand how it can be, but she knows it to be so. She can sense it is so,
and she can smell it is so, even in the air.*

*The black bitch tries the mass at several places before deciding on the
best spot to attack it. She digs and paws and scrapes and will tear the
whole mass apart if she must to reach what she is searching for. Suddenly
she is in. First her head burrows through. She struggles and manages her
whole body. She can see absolutely nothing, but she knows this is it. She
can smell the young human all around her, but she cannot hear the young
human as she knows she should.*

Jenny-Dog still hasn't found the child. Where is she? Jenny is in near panic. She wants to race and spin. Instead, she stands dead still, sniffs and listens. THERE! She discovers the second mound, softer and much smaller than the first. THERE! Jenny-Dog finds the best place and begins digging again. THERE! In the dark she can feel, but not see, the yellow bottoms of green rubber boots. THERE IS THE CHILD!

Jenny whines and creeps towards the boots. She nudges them but the little girl does not respond. Jenny nudges the boots again. Still, there is no response. DIG! Jenny-Dog paws at the mound. The snow is thick but soft. DIG! Jenny-Dog paws and scratches and digs. SOMETHING HARD! Jenny hits something hard. She can dig no further. TRY SOMEPLACE ELSE! She tries to penetrate another part of the mound. HARD, NO GOOD. TRY SOMETHING ELSE! She moves along the breadth and length of the snow covered hump. THERE! Jenny-Dog finds it. OPENING! She locates a small breech in the snow covered mound. The scent is strong. NO SOUNDS. DIG! She digs in the snow and enlarges an opening leading to a log, the object she was unable to penetrate before. INSIDE! She digs through more snow and partially uncovers a one-hundred-year-old maple log, dead for three years, down for two, hollow and cracked and covered by drifting snows. INSIDE! THE YOUNG HUMAN IS INSIDE!

Jenny-Dog barks, then squeezes into the log. The space is tight. She cannot see, but the scent is strong. Carefully, the ungainly bitch squeezes partly through the log. Finally, the unrelenting dog is rewarded. CONTACT!

The child's face is cold but soft and salty. There is no movement, but Jenny can smell the human is ALIVE. Jenny nuzzles the child. She moves slightly. Jenny-Dog nuzzles her again. The girl reflexively tries to turn her face. Lick, nudge, whine. NOTHING! Woof! The little girl opens her eyes. She sees nothing and closes them again. Nudge, nudge, whine, nuzzle, lick, Woof! The child opens her eyes again. Nothing. Something smells. Something warm. Jenny-Dog whines. TIGHT. TOO TIGHT.

Kelly Martin closes her eyes one last time.

Jenny-Dog continues to whine, nudging and licking the child peri-odically. Soon He will come. He will come and make all things well. Soon He will come. He will come soon. COME SOON!

The winds picked up and the going was rough. The snow was powder fine and needle sharp. It drifted into whorls and waves across the open field. Even when Joshua was able to skim through the powder his snowshoe tips would catch in the waves of the drifts and throw him off balance. It was rough on Joshua, but it was harder on Buck. He had tried to take a short cut and it had been a mistake. Now he had to rectify it. Buck fought and bounded through the deep snow. He had to pause every few yards to catch his breath.

"Find Jenny-Dog, Buck," Joshua encouraged. "Find Jenny." He knew they were losing time.

The great dog continued to struggle.

Joshua had trouble keeping his balance in the changing winds while following Buck through the drifting snow. He tried to float and skim across the snow, as his father had taught him, but his pack weighed nearly thirty pounds. Every time Buck stopped, the guide-rope went slack. One time when the rope went slack and the wind changed at the same time, Travis went down.

"How long has he been out there?" Steiner asked Sheriff Hanson, still standing by the window.

"About twenty minutes, maybe a half-hour." It seemed like more.

"How long you figure 'till we know something?" Peterson asked.

"Hard to say, Bill, especially with this guy. But given the weather out there, my guess is we'll know what he's found within an hour. Two at the outside."

The Martins looked at the clock. Steiner called it in.

"Buck, Come!" Travis called, trying not to panic.

The big dog worked his way back.

"Stay!" Travis commanded, using the hand signal as well as the command.

"Stay!"

Joshua used the rope to pull himself up against the resistance of the obedient dog. He didn't bother to brush himself off. The wind would do that for him. *God bless wool and down and Gore-tex. And you too, Buck.*

"Okay, Buck, now go find Jenny!"

Buck returned to his struggle in the lead. At long last, he regained the hard packed trail with only a foot of new powder. More importantly, it was the trail on which Jenny-Dog had passed.

Chapter Thirteen

It was no good being at the office. Her work and her colleagues were closing in on her. She couldn't think straight. She had to leave. Among the men who watched her leave was Nathan Goodman.

The cool, wet air felt good on Kristian's cheeks and neck as she left her office building on Montgomery Street and started to walk home. It was a long walk across several hills to the stylish townhouse on Pacific Avenue, but she wanted the exercise if not the pain. Stiletto heeled shoes assured her the pain. She wore them often, despite her natural five feet, ten inches. If men felt inadequate because of her height, that was their problem. But now they were her problem, and by the time Kristian reached Powell Street she was carrying her shoes, walking through the wet and the cold in her stocking feet.

Shit! She thought as she passed briskly through the light rain and dripping trees and awnings. *This wasn't supposed to happen.*

At the San Francisco Examiner, Bob Woods called Maureen Anderson.

"Hey, Maureen, we got some more on that Vermont story you were asking about. That guy from Wisconsin? The one they were trying to fly in? Well it turns out he made it. Doesn't look like it will make much difference though. It's so bad out there they've even ordered the snowplows off the roads. It looks like the kid is pretty much a goner."

"Did you get a name on the guy from Wisconsin?"

"Yeah, it's Travis. Joshua Paul Travis."

Anderson was awestruck. "Well I'll be damned," she muttered under her breath.

"We did a file search, and it turns out this guy has a pretty impressive record. You remember those canoeists up in the Boundary Waters, and that congressman's son and daughter-in-law out in Colorado? And there was that kid in the collapsed project in Chicago? Well that was all this guy. You think I should follow up on this story?"

Maureen was disappointed in herself. She had never made the connection. "Up to you." She did not tell him that that was exactly what she intended to do.

Joshua Paul *Travis*, she thought to herself.

Chapter Fourteen

Travis knew they had entered the woods. At ground level there was an illusory semblance of shelter from the treacherous winds. But high in the canopy the roaring air and snow raged in full fury, cracking off limbs and branches and felling mature trees, deciduous and conifers alike. Joshua had first hand knowledge of high winds and falling trees. He knew about broken spars and widow-makers. A chill ran down his spine. One not caused by the sub-zero temperature.

They had to be on one of the frequently groomed cross-country trails. No deer path would be that open or have such a firm base. There was much half-covered debris from the trees littering the trail. Joshua usually did not see it until it was too late. He had to negotiate the broken twigs and fallen branches carefully so he would not hang up or break his bear paws. When the wind let up or changed directions Travis could see the snow covered trees and the trail ahead. Then a sheet of snow would cascade down and he would be traveling blind again.

Buck was pulling hard. Joshua shortened the lead by one foot. He tried to listen for Jenny-Dog but he heard nothing. He did not think it would be long now. Travis knew he hadn't gone as far as it might have seemed, but he also knew that a six-year-old kid dressed in a snowsuit and kid boots would have a limited range, even under good conditions. When Buck pulled him off the trail and turned into the woods proper, Joshua Travis knew he was close.

"Hold up, Buck,"

Buck stopped and went into a half-sit. But he was too excited. He stood again and barked.

"Steady, buddy. This will just take a moment."

Travis didn't want to stop, but he knew he had to. In the woods, he would hang up for sure if he did not remove his snowshoes. He considered leaving them stuck in the snow by the edge of the trail but decided against it. He would need them to get back, and the chance of them blowing over and being covered by a drift was too great. He hated taking the time, but he removed his pack and rigged the snowshoes to it. Then he saddled up again and switched on the light attached to his chest.

"Okay, Buck. Let's go get Jenny and the kid."

Buck barked and lunged forward. He wound through the trees and climbed over the downed limbs and underbrush. The man followed with great difficulty. The fresh snow was shin deep and the boulders and logs were cold slick. Vibram cleated boots would have been better than mukluks, but there was nothing to do. He had to choose his steps carefully. Twice he slipped and fell. Three times he caught a snow-laden branch or an unseen limb in the head. But only once had they gotten so fouled that he had to get out of the pack to get clear. The trees groaned and creaked. Limbs cracked off and fell to the ground with a muffled *whomp*. He hated it. There was nothing he could do. Find the kid and get the hell out of the woods as fast as possible. It was all he could hope for. Seven minutes later Buck led him to the large mound. It was after eight P.M.

Travis inspected the mound with the light, but he was not sure what he was looking at. He whistled and called for Jenny-Dog. There was no reply.

"Buck, where's Jenny-Dog? Find Jenny!"

The big dog was already searching the area. It didn't take him long to discover the entrance Jenny had made, but Buck could not fit through, except for his head, and he got stuck. Travis eased him back out and had him stay. He took off his pack and utility belt and got out his field shovel and knife. Carefully, very carefully, he enlarged the opening. He still wasn't sure what he was dealing with, but Joshua knew he didn't want it coming down, whatever it was.

"Stay here," he told Buck as he crawled through with his lights and his belt. He stayed on his hands and knees. He still wasn't sure what he was dealing with. And he still didn't see Jenny. He whistled again. This time he heard a whine.

"Jenny-girl, where are you?"

Jenny whined again. Travis removed his goggles and turned both lights in the direction he had heard his dog.

"Jenny-Dog!" he called a second time.

She let out a sharp, "Yip!"

Joshua spotted the second, smaller mound. Then he saw the boots! Travis knelt down by the second mound and cleared away some snow. He discovered the log from which the child's boots were protruding. *Where's Jenny?* He wondered. Why wasn't she at his side?

Travis scanned with the light. He still did not see her.

"Jenny-Dog,"

Jenny whined. *Okay. She's okay but she'll have to wait.* He was afraid to call the little girl's name. He knew she would not answer.

Don't be dead, Travis muttered to himself.

"Easy now, Jenny. Are you okay? Just stay put a minute. I'll be right there." Joshua still wasn't certain what the circumstances were. He knew he had to see if the child was still alive. His first-aid training had taught him to be careful to avoid sudden jarring or motion. A cold heart is especially prone to ventricular arrhythmia, even a young one. He carefully attempted to withdraw Kelly from the log.

Her jacket snagged. He could not dislodge her.

Travis knew that time was of the essence. If Kelly Martin wasn't already dead, Joshua knew that her soul might slip from her body at any second. But he also knew that now, more than ever, he had to do things by the numbers. No mistakes.

Joshua removed his overmitts and set them aside, leaving on only his woolen gloves. He cleared snow from the log with his knife and hand-ax. He scanned the log with the light, searching for a seam. Cautiously, the experienced woodsman wedged the knife into the seam. He tapped it with the butt of the ax and wiggled it side-to-side with his hand. The seam widened. Travis repeated the procedure, not knowing the thickness of the wood, fearing for the safety of the child.

After several wedgings with the knife, Travis could follow the line of the seam close to the end of the log where the little girl's feet came out. With one deft swing of the small ax into the edge of the log the wood split. Access to the child was attained. Using the ax as a lever, Joshua split the log further and cautiously removed Kelly Martin. Jenny-Dog freed herself and raced to him.

"Over there, Jenny. Stay!" Jenny-Dog felt slighted, but she did what she was told.

Travis picked up his goggles and wiped the lens with his hand-kerchief. He held them in front of the girl's face, close to her nose and mouth. He flashed the hand lantern on the lens.

"C'mon, sweetheart, breathe." He had to see if the child was breathing on her own. If not, Joshua would start CPR even though he did not think it would do much good. *Not again,* Joshua prayed. *C'mon, Big Guy, help us out.* Maybe Jesus Christ or the prophet Elisha or Guy Macauley could breathe life into the dead, but Joshua Travis did not think he would be able to. He didn't want to have to put his lips to the cold lips of the child. He had been that route before.

Either God or Guy Macauley answered his prayer. A tiny mist

formed on the goggle lens.

"Jenny! Come here, girl!"

Jenny-Dog raced to his side again, the insult forgotten.

"Down!" Travis ordered. He lay the unconscious child alongside the dog, her head on the dog's ribs. "Stay still, Jenny. I'll just be a moment."

Joshua quickly shined the light around the interior of the large mound and crawled back through the entrance.

"Easy, Buck." Buck had already dug out and curled into the snow. Travis knew he would be all right. He grabbed his backpack and dragged it through the opening into the shelter. He unzipped the pack's back pocket and spread out the foil *space blanket* on the ground. Next, he undid the roll of closed-cell foam strapped to the top of the pack. He opened the bottom compartment and removed the down sleeping bag from its compression sac. Travis carefully shook the sleeping bag to restore its loft, then he lay it out on the foam and opened it up. Now he was ready. He knelt down and took up the child in his arms.

"Over here, girl," he called to Jenny. "Lie down on the bag."

Jenny-Dog was in heaven, but Travis had more in mind than reward. He lay Kelly Martin next to the dog in the sleeping bag and gently removed her boots. He zipped the little girl and the dog into the tapered bag.

"Stay still, Jenny. I know you might get warm but just hang in there and stay." The dog did not like the bag over her, but she did what Joshua told her.

Travis didn't check the girl further. Not yet. But every second was critical. He called Buck.

Buck nosed into the large mound opening, not so far that he would get stuck again.

"C'mon buddy. I'll help you in."

Once inside, Buck shook the snow off and raced over to

Jenny-Dog, licking her face. Jenny looked up and whined.

"Steady, girl. Buck, come over here." Joshua ordered.

The giant dog came around, and Travis had him lie next to the child but outside the sleeping bag.

"Stay! And don't lick her, either of you."

Travis took out the two homemade tin-can reflector candles and lit them. He placed them on the diagonal corners of the space blanket, turned off his breast light and quickly shined the other lantern around. He tried to assess what had happened and exactly what their situation was.

"Well I'll be darned," he murmured quietly. "So that's how you made it."

The trunk of a large maple tree, at least one hundred and fifty years old, stood a few feet away. A second old sugar maple and a couple of widowmakers, or maybe they were young trees, had lodged in the main crotch of the great old tree. Over the years, shrub vines, probably blackberry, maybe some poison ivy, had woven their way through and around the fallen trees, forming a natural wickiup. The winter's snow had enveloped the loosely woven structure, sealing it against the storm, providing protection from the wind.

The snow covered log where the child had been found Travis knew to be some animal's lair. The tuffs of fur and smears of fecal pellets on Kelly's jacket testified to that. What Kelly was doing there he could not even begin to guess. It did not matter. It had saved her life. It had turned out to be a night for miracles after all. Joshua knew they would have to keep coming.

He could still hear the storm raging above. He didn't take time to wonder if the shelter would hold. Instead, Joshua Travis dug out the small white-gas stove and a bottle of fuel. He pumped the bottle, primed the pan with paste, and lit the stove. He placed it as close to the child and the dogs as he dared and carefully poked two small holes through the snow covered mound for ventilation. He closed the entrance to the mound with his pack. Joshua Travis had done all he could to raise the temperature of the surroundings. Now it was decision time.

He again surveyed the interior of their *wickiup* and approximated some measurements. It would be tight but he thought he could set up his tent within the shelter. That would further conserve heat and put one more layer between them and the elements. Travis knew that most of the structural protection the tent would afford them would be psychological, but he also knew that an important part of survival was psychological.

The tent had a height of forty-nine inches. That wouldn't be a problem close to the maple trunk. The tent's base was one hundred and four inches by eighty-four. The one hundred and four inch dimension might be close, but Travis felt he could make it work. He didn't know about the fly.

Joshua wanted to get the tent set quickly, but he knew that if he tried to rush things it would only make matters worse, especially in the poor light and cramped quarters. He forced himself to be as methodical as possible. All the while he spoke to the unconscious child and the dogs.

"Buck! Over here, boy." Working from his knees, or a squat, he slid the sleeping bag with Jenny and the child as close to the leeward perimeter of the shelter as possible. He placed the stove and tin-can candles nearby.

"Okay, Buck, back down."

He had the big dog lie on the edge of the bag once more. Then Travis unstrapped the tent from his backpack and shook it from its compression sac.

"Hang in there, sweetheart. Everything's going to be just fine."

He assembled the shock-corded Easton aluminum poles and spread out the tent, approximating the best orientation.

"Things are getting nice and warm. Everything's going to be

okay. Just a few more minutes and we'll be snug as a bug in a rug," he told the still unconscious child.

He threaded five poles through the sleeves he had specially color coded, and secured the ends with the securing pins.

"Here we go, honey. Slick as a whistle. Hmm, it's going to be tight here but we can make it." He re-oriented the tent and bent one Easton pole to accommodate the limb.

"There we go, guys. All done. Buck, kennel!" The big dog entered the tent. Travis had yet to remove the harness and lead.

"Okay, Jen, steady now. I'm just going to slide you guys inside." He slid the child and dog filled sleeping bag into the tent and hung the tin-can candles from suspended hooks fastened to the interior top, their flames protected by the can lids. The white-gas stove had to remain outside the tent. Joshua moved it close by.

Joshua shined the light on Kelly Martin's face. She was still bundled in her filthy snowsuit, its hood secured over a wool hat. Her eyes were partly open but she had a glassy, apathetic stare. Joshua couldn't be certain in that light, but he thought there might be some discoloration in the exposed parts of her cheeks. He knew the signs well. And he knew there would be no returning to the lodge before he had warmed and stabilized the child. If he *could* stabilize the child.

Travis opened the sleeping bag as little as he had to and removed his gloves. He carefully unzipped Kelly's snowsuit and gently reached beneath her layers of clothing. She wore a sweater over a sweatshirt which itself was over cotton duo-fold long johns. *Way to go, Mama. Cotton's no good, but your over protectiveness probably saved your daughter's life.* Kelly's long johns were moist. Her skin was cold and clammy. Joshua could smell urine. He knew her socks were damp. Jenny-Dog whined.

"Take it easy, girl. You've done your job. Now let me do mine. Just stay still a while longer so's I can get her changed."

Buck looked up from his curl, not wanting to be left out.

"You too, Buck. You did a good job too." Travis told the dog as he went to his pack. The big dog's head went back down on his paws.

Joshua returned to the semi-conscious child with two pair of his woolen socks, a navy wool/poly blend T-shirt, a heavy Woolrich lumberjack shirt, a spare wool watch cap and a towel. He laid the items on the sleeping bag, along with the little girl's pajamas that he carried in his pocket, taking care not to get any snow on them.

"Buck, move over here." He pointed to the foot of the sleeping bag. The big dog reluctantly got up and repositioned himself.

"Okay now, honey, let's get you dry and warm."

Travis opened the sleeping bag part way. He carefully removed Kelly's mittens and gently examined her fingers. They were cold but the color did not look too bad. Good sign, Travis hoped. He quickly, but cautiously, removed the girl's jacket, sweater and sweatshirt, trying not to make contact with the child's injured cheeks as he worked. Then he removed the girl's undershirt and replaced it, first with her pajama tops and then with his own extra large T-shirt. He didn't bother trying to bring Kelly's arms through the sleeves. He wrapped the little girl in his large wool shirt, buttoning the front and tying off the sleeves. He removed her soiled hat and placed the watch cap over the girl's head, again being careful of her cheeks. He covered her hands with dry socks.

"Looking good, sweetheart. How you doing?" The child did not answer, but the wind outside roared. Even within the shelter, the tent shook.

Next, he removed Kelly's socks and looked at her feet. They didn't look good. Her feet were white and cold. The tips of her toes looked waxy. Joshua hoped it was just the light. He unzipped the sides of her snowpants and very carefully removed them, her sweatpants and the cotton long johns. The underpants and sweatpants were soaked with warm urine. Joshua was not surprised. He was glad it was still warm. Had she soiled herself sooner, she would have died. He wiped the child dry with his towel. He carefully slipped on the child's pajama bottoms and gently pulled one of his thick woolen socks over the girl's right foot and leg. The sock went up to her thigh. Joshua covered the left foot also. All the time he was working, he took care not to jar or move the child more than he had to.

"Kelly, how you doing? Can you hear me?"

The child did not respond, but her eyes opened a bit more and he thought hc saw them blink.

"Kelly, it's time to wake up. Can you hear me sweetheart? Time to open those eyes."

Joshua stroked the once moribund child. She blinked her eyes again.

"That's the girl. Come on back. Everything's going to be just fine. It's getting nice and warm in here. Soon you'll be just fine. Can you hear me?"

The disoriented child nodded, once.

Good, deal.

Chapter Fifteen

"Sam, George Hoffman wants to assemble everyone in the dining room to inform them of emergency procedures," Andy Johnson informed the sheriff.

"Good idea." Hanson looked at the clock. It was 8:30.

"I talked to Sarah on the phone," Johnson reported. "They're holding down the fort. So far, just the usual mishaps. Most people are staying indoors, thank God. But she said the weather forecast don't look good."

"Tell me something I don't know. How are the Martins holding up?"

"Not too well, but they're quiet now. I think the doctor slipped them a mild Mickey in some hot cider."

Hanson nodded.

"George thought it would be a good idea if you would be in the room when he laid out the emergency procedures. Help keep people calm."

Sure, why not? Hanson thought as he left his post by the window and walked across the lobby to the dinning room.

Kristian entered her townhouse and hung her wet raincoat on the brass coat tree. She poured herself a drink, Scotch this time, and carried it into the master bath. She took out a clean bath towel and dried her dripping hair. With the towel still over her shoulders, Kristian looked at herself in the large wall mirror. *Well, aren't you a picture. Come on now, get a grip. You've been here before. Don't go to pieces. Don't lose it. Just like a bad trip. Don't lose it. You know what to do.* She walked into the master bedroom, changed into jeans and a sweatshirt, and telephoned Jane.

Her friend, Jane, was a buyer for I. Magnin. Kris knew it would be hit or miss, but she tried her office first.

"I'm sorry, Ms. Sloan is out of the office until tomorrow. May I take a message?" Jane's secretary informed Kris.

"Is she out of town?"

"I'm sorry but we can't give out that information. May I take a message?"

"If she checks in, ask her to call Kristian. She'll know who it is. Tell her I'm at home and it's urgent. Thank you."

Kristian hung up. She decided to try Jane's home number. She knew Jane kept her own hours and often took long weekends after grueling business trips. She got her machine.

"Jane, it's Kris. Give me a call as soon as you get in. It's kind of an emergency. I need to talk to you. Bye."

Now what do I do?

Kristian returned to the bathroom and looked for the Librium in the medicine cabinet.

"Folks," George Hoffman began, "can I have your attention, please."

The guests and staff assembled in the restaurant continued their conversations and speculation but eventually settled down.

"We want to bring you up to date on the storm situation and to fill you in on some procedures we're going to institute until the emergency passes. We're going to need everybody's cooperation, but if we all pitch in I think we can weather this thing without too much hardship or discomfort." He glanced over at the Martins and bit his tongue, but they did not react. Jim Beard would give the update on the weather. Beard confided to Sam Hanson that the report would not be good news for the Martins.

"Can't be helped," Hanson replied. "Besides, I believe the doc's got things pretty much under control." He looked at Doc Whitman. Whitman nodded casually. "Just don't exaggerate things."

"That would be hard."

Jim Beard addressed the assembly. "Ah, folks, the latest weather report shows that we're in for one granddaddy of a snowstorm. It looks like we're going to be stuck here for a few days, so we might as well settle in and make the best of it.

"This current storm is caused by a low pressure front coming up from the south, picking up moisture over the Atlantic and then running into a blast of high pressure Arctic air off the coast of Newfoundland. The cold high front forces the moist air back south, causing the high winds and snowfall. Right now it's snowing one to three inches per hour, but the worst part is the wind. We've got gale strength winds, which for those of you who don't sail is 32 to 63 miles per hour. Some gusts have been reported in the seventies. Obviously the snow is drifting. The current temperature is five below zero. Any questions?"

"Is that temperature with, or without, the wind?"

"Good question. Five below zero is the actual temperature. Factor in the wind and your looking at forty to sixty below, maybe colder." Murmurs and whistles filled the room.

"How long is this expected to continue?"

"The weather service is predicting at least one more day of it, possibly two, with intermittent respites possible, but not guaranteed. They're predicting two to three feet of new snow with drifts over ten feet high... One more thing. The satellites have spotted another storm building over the northern plains that's heading for the Great

Lakes. It's too early to tell, but it's possible that storm may move into this region once this one moves out. Anything else?"

"We're not going to be charged extra for staying past our intended departure, are we?"

"I'll let George Hoffman fill you in on the logistics for the next few days."

Nancy Grady made her way over to Sheriff Hanson, whispered something to him and pointed to Mrs. Martin. Hanson walked over to Doctor Whitman and spoke softly to him. The two men walked over to the little girl's mother. Despite the sedatives surreptitiously administered by the doctor, when Diane Martin heard Jim Beard's report she fainted.

George Hoffman returned to the microphone to inform people how food and energy would be rationed during the emergency and how the emergency generators would apportion electricity in the event of a power failure.

"Heat will be lowered to conserve gas, and wood will be used as much as possible. Guests will not be charged for unintentional extended stays, and lift tickets will be refunded if they cannot be used, or they may be used at any time in the future. Rationed food and beverages will be free and no one can buy extra food, but there is plenty to go around. Most of the stores were set in for the weekend and fewer people are here than we would normally expect for a Friday and Saturday. The bar is open for business, but please, folks, don't get drunk. The last thing we need is to have to deal with a drunk. Are there any questions?"

Diane Martin was carried to her room.

Chapter Sixteen

"Kelly, how're you doing? Hang in there, kid. Everything's going to be fine." He got no response from the child, but her eyes were open and blinking. After roughly twenty minutes of first-aid, Kelly began to shiver and shake. Then she let out a moan.

"C'mon, Guy. Help me out," Joshua prayed as he worked on the girl. He hoped the shivering was a good sign, but he wasn't sure. He raised her by the shoulders, his arm around her back.

"Kelly. How're you doing?"

Her breathing was stronger, but it shook with her shivering. Her eyes were open and blinking. This time she moved her eyes and whispered, "C,c,c,cold."

Joshua smiled.

"Yes, sweetheart, it's cold. But it's getting warmer now. You're going to be just fine. Soon you'll be warm and then everything will be fine."

Kelly said nothing.

"I've got some nice warm Gatorade. How about a sip? Just a second now."

Joshua went back to the pack by the shelter opening and returned with the red Thermos, the one filled with hot Gatorade. He poured off half a cup and tested it. It was sweet and it had cooled considerably, but it was still too warm. Travis knew that for the girl temperatures even approaching normal body heat would feel hot. He mixed in some snow and tested it again. *Better.*

"Here you go, sweetheart. Just take a sip of this." He poured a few drops into the girl's lips. Kelly moved her tongue and tried to swallow.

"Good deal, honey. Take it nice and slow. Just a few sips." He poured in a few drops more. "That's the way. Nice and sweet and warm." He watched to see if she would keep it down. When she didn't upchuck, he poured in a few more drops.

"Good girl." Joshua told her. Her shaking was less violent now, but he knew Kelly wasn't out of danger. He had to replace the fluids and electrolytes Kelly had lost through hours of respiration in cold, dry air.

Travis also decided to risk turning off the little white-gas stove. He only had two small bottles of fuel. Their tent was warming nicely, thanks to more than four hundred pounds of man and beast, and he knew he would need the stove later if they had to stay put much longer. Joshua hated the thought of staying put. He flinched every time he heard a tree crack or a limb come down. Given Kelly's condition and the sound of the storm outside, staying put was his only option.

Joshua turned off the stove and gave the little girl a few more sips of the tepid Gatorade. He lay her back down and began to work on her feet.

"This may hurt a little but don't be scared, sweetheart. It'll just hurt for a bit."

As he began to administer first-aid, Kelly began to cry, softly at first and then louder and louder. Kelly Martin was in pain, she was disoriented, and she was frightened. Joshua Paul Travis said a little prayer of thanks.

The telephones rang in Kristian's townhouse. She prayed it

would be Jane, although she knew it probably wasn't. She took it in her studio.

"Hello?"

"Hello, Kristian? It's Nathan."

Nathan Goodman was an important client of the firm. In his late thirties, trim, fit, tanned even in February, the waterfront developer had soft, straight, sand colored hair that set off his bright blue eyes. He was no taller than Kristian, but if he was self-conscious about his height, he did not show it. They had discussed business over drinks and dinner a few times, and they had gone to a show once and the ballet a couple of times. Just coming out of a painful divorce, Nathan Goodman had never hit on her. Kristian liked him. She liked him a lot.

"I was at Wheaton's this afternoon and I saw you leave. Laura said you didn't look well. Is everything all right?"

Kristian knew his concern was genuine. She did not want to lie to him.

"Something I saw on the TV at lunch disturbed me a little. That's all. I'm fine." She didn't sound fine.

"Are you sure? Anything I can do? Anything you want to talk about?"

"I'm sure."

"How about joining me for a bite to eat? Nothing heavy, maybe just coffee and a sandwich at Theo's. Or how about pizza and beer at Caruso's?"

Kris gave his invitation some thought. It actually sounded pretty good. She wasn't very hungry, but she desperately needed to be with a friend. Too desperately, she knew.

"Thanks, Nathan. I appreciate the offer. But I have some work I have to catch up on. How about a rain check?"

"It is raining."

Kristian smiled.

"Some other time, Nathan. Okay?"

"Sure, Kris. Some other time." And then he added, "Kris, are you sure you're okay?"

"I'll be okay," she assured him.

"If you need to talk to anyone, or to be with anyone, no strings attached, give me a call. Will you?"

Kristian knew he was sincere. "I will. Thank you, Nathan."

Kristian hung up the phone. *That had been close.*

Joshua's shirts were longer than Kelly. That worked out well. It enabled him to work on her feet without exposing any unnecessary skin, but he had to open the sleeping bag further. He did not want Kelly to lose any heat, so he took off his down parka and wrapped the child in it. He was surprised how comfortable he was without his jacket. *Good deal!*

Travis removed his sweatshirt, raised his own wool sweater, and unsnapped his Pendleton shirt. Gently and carefully, he placed Kelly Martin's left foot inside his wool shirt, beneath his armpit. The moist body temperature air, wicked by his wool/poly undershirt, surrounded the child's frozen toes. Joshua took care not to make but the lightest contact with the frozen flesh. After several minutes of ministering to the left foot, Travis placed that foot in the remaining wool sock and went to work on the right one. He alternated between feet every four or five minutes.

Kelly was screaming bloody murder, but her feet were looking better. Her toes had lost some of their waxy look and were regaining some color. There were a few blisters but not many. Kelly jerked her legs as Joshua tried to work. The good news was, she was able to wiggle her feet. Joshua needed to dress them, but Kelly wasn't making it easy.

"Easy now, sweetie. Just let me bandage your tootsies, okay?"

"It hurts!" were the lost child's second words. Joshua took it as a good sign.

"I know, sweetheart, but this will make it better. You'll see. I promise." He knew her painful cries were an encouraging sign. They still broke his heart.

Travis needed to dress the injuries, but the girl's crying was too intense. Now it was out of control and Travis knew her screams were more than pain; they were fear. He had to calm her. He did not want her going into shock.

He covered her feet and gently lifted her to his lap, his arm around her.

"It's okay, Kelly. Everything is okay. My name is Joshua and I'm a friend of your mommy and daddy. They asked me to find you and to bring you back to them. You *are* Kelly Martin, aren't you? I want to be sure I have the right little girl."

The little girl continued to scream but she managed to inform him, "*I'm* Kelly Martin" in no uncertain terms.

"Well, I'm pleased to make your acquaintance, Kelly Martin. This big guy here is Buck and this one over here is Jenny-Dog. She's the one who found you."

"Do they bite?" Kelly cried. She was gradually calming down.

"Oh, no! They would *never* bite you. They're just a couple of big ol' teddy bears. Say, that reminds me of something. Let's take a look in the pocket of this jacket we've got wrapped around you. I think it's in this one right here. Why if I'm not mistaken, this is a friend of yours." Travis dug out the little girl's teddy bear that he had taken from her room and had used to give the dogs the scent.

Kelly grasped the small stuffed animal with both hands and clutched it to her chest.

"Careful of your cheeks, now." Joshua tried to warn.

"Grizzle-Bear! This is Grizzly Grizzle. Grizzle-Bear."

Travis was amazed at the child's resiliency and how quickly she had gained her composure.

"How about a little more Gatorade?"

Kelly nodded. Travis mixed some more Gatorade with a little snow and tested it.

"Here you go. Careful, now. Let me know if it is too hot."

Kelly tasted it. She was still shivering, but this time she actually sipped a couple of ounces by herself.

"Good girl. Okay, sweetheart, now why don't you just lie back down here and let me put some gauze on your feet."

"It'll hurt," the girl worried. She started crying again from fear, but this time it was just a child's normal fear of pain.

"Nooo... Don't you worry. Why I'll be as gentle as I was the time I mended a little nuthatch's broken wing."

Kelly did not say anything. Joshua went to the pack and brought out his first-aid kit. He cut eight small squares of gauze from two gauze patches.

"Yep," he said as he worked, "this tiny little nuthatch had flown into the barn and caught his wing in one of the rafter angles." He placed the patches carefully between the child's toes.

"Ol' Molly-cat was just getting ready to have that poor little guy for dinner when Kris happened to come along and shooed Molly-cat away." He lightly wrapped each foot in gauze from the roll and secured it with adhesive tape.

"I had to use a popsicle stick to splint the bird's wing. We made a cage out of some old screening." Joshua replaced the woolen socks over Kelly's bandaged feet.

"Molly-cat was so mad, she wouldn't look at Kris for a week, even when Kris brought a peace offering of milk. There."

"Is it going to hurt?" Kelly asked again, not realizing the procedure was finished.

"No, sweetheart. It's not going to hurt. How about a little more

Gatorade?" Travis removed his parka from the child and re-covered her with the sleeping bag.

"You stay there, Jen. I still want her plenty warm. Buck, you come back here too."

Travis put on his parka and sat back on the end of the sleeping bag. For the first time since he found the girl, he allowed himself to ease up just a bit. Then he exited the tent.

He surveyed with satisfaction the interior dome of their little shelter. It was tight, especially now with the tent set. The big man had to hunch over or kneel in most places. Only right next to the big maple could he actually stand up, and even there the twisted and hanging vines filled with snow would not accommodate his full height. The innermost snow covering the form was glazing over. That would add strength. Joshua reopened the holes he had made on what he took to be the leeward side. He would have to do that periodically. They would need ventilation, especially if they had to cook. He hoped they wouldn't. He wanted to get the little girl out of the woods and back to the lodge as soon as possible.

"How are you doing?" he asked Kelly. Her shaking had stopped and her shivering was barely noticeable.

"I'm cold."

"How about some more warm Gatorade?"

She nodded. This time he did not cut it with snow.

Travis tried the walkie-talkie. As expected, he got no response.

"I have to go outside for a minute. These guys will keep you company. Okay?"

Kelly nodded, okay.

"You're not scared of them, are you?"

She shook her head tentatively.

"They won't hurt you. And they won't let anything else hurt you. They'll just keep you warm. They're our heaters. I'll be right back."

When he moved the backpack by the opening they had used,

Travis found drifted snow obscuring the way. Rather than reopen that passage, he packed the snow tight. He took his knife and trenching tool and burrowed an exit through the opposite side of the wickiup, the side away from the wind. Joshua brought his pack over to the new opening to use as a seal. Unless it was absolutely unavoidable, he did not want any heat escaping from the shelter.

Travis secured his hood and put on his gloves. The dogs perked up.

"You guys stay here. I'll be right back. Keep Kelly warm." He zipped closed the tent door.

Travis took the lantern and crawled backwards through the newly dug opening, pulling the backpack into the breach as he went out.

Outside, the cold hit him with a crack. The wind tried to race through his body. The difference between conditions inside and outside the shelter was incredible. The storm raged on. Snow was coming down in sheets, even in the woods. The frozen tree crowns rocked and shook and sometimes shattered, sending giant wooden shards crashing to the ground. These woods were not a safe place to be, but he knew that the child would never make it back to the lodge in the shape she was in. Not under current conditions.

He shined the light over the exterior of the mound and discovered that a large Norway spruce spar had come down and lodged in the crotch. This spar was fresh fallen, the result of the current storm. Good deal, Joshua thought, the more strength, the better. He looked over the rest of the mound. It was difficult to assess its structural integrity, but he tried. Barring a direct hit from a large limb or a tree, Travis thought it would hold. He tried the radio again to no avail.

Travis carefully considered his options. He could leave the girl in the shelter, with Jenny-Dog and the white-gas stove, while he and Buck tried to make it to the ski lodge to fetch help. One to two hours, perhaps longer, was the best he could hope for, assuming he could make it at all, which in this storm was problematic. He would have to lead any rescue team back by foot, regardless of equipment available, so that Buck could find the trail. That too was problematic. Better to wait it out where he was, with the girl, until the child stabilized and the storm let up. As soon as Kelly was in better shape and the storm eased, he, or they, would make a dash for the lodge. Based on the forecasts he had heard, twelve to twenty-four hours was his best guess, less if they were lucky, more if they were not. They could handle that, he thought. He was unaware of the storm building in Manitoba.

Joshua Travis looked around one last time. He checked the vent holes on the leeward side and drilled another one low on the structure, perpendicular to the wind. Joshua thought about his options one more time. He looked up at the swaying trees. Even without Kelly, he doubted he could make it back to the chalet trekking into the wind. Despite his fears and misgivings, he decided to remain at camp.

"How are you doing, champ?" Joshua asked Kelly as he re-entered the shelter.

"Okay," she whispered, not really sure. Since Travis had left her, she had not taken her eyes off Buck. She didn't trust him. She liked the big, warm black one in the sleeping bag with her. That one was funny with her brown Bambi eyes and her floppy ears and funny noises. But the other was too wild looking. She had seen animals like him in story books.

"How are you feeling?" He took off his jacket and knelt beside her.

Softly, she replied, "Okay."

"Are you still cold?"

"A little."

"How do your feet feel?"

"They're okay. I can't feel them."

Joshua hoped that meant they didn't hurt. He didn't press it.

There was nothing more he could do at the moment, but he would have to keep an eye on them. If they started to become gangrenous, he might have to make a break for the lodge regardless of the storm.

"We're going to have to stay put for a bit, so we might as well get comfy. How about some hot chocolate? Do you think you can keep some down?"

Kelly nodded yes. Travis opened the second Thermos and helped her drink half a cup.

"Want some more cocoa?" he asked. Kelly shook her head, no.

"How about a Hershey bar?"

Her eyes lit up and opened wide.

"When are we going to go home?"

"Just as soon as we get you warm and the storm lets up a little. For now, we'll just have to get cozy. Are you hungry? I have some granola and I can cook up some oatmeal."

Kelly shook her head again.

"How'd you happen to find this place anyway?"

Chapter Seventeen

"Sam, it's 9:30." Andy reminded the sheriff.

"So?"

"You need to get something to eat. You standing by the window won't make him appear."

Hanson knew his deputy was right, but somehow it seemed wrong to desert his post.

"Anything over the radio?" Hanson asked.

"Just static."

Hanson went over to check for himself. He felt that was a legitimate reason for leaving the window. He grabbed a sandwich on the way. He also felt a tug on his pants pocket. Sam Hanson looked down and saw Sharon Grady.

"I'm scared," the little girl implored, looking up. Hanson was past being scared, but he wanted to help the child.

"Now don't be scared, honey. I'm sure this storm will pass soon, and we'll find your friend, and everything will be all right." Dammit, sometimes you just had to lie to kids, plain and simple. Sharon shook her head. There were tears in her eyes.

"I'm scared for mommy."

Now Hanson was worried once more. He knew Nancy was taking the situation hard and blamed herself for the missing child.

"Where is your mommy, Sharon?"

"She's up in our room, crying."

Hanson took the child by the hand and made for the stairs. Along the way he told Andy Johnson to find the doctor and have him meet them at Nancy Grady's room.

Hanson knocked when they got to the room but received no reply. He knocked again and then tried the door. It was locked.

"Do you have a key, Sharon?" the sheriff asked the child. She shook her head no.

Hanson knocked again. Again there was no answer from within. He spotted a house phone in the hall and hurried to ring the front desk.

"This is Sheriff Hanson. Send a key up to room 307 immediately. We might have an emergency."

He returned to the room door and knocked again. Andy Johnson arrived with Doc Whitman.

"What's the problem?" the doctor asked.

"Nancy's not answering her door."

"Are you sure she's in there?" Andy asked.

"Hell, I'm not sure of anything anymore."

"Do you want to try to break it down?"

The hardwood door looked fairly substantial.

"I've got a key coming up."

Moments later George Hoffman arrived with the key. They unlocked the door. Nancy Grady was sitting on the edge of her bed, doubled over, crying inconsolably. Sam Hanson looked at the doctor. Then they both went to her and sat at her sides. Sam put his arm around her.

"Hey, what's all this?"

Nancy wept in his arms.

"Nancy, Nancy, pretty and fancy. C'mon sweetheart, you can't give up hope."

"Sam, it's all my fault. It's all my fault," wept the despondent recreation director. "I let that little girl get killed. Sam, I'm so sorry. I'm so sorry."

Hanson looked at the doctor.

"Hey, who said the little girl was dead? Beard just picked up something on the radio. It was pretty broken up and garbled with static, so's he had a hard time makin' it out, but we think Travis may have found her. She may be all right." *Damn,* he thought, *this lying bullshit is getting too easy.*

Nancy looked up. "Really?"

"Hell yes, really! We think they're just waiting out the storm. Now we can't be sure, mind you, and things are probably pretty hairy out there, but this Travis fellow is one hell of an outdoorsman. If anybody can bring her back, he can. The fact that he's still out there is a good sign, not a bad one. Understand?"

Nancy Grady nodded. Deputy Johnson gave the sheriff a hard look. Hanson ignored it.

"So buck up, kid. Things might turn out all right after all. Besides, however things turn out, it's no one's fault. You got that? Now let the doc here give you a little something to calm your nerves. Remember, you've got a little girl of your own to take care of."

"Kelly isn't much older than Sharon, Sam."

"All the more reason for you to hang in there. Now Sharon's scared shitless, so go on over to her and give her a hug, and tell her that everything is okay. Tell her some nice story or something and put her to bed. Then you get some sleep yourself. Okay?"

Nancy smiled weakly. "Thanks, Sam." She went to her daughter and hugged her for dear life. Doctor Whitman prepared some Ativan for her.

"Andy, you and the doc go through her medicine cabinet and dresser before you leave. Get rid of all blades and drugs. Understand?"

"Got it, Sam."

Doctor Whitman nodded.

"George, can you get one of the girls to stay with her?"

"I'll ask Pam. They're pretty tight."

"Good." Hanson replied. *We've lost enough people for one damn night.*

The telephone in Kristian's townhouse rang again.

Oh God, please let it be Jane, she hoped as she carried her drink into her bedroom. If it was, she could lie down and talk things through. Maybe that would help her feel better. Perhaps she could even spend the night at Jane's house in Marin.

"Hello?"

"Hello, Kristian? It's Maureen."

Damn. "Hi, Mo."

"Kristian, I got some more information for you."

Kristian sipped her drink. She said nothing.

"You know who it is, don't you?"

"Yes. It's Joshua." Her lips quivered.

"Kris, Zabrieski asked me to find out if there was a story here. I think he's looking for a San Francisco connection. You know, that kind of thing. What do you want me to tell him?" Zabrieski was the news editor.

"There's nothing to tell."

"What's your relationship to this guy. Is he related to your ex....? Oh my God! Don't tell me he *is* your ex!"

Kristian quietly explained, "He's my husband, Mo. We never divorced."

Now silence on the other end.

"What?" The writer was stunned.

"We never divorced. Technically, Joshua Travis is still my husband."

Maureen Anderson was at a loss for words. At one time she and Kris had palled around together. The two statuesque women had even picked up some guys together, Kristian with her chic, short, sunrise blond hair and healthy tan, Maureen with her alabaster skin and flowing flame red hair. When the two women walked together they stopped traffic. Maureen had no idea. Then she recovered.

"Look Kris, I don't owe Zabrieski anything, and I sure as hell don't need the few hundred dollars he'd throw my way. But I gotta tell you, you're blowing my mind. What the hell's going on?"

Perhaps it was the Librium, combined with the whiskey. Mostly, Kristian knew, it was that she did not want to be alone that night, and she sure as hell didn't want to wind up with some guy.

"Why don't you come over, Mo, and we'll talk."

Chapter Eighteen

"I followed a Peter Cottontail," Kelly told Joshua in response to his question.

"What?"

"I saw a Peter Cottontail and I followed him!" she explained again, exasperated by his thick headedness. "Me and Sharon and Patti Nickelson were making a snowman, but it was too hard because the balls wouldn't roll. Then I saw a Peter Cottontail but he was way over. I went over to watch him better and he rand away, but I could see his feets in the snow so I followed where he went."

Damn foolish city folks, Joshua thought. *They must have fed the wildlife regularly to entice a rabbit out in mid-day. Kid must have pretty good eyes.* "You must have followed for a long time. Weren't you afraid of getting lost?"

Kelly shook her head bravely.

"I got scareded when I came to the woods and it was snowing, but I wanted to see where he lived, so I just followed his foot prints."

"And he came in here and went into his hutch," Joshua surmised.

Kelly nodded. "I thought it was his house so I went in. I wanted to see if he had any baby bunnies."

Travis nodded his understanding.

Kelly continued, "But when I got inside, I couldn't see much. I called for him, but he didn't come out. And I heard the wind blow and something went BANG! And I couldn't get out and," she told Joshua, with some embarrassment, "I started to cry."

"I'm not surprised," he tells her. "I probably would have done the same thing myself." Joshua looked around the tent. Its yellow walls glowed orange/gold in the candlelight as it shook with the pressure changes caused by the wind. It was starting to smell a little doggy, but that was small price to pay. He was glad he had brought the dome tent. Joshua had worked on the tent design with Kristian and North Face, the manufacturer. The material was rip-stop nylon. The poles were Easton aluminum, O.D. .370. The color coded sleeves were his idea. Pound for pound, it was the strongest tent available, and Joshua could set it in his sleep. It had been awkward, working in the enclosed area. Travis had to re-orient its base and bend one rod slightly to accommodate the fallen trees, but it was worth the effort. With or without the fly, they would be plenty warm. He opened the sleeping bag and called Jenny out. He did not think the little girl would need her in the bag anymore. Jenny-Dog was thrilled to be free.

"You did a good job, Jen," Travis told her. That was all she needed.

"How are you doing now, Kelly? Want some more cocoa? How about a little something to eat? Are you hungry?" Travis wanted to get some warm food into the little girl. She needed to be warm on the inside as well as the outside.

"I'm not *too* hungry," was Kelly's reply. Joshua suspected she was holding out for another chocolate bar.

"How about if I cook up a little of my world famous maple oat-meal? We can eat that for supper and have candy bars for dessert. What do you say?"

Kelley nodded agreeably. Joshua dug out his mess kit, re-lit the white-gas stove and melted snow to mix with the pre-mixed instant oatmeal and powdered milk that was laced with maple sugar. Two cups of snow, one of cereal, a cup of warm cocoa split between them and a Hershey bar apiece. Joshua also ate a one-inch slice of summer sausage. That would hold them until morning as long as there were no problems.

"I'd better keep our heaters stoked," he explained to the child. "Buck, you stay! C'mon, Jen. Come with me." Kelly hid within the sleeping bag. She still didn't trust Buck not to eat her.

Travis adjusted his ski mask. He put on his mitts and parka and led the dog outside.

"Go park, Jen," he told her as he once more examined their shelter from outside. The wind and cold were piercing. Snow battered his parka. The trees creaked and moaned eerily. Joshua tried the walkie-talkie again, but there had been no improvement in conditions. To make matters worse, the cold was causing the batteries to drain faster than expected.

Travis was happy to be back within the *wickiup*. The lights from the tent glowed, but outside the tent the lantern was still needed. He fed Jenny-Dog a piece of sausage and then had her exchange places with Buck. He did not want more than one dog out of the tent at a time. When both dogs had been taken care of, Travis returned to the tent and set the fly. It was time to hunker down and settle in. Before he did, though, he wanted to check Kelly's feet one more time.

"Would you like anything more to eat or drink, sweet pea?"

Kelly shook her head.

"Do you have to go potty?"

Again, she shook her head no.

"Be sure you let me know if you have to go potty. I'll help you, okay? We don't want to have any accidents if we can help it, okay?"

"Okay," and then meekly, "did I have a accident before?"

"Just a little one. No big deal. We just don't want any more if we can help it. So you let me know. Okay?"

Kelly nodded.

"Good deal. How're you getting on with ol' Buck? You're not still scared of him, are you?"

Kelly hedged her answer. "He sure is big."

"He sure is. Why one time my tractor broke down and our horses were lame and I still had this field to plow, so I just harnessed up old Buck to that plow and, you know, we finished off that old field in half the time it normally takes."

Kelly had no idea what Joshua was talking about, but that didn't stop her from being duly impressed. She liked it when he told stories.

"I want to take one more look at your feet. Okay? Then we can go to sleep."

"Is it going to hurt?"

"I'll try to be careful," he assured her as he opened the sleeping bag and tentatively removed the woolen sock covering her right foot. Gently, he unwrapped the gauze surrounding the foot.

"Hmm, not too bad. Can you wiggle your toes?"

Kelly could and did. Joshua replaced the right sock and examined the left foot. A pang struck his gut. *Damn*, he whispered to himself as he noticed the blue/black discoloration on the tips of her middle three toes. *Maybe it's just bruising* Joshua hoped as he closely examined the toes under the lantern's light.

"Can you wiggle these toes?"

"They hurt."

"Try, sweetheart. Just a little."

"Ow! They hurt!"

"Okay, sweetheart. They're looking good. We'll check them again in the morning." Joshua wondered what more he could do.

"Well, I guess it's time to go to sleep. Are you tired?"

Kelly snuffled, "yes."

"Sure you don't want to go potty first?"

Kelly shook her head. Joshua removed his boots, sweatshirt, coveralls, woolen pants and socks.

"You guys are going to have to move over," he told the dogs. They begrudgingly got up and repositioned themselves.

"Got any room in there for me?"

Kelly nodded.

"Okay, now we're snug as four bugs in a rug. We'll just wait for this old storm to settle down a bit, and then we'll high tail it back to the lodge."

"Five bugs inna rug," Kelly corrected him.

"Huh?"

She holds up Grizzly-Grizzle Bear.

"Why by golly you're right. Five bugs in a rug."

Kelly smiled and hugged her bear. She turned towards the large warm man next to her. "Tell me a story."

"What kind of a story would you like?"

"Tell me another dog story."

"Another dog story. Hmm, I'll have to think about that. I have lots of dogs, so I could probably tell you dog stories all night long. Hmm, let's see...."

"Tell me a story about the other dog."

"About Jenny? Okay, I've got a good one. This happened a long time ago, maybe ten, eleven years ago. Kris and I were traveling across the country in my pickup truck and..."

"Who's Kris?"

Now there was a good question. Just who was Kris? Travis thought to himself.

"Kris was my wife. Anyway, Kris and I were traveling across the country with Jenny-Dog and we stopped outside Boseman, Montana to get some..."

"What happened to her?"

"To who?"

"To your wife?"

"Why nothing. What do you mean?"

"You said she *was* your wife. Is she dead?"

Joshua saw her point. *Bright kid.*

"No, sweetheart. She's still alive."

"Then why did you say she was your wife? Isn't she still your wife."

Joshua had to think about that one. He decided to put it to rest.

"Yes, honey, she still is my wife. I just misspoke." Kelly accepted that.

"Now, do you want to hear the rest of this story, or not?" Joshua smiled. He was happy she was so alert. Kelly nodded.

"So anyhow, we had stopped outside Boseman, Montana to get some breakfast, and I let Jenny-Dog out of the truck to stretch her legs. I left her outside while we went in to eat, and, don't you know, a few minutes later we heard her barking to beat the band. Kris and I ran outside to see what the problem was, and, would you believe, there was Jenny barking at one of those mechanical horses that they have for kids where you put a dime in them and they go up and down and make you sick. Well, it turns out that some smart-a..., smart-aleck cowboy had put a dime in it to see how Jenny would react, and sure enough, ol' Jenny-Dog was doing her level best to herd the *critter* away from our truck."

Joshua was surprised Kelly had not interrupted with any more questions. He looked down at her and saw she was fast asleep.

"God bless you, Kelly Martin," he spoke softly.

He settled back, his arm around the sleeping child, and listened to the raging storm. Every now and again he could hear a cold brittle tree crack and break. Falling trees and widowmakers were his biggest fear. Widowmakers and gangrene. He knew the best thing to do was to get some sleep. There was nothing else to do. But he knew he would not. He wanted to listen for any let up in the winds. Perhaps the storm would have an eye, a window of opportunity to make a break for the lodge. He didn't want to miss it.

Joshua lay back and listened to the trees and the storm. He hoped it would blow through in a few hours.

Who was Kristian. He thought. *Now that was a really good question.*

Chapter Nineteen

The night sky had clouded up in Lincoln County, Wisconsin. The temperature hadn't dropped much from the daytime but the barometric pressure had. Noticeably so. Jonathan VanStavern drove out to the Travis place to check on things. As he approached the homestead, he could see bright lights burning in the barn. An old gray Chevy station wagon was parked near the entrance to the outbuilding. VanStavern let his breath out, relieved that Gerry Nelson and his son were taking care of the chores. The barn felt warm and moist as the sheriff walked in. It had the sweet/sour smell of hay and manure.

"Evening, Ger. Any problems?"

"Hi, Jon. No, everything's under control."

"Have any trouble with the dogs letting you in?"

The dogs had free range of the fenced yard and access to the kennel.

"No. They know us okay."

"Even Butch?"

Butch was relatively new. An unwanted cross between a Rottweiler and a boxer/lab mutt, Butch was a hundred and fifty pounds of tooth and muscle that looked like a brindled bull mastiff that pumped iron.

"Yeah, even Butch. You know the drill Josh puts new dogs

through. Butch and the rest know us well enough. They were just a little excited because we were a little late getting out here."

VanStavern did know the drill. Whenever Joshua picked up a new dog, the first thing he would do would be to take him on the "campaign trail," as Joshua called it. Joshua would bring the dog over to neighbors' houses and take it into town with him just to see how it would react to people. He would give the dog a chance to meet different people in different situations. He especially watched how they were around children. Then he would ask his neighbors and friends to be sure to drop by so that the dogs could see that these people were welcome on the property and in the house. Next, Josh would ask a select few to help him feed the dogs for a few days. This ensured that the dogs would take food from people other than he, and it helped cement the relationship between the dogs and the neighbors. Finally Joshua would ask the neighbor or friend to feed the dogs without him being there. For this, Joshua would always borrow a walkie-talkie from VanStavern just in case there was a problem when he drove off and parked down by the lake. There never was. Joshua had a good eye for temperament in dogs and people. By the end of the first leg of the drill, Joshua could usually spot any dog that might present a problem. Any dog that didn't measure up was history. There were very few.

Joshua's neighbor was mucking out the first stall.

"Where's Nick?" Jonathan asked.

"He's feeding the dogs and the chickens. How are things going with you, Jon?"

"About as usual."

"We got out a little late 'cause my old clunker blew a radiator hose, dang old jalopy. Any news about Joshua?"

"Nothing yet. We've got our fingers crossed, but this one looks to be a tough one."

"Hmm. Well, I sure hope things turn out all right. Ol' Josh

doesn't handle losing real well."

"Not when there's a kid involved, that's for damn sure. You need a hand?"

"No. We're almost finished here."

"Well, I really appreciate you and your boy doing this. I know Joshua appreciates it too. Tell Nick, will you, Ger'."

"Sure. No problem, Jonathan. We're happy to help out."

"Make sure that you tell Nick. How's Laurie?"

"She's doing fine. Getting big."

"When is she due?"

"The doctor says April. I say any day from the looks of her."

"Well tell her Margaret and I were asking for her. Tell her not to hesitate to call if she needs anything."

"I sure will, Jonathan. Thanks." Gerry Nelson walked the sheriff to the door. "Has it started to snow yet?"

"Not yet," VanStavern answered. He looked into the sky. "Looks like it might."

"Feels like it."

It was snowing in Vermont. The temperature had dropped to minus fifteen, not counting the wind. The winds were still gale strength. Outside the shelter, human flesh would freeze in seconds. Inside the shelter things were warm and cozy. The interior temperature had almost reached a toasty thirty-two degrees.

Joshua lay awake, listening to the wind and the trees. Kelly was asleep. For the moment they were comfortable, deceptively comfortable given the true danger around them. Joshua's instincts had been proven right. This one was like Cody in more ways than one.

In both rescues, finding the lost parties was only half the battle. Getting them and himself out alive was the hard part. The Wyoming rescue had been in a forest-fire; this one was in a sub-zero blizzard. But for Travis those were only minor details. In both circumstances one bad decision or one freak accident could mean agonizing death. In both circumstances success, indeed survival, had been beyond his control. All he could do was his best. And pray a lot. The rest was up to God and Mother Nature, he knew, but that did not stop him from running the possibilities and the probabilities through his mind, over and over, in an endless search for the right decisions.

Like the fire rescue, this one involved high winds and falling timber. The winds in Wyoming hadn't been quite as strong as the winds were now, but they had been just as deadly. Joshua lay on his back, listening to the wind and the trees, comparing them to the sound of the wind and the trees on that horrible night five-and-a-half years earlier. It was the same wind. The same incessant roar. The same terrifying, raging air carrying death.

The trees, however, were different. In Wyoming they had crackled and popped and hissed as they yielded inevitably to death by fire. In Vermont the trees were resisting with all they had. Their cold-brittle limbs and trunks moaned and cried as they swayed to and fro, locked in a life-and-death dance with the storm. Sometimes a branch or a limb would crash down, a tactical retreat, a sacrifice for the good of the whole. Sometimes entire individual trees were lost, necessary tribute to the same weather patterns that also brought life giving water to the Northeast. But in the end, most of the trees would still be there. Some animals would die, but most would survive. There would still be life and beauty. In Wyoming there had only been scorched earth.

Joshua looked down on Kelly Martin, sleeping fitfully beside him. His own child would have been about her age, maybe a little older, had Kristian been able to carry her, or him, to term. He could only imagine what the child's parents must be going through. He regretted not being able to contact the lodge with the radio. At least let them know she was alive. But perhaps it was for the best. Kelly Martin was not safe yet.

Joshua Travis lay back and listened to the wind and the trees. He knew he should get some sleep. He had done all he could for now. Rest and conservation of energy were important. But the wind and the trees would not let him relax.

It was funny, he thought, how Kelly had gotten him talking and thinking about Kristian. He had tried to minimize that over the last few years. Now she was back in the forefront of his thoughts. During the Wyoming fire rescue it was the thought of Kristian and getting back to her that had helped pull him through that eternal night of hell. Now, all he could do was wonder how she was and what she was doing.

"Hi, Kris."

"Hello, Maureen. Come on in. Here, let me take your coat." The two women hugged briefly.

"Watch it, it's wet. Just hang it any place." The freelance writer looked around. "Wow! This is some place you have here. I love all the wood. And that view is spectacular. God, you even have a balcony."

"Thanks. Would you like something to drink?"

"Hot coffee would be great if you have some made. Otherwise a Coke will be fine."

"I'll put some on."

"Don't bother."

Kristian went to the kitchen and ground some French roasted beans. She filled the two-cup, stainless steel espresso maker she had picked up in Italy. She was happy to see Maureen Anderson. She had been sorry their friendship had lapsed.

Maureen was easy to talk to. She was intelligent and well read. Most importantly, she knew how to listen. Kristian knew she would have to be careful. If she wasn't, Maureen was liable to write a book about Joshua and her. But if she played her cards right, Kristian knew, she would be able to keep Maureen mesmerized until morning. That was what she wanted. Things would look brighter in the morning, she hoped.

"I've forgotten, Mo, do you take sugar or cream?"

"Just cream, Kris. Thanks. So tell me, what the hell's going on? I mean, are you really married to this Joshua Paul Travis guy?"

"I could never quite bring myself to file the necessary papers."

"How long have you been married?"

"It will be ten years in November."

"Jesus, I had no idea, Kris. You never mentioned it when we did that series of articles."

"It wasn't relevant."

"Perhaps not, but the publicity might have gotten you noticed sooner."

"We did just fine, Mo." Kristian's eyes drifted around her home. Everything was exactly what she wanted, from contemporary restorations and renovations to the plain line hardwood furnishings.

"I did a little research on this guy..."

"Joshua," Kristian interjected.

"Sorry. I did some research on Joshua. He has quite a track record when it comes to this sort of thing. I can see why they would want to get him involved."

"You don't know the half of it."

"I mean, it sounds like he's the best there is when it comes to this sort of thing."

Kristian mused for a moment. "He's better than the best. I know that sounds hokey, like some stupid oxymoron used by some jock coach trying to pump up his team. What I mean is that he is different from the others."

"How so?"

How so, indeed? Kristian chose her words carefully. "Well for starters, Joshua's live find rate is about twice as high as most search and rescue teams."

"Live find rate – that's when he finds whoever he's looking for alive?"

"Exactly. Jon VanStavern once told me that the average rate for live finds is less than forty percent. More than sixty percent of the time most teams either don't find anybody or they find a body."

"Who's Jon VanStavern?"

"He was the sheriff back in Wisconsin. Probably still is."

"And Joshua did – I mean does – better?"

"Joshua's live find rate is above eighty percent. The only time he doesn't find someone is if they're not there."

"Sounds impressive. So how does he do it?"

"It is impressive. Part of it comes from the fact that Joshua never intentionally has his dogs do cadaver work, even in natural disasters like that earthquake in San Paulo. He has his dogs focus on finding survivors. But it goes beyond that. Joshua had a special relationship with nature, *has* a special relationship with nature," she quickly corrected herself, "with nature and with animals."

"Really? In what way?"

"It's difficult to explain. But Joshua is in tune to nature and to animals on a different level than most people. A lot has to do with his parents and his upbringing. His father was an avid outdoorsman who used to hunt and fish with Aldo Leopold. Joshua knew Leopold also, when he was a boy."

" Who?"

"Aldo Leopold. He was a well known naturalist. He wrote *A Sand County ALMANAC*. Josh's mother was from northern Quebec. She was pure *Quebecoise*, if you know what I mean."

"Is that where his special talents come from?"

"I don't know. Like I said, it's difficult to explain. Part of Joshua's abilities come from the fact that he works at things harder than most people would. He and his dogs train like champion athletes. And once he gets involved with a problem, or takes an interest in a subject, he studies it from all angles and keeps at it until he gets it right... It's not that he's smarter than most people, it's just that he doesn't let his ego get in the way of trying something different, or asking other people's opinions, or making a mistake. And he always learns from his mistakes..... Well, almost always."

"It sounds to me like he *is* a lot smarter than other people. Other men for sure."

"But even those qualities don't fully explain everything."

"What do you mean?"

"Let me tell you a little story, and I'll let you draw your own conclusions." Kristian rose to get the coffee.

"This is getting good. Do you mind if I tape record it?"

"I'd rather you didn't." Kris brought the coffee into the living room.

"May I take some notes?"

"I'll be honest with you, Mo. I invited you over here because I like you and because I need someone to talk to. I'd rather the things I tell you don't appear in some newspaper article."

Maureen Anderson put away her notebook. Why not? She liked and respected Kristian. She didn't care about Zabrieski or a crummy newspaper article. Her instinct was starting to feel that there might be more here than meets the eye. For now, she would let Kristian tell her story. Maureen would take mental notes and decide what to do with them later.

"Go ahead, Kris. I'll just listen."

"Thanks, Mo. I'd better warn you. Some of this is pretty wild."

"Terrific."

"I knew Joshua was special as soon as I started going out with him. That was back in 1967. But the first glimpse I got of just how special took place when we left California on our journey to Wisconsin."

"That's where you're from, right?"

"That's where he is from. I'm from Monterey, originally."

"That's right. I forgot. Is that where you met?"

"We met in San Francisco. He was working construction, and I was a new associate at Borsos Building Design. God, he was beautiful."

"I see, now it's still 1967?"

"Yes. We were in Josh's pickup, traveling a jagged path east and south and north, working our way towards Merrill, but taking the time to see places we wanted to see and visit people we wanted to visit, mostly friends or acquaintances of Joshua. We had just left some friends in Prescott, Arizona and stopped off to see the Grand Canyon. It really is marvelous. Have you ever seen it?"

"Only in pictures and from the air."

"It's absolutely breathtaking, and I'm not easily impressed. You know, the Southern Paiute say that it was formed when the Great Spirit rolled a mad, raging river into the gorge that would engulf any that might enter."

Anderson wondered where that came from.

"Anyway, after we visited the Grand Canyon, we drove to the Shongopovi pueblo, even though it was out of the way. Tom, our friend in Prescott, had said the Indians there were holding their biennial Snake Dance, and that it was truly a spectacle to behold. Joshua was concerned about the heat and Jenny-Dog, but I was in-terested in the ancient architecture, and Laura told us we shouldn't miss it, so we made the trip and, believe me, it really was a trip."

"Who's Jenny-Dog?"

"She's this dog that Joshua had back then, maybe still has. God, I wonder if she's out there with him." She looked at Maureen plain-tively. The writer was sorry she had interrupted.

"Tell me what happened at the pueblo."

Kristian regained her composure. "It was high on a baking plateau, under the August sun. There were a thousand or more spectators watching whirling Hopi Indians dance with live rattle-snakes clenched between their teeth."

The last snake is placed in a special kiva. The ceremony is almost complete. An ancient medicine-woman arises from her place of honor to give the final benediction. She proceeds slowly towards the center of the ceremony, attended by her granddaughters, when, inexplicably, she stops and abruptly turns towards the crowd. She looks directly at Joshua.

"Maahaaamahaaayahaiahai!

"Maahaaamahaaayahaiahai!

"Conway qoayangwunkuiwahai

"Conway sikangwunkuiwahai

"Mahaahahahaiahai

"Mahaahahahaiahaha," the medicine-woman shouts.

The crowd parts around Joshua and Kristian like a Red Sea of tourists parting for an Indian Moses, and the old woman walks slowly and deliberately directly towards them, her procession growing as it approaches.

"What the hell is going on?" Kristian whispers to Joshua.

"Darned if I know."

The old woman stands for a long minute in front of Joshua, looking directly into his eyes. The crowd falls silent.

"You are from the East," she tells Joshua.

"Wisconsin, ma'am," Joshua replies.

"It is East," the woman affirms. "You have a flute," she continues.

"A small wooden one," Joshua nods. Kristian is aghast.

"You travel with Fair Maiden."

Joshua looks at Kristian, smiles, and nods.

"Another one," the Indian explains. "One of the Dog People, she is also called White Wind."

"We do have a dog, ma'am, but her name is Jenny-Dog and she is mostly black."

The medicine-woman looks at Joshua, unblinking, and nods. "White Wind. White Spirit." The ancient Indian hugs Joshua three times and

then steps back. "The dawn has appeared. I will accept its radiance," she
proclaims.

A murmur goes up among the Indians. The medicine-woman returns
to complete the ceremony.

Maureen Anderson shivered. "Jesus, Kris, that *is* wild."

"You're telling me? That old Indian woman hugging Joshua like
that was the damnedest thing I had ever seen, and it has haunted
me many times in the years since. It still haunts me today. After she
hugged him, it seemed as if every Indian from that pueblo wanted
to shake Joshua's hand or pat him on the back or just touch him
anywhere they could. Whatever that old woman had said obviously
wasn't bad, but it was eerie how she seemed to know Joshua, and the
way people looked at us afterwards made Josh uncomfortable. We
beat a slow, but determined retreat, amid copious offers of water,
fruit, and melons, and Joshua breathed a sigh of relief as we drove off
the reservation and began our journey north. But I was totally blown
away. What the hell was that all about? I kept asking myself."

"Did you ever find out?"

Kristian paused. "Not exactly." She hesitated again, reflecting,
then she continued.

"After we left the village, we stopped at a small adobe restaurant
near Tuba City. Interesting little place, dark and cool even without
air conditioning – didn't seem like it saw many tourists, even on
a good day. We ordered a couple of Coors, that were served with
wedges of lime, and we were looking over a menu that was mostly in
Spanish with some English scribbled in pencil in the margins, when
a large Native American man walked in, approached us, and asked
if he could join us."

"Who was he?"

"He introduced himself as Professor Pojoaque and told us he was
an associate professor of anthropology and linguistics at Northern

Arizona University in Flagstaff."

"Interesting. What did he want?"

"Are you sure you want to hear this? This is where it really gets weird."

"Are you kidding? This is great."

In black cowboy boots, the middle aged Native is almost as tall as Joshua and considerably heavier. His cheek bones are high, his nose is broad, and his dark almond eyes are set deep. Straggly gray and black shoulder length hair swept into a ponytail confirms the impression given by the cracks and wrinkles on the man's face of a life spent outdoors. The man is wearing Wrangler jeans and an embroidered black shirt with mother-of-pearl snaps. Over the shirt he wears a gray Harris Tweed sport coat – at odds with the rest of his apparel. Silver and turquoise on his leather belt and black string tie match the handmade bracelets clasping his solid wrists. He is unsmiling.

"May I sit down?"

Joshua looks at the man and nods.

"I saw you at the Snake Dance today," the Indian comments. "You made quite a stir."

"That was the darndest thing I've ever seen. The old woman seemed to know me, but I know I've never seen her before."

"Maybe it was just done for affect," Kristian suggests. "You know, like those rigged "mind readers" you see in 'Vegas or on TV. She could have made lucky guesses about us, or even had somebody snoop through the truck and feed her information."

"Maybe," replies the Native. Even Kristian doesn't believe it.

"What did you feel when the woman embraced you?"

Joshua looks at Kristian before speaking. Then he turns towards the Indian. "It was strange. I was nervous as the woman and her attendants approached us. And I was uncomfortable after she left us – embarrassed, I guess..."

The large Indian waits patiently. He knows there is more.

"...but at the moment that the old woman embraced me, I felt good. I felt safe. I felt like..." Joshua pauses, looking for the right words. "I felt like I knew at that moment that everything would work out."

The Indian nods. Kristian shudders.

"Are you Hopi?" she asks.

"Tewa," is his reply. "We're cousins."

Kristian presses. "Do you know what this is all about?"

Now it is the Indian's time to pause. Finally he replies, "Maybe."

"Jesus, Kris," the writer told Kristian in a hushed voice, "you are right. This *is* weird. I love it. What else did he tell you?"

"We ordered some more beer. It came with salsa and guacamole and two baskets of corn chips – white corn chips and blue corn chips. Joshua asked the man with us if he could recommend anything from the menu. The Indian didn't even look at the menu. He spoke fluent Spanish to the waiter and ordered for all of us.

"While we were waiting for the food to come, the anthropology professor picked up a blue corn chip, but he didn't eat it. He didn't even dip it in anything. He just stared at it."

"Blue corn holds a special place in Hopi culture, Hopi religion," he tells them. "The medicine-woman is called Blue Corn Woman. They also call her Sowuhti. It means grandmother. The Traditionals – the old Traditionals – call her Gogyeng Sowuhti, Spider Grandmother."

Joshua and Kristian listen intently. Kristian recalls the old woman's amazingly wrinkled face. "Is that a good thing or a bad thing?".

The Tewa explains: "Spider Grandmother, or Spider Woman, is one of the prime creators in Hopi creation stories. She often appears in other myths and legends. She helps people with magic. She gives people advice. Sometimes she turns herself into a spider and climbs up on someone's ear. Whispers advice into it."

Joshua and Kristian are intrigued but puzzled. "What does this have to do with us?"

"The Traditionals say Blue Corn Woman is a povoslowa, a diviner.

They believe she can see things others can not. They believe she can recognize things inside a person's soul that they themselves may not be aware of.

"*The Hopi believe that in the beginning all the good people climbed up from the Third World and entered the Fourth World, the world we live in today. All the powakas – the sorcerers and witches – were supposed to be left below. But one powaka made it to the Fourth World.*

"*When the time came for the clans and the tribes to disperse, all the tribes and clans refused to allow the powaka to come with them. All except for the Pahanas, the White People. This gave the Pahanas special powers, special magic, but it also gave them the knowledge of evil. The other peoples were counseled to avoid the Pahanas.*"

"*I still don't see what this has to do with us,*" *Kristian insists.* "*Why would a medicine-woman embrace a white person if Indians are supposed to be wary of them?*"

"*The legend prophesies that, despite having accepted the powaka, at some time there would come from amongst the Pahanas a Special One. A special hero or messenger who would show the people how to pray and how to live.*"

Joshua smiles, embarrassed. "*I'm afraid the Grandmother has missed the mark with me. Sounds like some Christian missionaries may have influenced the legend.*"

Kristian is silent.

"*The legend is pre-Columbian. It may pre-date Christianity. The Special One is to come from the East. You are from Wisconsin. East. The Special One is to have a flute. You have a flute. The Sowuhti knew these things. They say she is a povoslowa. They say she can see things others cannot.*"

"*What was it she cried out when she first saw us? Did you understand what she said?*" *Kristian asks.*

"*Hmmm,*" *reflects the Indian.* "*That was interesting. The words are from a song chanted by initiated members of the Owaqol society, an ex-*

clusive women's society. It is a song used in a ritual at the Corn Dance. It was very strange to hear it used at the Snake Dance. Rough translation:

White Dawn has appeared.

Yellow Dawn has appeared.

I embrace your radiance."

Kristian and Joshua look at each other. Neither knows what to say. Finally the food arrives, chicken flautas and tostadas, quesquedilla, a special black bean salad. Kristian takes a swig of beer.

"What was that business about fair maiden and white wind? The old woman was wrong about that."

"Maybe," the Tewa replies.

The ex-reporter in Kristian's living room was speechless. Finally she recovered her voice. "What are you telling me, Kris? You're married to an Indian god? Or is he just a mythological hero?"

Kristian smiled. "You might not be so quick to dismiss the idea if you knew Joshua," Kristian laughed, "but no, that's not what I'm saying. A few days later we were camping up in the Tetons and I had an amazing experience that helped me put the medicine-woman incident into perspective."

"Really? What happened?"

They are high in the Teton Mountains. They have hiked in. The air is fragrant and cool. Late summer wildflowers and grasses blossom in the high mountain meadow. Nearby is a cold, clear lake. Wildlife abounds. A fast flowing stream, just out of sight, can still be heard, background for the cry of the hawk. While Joshua and Kristian make camp, Jenny-Dog chases ruffed grouse. This is the way it's supposed to be, Jenny-Dog thinks to herself.

"This is wonderful, Kris."

"We saw tiny blue wild flax and magnificent lodgepole pine. There were golden eagles, elk and even an old grizzly. Jenny-Dog loved every moment, but she had to repress her natural instincts because of her unflinching devotion to Joshua. She would trot ahead

FROZEN MOON

and then break into an easy, happy lope, only to check over her shoulder and slow back down to a trot to wait for us.

"I don't know how he does it, but I've never seen another person who has such a way with dogs or other animals or even with people, for that matter. I once asked him about it and he just shrugged, but there's something special going on." Kristian thought back while she considered how much to confide in the writer. Then she continued, "And you know how I told you how all the Indians wanted to shake Josh's hand and pat him on the back after the Snake Dance?"

"Yes..."

"Well, whenever Joshua came in from a rescue, there were always people doing the same kind of things. And I would flash back to that day on the mesa, and I always had a weird feeling that somehow that old Indian medicine-woman and Joshua really were connected. Crazy, isn't it?"

"Kristian, this is absolutely amazing. I can't get over it..."

"There's more. Remember how I told you that the Indian woman had been wrong about knowing our dog's name...?"

"Yes," the writer replied, warily.

"Well, when I was pregnant, I was thumbing through one of those name books. You know, the ones that tell you the meaning and derivation of various names?"

"Yes.....?"

"Well, we were thinking about the name, Julia, if it was a girl, so I was leafing through the J's and came across Jenny, or at least Jennifer. And it turns out that the name goes back to the ancient Welsh. The meaning it had listed was *Fair Maiden*. It also listed an older meaning – *White Wind.*"

Anderson was stunned. "My God, Kris, this is absolutely unbelievable! So you actually think Joshua might find that little girl in Vermont and bring her back alive?"

"I don't know, Maureen. I hope so. I do know this much: If he can't, he won't come back either."

Anderson looked at her. "Why do you say that?"

"I just know."

The Snake Dance is over. The sun is almost down. The first stars have appeared. The old woman is sitting in front of her house. She gazes into the evening.

"*Grandmother, who was that man today?*" *inquires a young granddaughter.*

"*I cannot be certain,*" *replies the sowuhti.*

"*Was it The Pahana?*"

"*He was a Pahana. I do not know if he was The Pahana.*"

"*Grandmother, who do you think he was?*" *persists the child.*

The povoslowa considers the question. With ancient hope, she answers.

"*I think he may be the Son of Light.*"

Chapter Twenty

Joshua Travis lay back and listened to the wind and the trees. He looked over at his dogs sleeping peacefully. Did they really not have a care in the world, or were they just exhausted? Maybe the storm will blow through in a few hours, he hopes, or maybe there will be an eye that will give them a chance to escape. But the storm doesn't blow through in a few hours; it just continues and intensifies through the night. And if there is an eye, it's about the size of a needle's.

Well past midnight, Joshua's heavy eyes closed, only to be laced with competing images of fire and snow and Jenny-Dog and Kristian. A grieving mother. A dead little girl.

The old woman in the Shongopovi pueblo lies calmly now. Her shivering has ceased. Her closed eyelids flutter rapidly.

"I'll watch her now," the mother tells her daughter. "You get some rest."

"Mother," the daughter asks, "is grandmother going to live?"

"I do not know. It is too early."

Long ago, the fate of Gogyeng Sowuhti's village was to be determined by a foot race. A single child was chosen from her village to compete against all the runners from a neighboring village. The day before the race, the child was brought into a special kiva. Spider Grandmother took a bowl from her bag. She placed special leaves and bark in the bowl and mixed them with water.

"Drink this," she told the child. "It will keep the powakas away."

Then she put medicine powder into the bowl and mixed it with the other ingredients.

"This is to protect the child from sorcery."

Spider Grandmother rubbed the medicine on the child's legs.

"Now the child must sleep."

Gogyeng Sowuhti sang softly to the restless child.

Go to sleep, little one.

Mother is making piki.

Tomorrow you will have a treat.

The next morning the child awoke rested and strong. Still, the challenges to be faced were daunting.

The lodge was hunkered down for the night. Three people were sedated. Four had been treated for minor frostbite. Lights were dimmed. Room temperature had been lowered to 65 degrees. The phones were out, but, miraculously, the power was still on. Sam Hanson slept in an overstuffed leather armchair near the window. He was covered with his parka and an old plaid woolen blanket provided by George Hoffman. Andy Johnson slept on the couch by the fireplace. Jim Beard read hunting magazines by the radio receiver. Nothing but crackling static had been picked up all night. Hanson had coached Beard to be ambiguous if anyone asked him for news.

At 4:57 A.M. the power failed. The emergency generators kicked in.

The painful crying and incoherent thrashing of a little girl, only half awake, jolted Joshua Travis back from his uneasy visions and semi-sleep. He switched on the lantern and held the light towards the inexplicably tortured child. Her face was flushed and moist. Her hair was damp. They had managed to raise the temperature in the tent considerably, but not anywhere near a level to account for the child's discomfort. She was burning up.

Travis opened the sleeping bag and held the child in his arms. He hoped her fever was only her body's regulating mechanism trying to play catch up, confused by the unexpected warmth. Of course, it was always possible that Kelly had been exposed to some virus prior to becoming lost. The trauma of the ordeal could have lowered her resistance enough to let the symptoms manifest themselves. The third set of possibilities that Travis could think of was the one he feared the most: thrombosis, cellulitis, or gangrene.

"Kelly, Kelly, what's the matter sweetheart?"

The child did not respond to his questioning. She kicked and thrashed and cried. Except for the fever, Kelly almost appeared to be having a seizure, but Joshua did not think that was the case. A semi-conscious, pain induced tantrum was more apt to be the situation, or so he hoped. He held the struggling child so she would not hurt herself and tried to calm her. Buck growled and moved out of the way. Jenny-Dog whined and repositioned herself also.

"Easy now honey. Everything is all right. Take it easy now.... Can you tell me what's the matter?" He still got no reply from the little girl other than uncontrollable sobs and crying.

"Kelly, honey, wake up. Tell me what's the matter. Try not to kick your feet." He did not want her injuring her toes.

"It h,h,hurts!" cried Kelly through her tears. She continued her thrashing. Joshua tried to control her legs.

"What hurts, sweetheart? Can you tell me where it hurts?"

"It h,h,hurts!" she cried, "It hurts! It hurts."

"Where does it hurt, sweetheart? Tell me where it hurts. I'll make it all better."

"It hurts! It hurts m,m,my f,f,feet! My feet!"

Joshua was frightened. He reached around and grabbed his first-aid kit.

"Okay, honey, it's okay. Try to calm down. That's it, easy now. Everything's going to be okay. I'll make the hurt go away." He hoped he would be able to keep that promise. Kelly continued to cry, but her spastic kicks eased. Joshua opened the kit and illuminated its contents with his light.

The first-aid kit was well supplied. Old Doc Lieberman had seen to that. Joshua wanted something that would relieve Kelly's pain and bring down the child's fever. He thought about aspirin but remembered reading or hearing something about some children in Michigan who went into comas after taking aspirin during a high fever. He went on to Tylenol. Tylenol should help with the fever, but he did not know if it would be enough for the pain. *Come on,* he thought, *give her something. No,* he told himself. *Don't make a mistake. Whatever you give her now is all you'll be able to give her for a spell. Choose carefully.*

He searched through the small bottles of pills and liquids. He had antibiotics. He even had a syringe and a vial of morphine. Joshua prayed he would not need that. He settled on Tylenol with codeine; codeine for the pain and to sleep, acetaminophen for the fever. He estimated Kelly's weight and gave her one tablet, 325 mg., dissolved in tepid Gatorade.

"Here we go, honey. Drink this." He held the still sobbing child in a half-sitting position with one arm. His free hand held the cup.

"Come on now, Kelly. Just a little at a time. It will make you feel better."

He wrapped the child once again in his down parka so he could hold her without her getting chilled. He knew he would have to check Kelly's pajamas to see if they were wet and then examine her feet, but first he had to calm her.

"Easy now, hon. Just take it easy. The medicine will make you feel better, just give it a chance to work."

Kelly continued to cry and sob. Joshua sat her across his lap and rocked her. He tried to think what his mother would have done had she been present.

What would she do? What had she done? What was that song she used to sing?

Joshua sang softly as he comforted the child,

Fais dodo, ma petite fille, Kelly
Fais dodo, t'auras du lolo
Maman et en haut
Qui fait du gateau
Papa est en bas
Qui fait du chocolat.

Fais dodo, ma petite fille, Kelly
Fais dodo, t'auras du lolo.

Then he sang it in English.

Go to sleep, my little girl, Kelly
Go to sleep, and you'll have a treat
Mama is upstairs
Making a cake
Papa is downstairs
Making chocolate.

Fait dodo, ma petite fille, Kelly
Fait dodo, t'auras un lolo.

After twenty minutes of singing and holding and rocking, the child was asleep. Now he had to work quickly. Joshua felt the girl's chest and back and the blue pajama tops. They were wet with perspiration. The pajama bottoms, thank God, were not too bad.

Joshua found his last dry T-shirt in his pack and quickly re-placed the pajama tops with it. He re-wrapped the child in his shirt and parka and lay her in the open sleeping bag. With trepidation, he examined Kelly's legs and feet.

Travis removed the woolen socks from the girl's feet one at a time. With his knife, he carefully cut the tape securing the dressings. He shined the lantern on the foot and toes and very cautiously felt the skin. The right foot seemed okay. Color was good and the skin felt warm and supple. He re-bandaged the foot, just to be sure, and placed the sock back over it.

The left foot wasn't in as good shape. The toes were bruised, as before. Perhaps they were darker. It was difficult to judge in the poor light. As best he could tell, they were hard and cold but they seemed dry. Joshua saw no evidence of cellulitis. That was a good sign. He bent over and smelled the toes. They smelled like dirty feet, but there were no foul or sweet/sour odors. That was another good sign. He wasn't certain about edema.

He slit the cuff of Kelly's pajamas with his knife and examined the child's leg. The color was good and the leg felt warm and soft except for one spot on the quadriceps that Joshua thought might be tighter and harder than usual. There were several possibilities, some worse than others. Given the appearance of the rest of the leg and foot, Joshua diagnosed a simple muscle spasm, a Charley-horse, not the more serious problem of cellulitis or thrombosis. Joshua gently massaged the little girl's leg muscle and hoped he was right. He wasn't sure what to do about the toes. He carried antibiotics, along with a crib sheet provided by Lieberman, and could begin a course as a prophylactic treatment. That would also probably help if indeed there was wet gangrene or cellulitis. But Joshua had found no good evidence of wet gangrene. Dry gangrene was still a possibility, but its ramifications weren't as serious. He decided to hold off on the antibiotics for the time being and re-evaluate the situation in a few hours. He was afraid of an allergic reaction. *Damn, why didn't I check with the girl's parents?* Joshua re-dressed Kelly's foot and zipped the child back in the sleeping bag. She was fast asleep. The time was 5:29 A.M.

Travis decided to check the condition of the shelter and the weather. He pulled on his trousers and laced up his soft moosehide boots. It was a bother but he struggled with his bib-coveralls also. He didn't want his trousers getting wet, wool or no wool. Joshua put on his parka, mask and gloves and crawled out of the tent. From inside, the shelter appeared secure. Joshua wiggled the stick he used to clear the air holes. The two on the leeward side were open. The one perpendicular to the wind was clogged. He might have to reposition that one.

As long as he was up, he decided to relieve himself and to let the dogs out. He opened his parka and dropped his coveralls. He had to squat and hunch over even to urinate, which he did into a plastic baggie. It was awkward, but Travis knew it would be difficult and dangerous to try to do it outside the shelter. By disposing of the filled baggie he would prevent fouling their nest.

Joshua dug out the leeward exit, near the base of the maple, that he had sealed with snow. One at a time, he let the dogs out. Jenny-Dog returned quickly. Travis went out with Buck. Outside, conditions were as furious as before. The temperature was the lowest it had been, and the wind screamed through the trees. Joshua wished he had put on his sweatshirt, but he wasn't planning on staying out long. It was difficult to tell if it was still snowing, but it hardly mattered. The air was filled with choking, blinding snow.

Joshua looked over the snow covered *wickiup*. It appeared to be intact and sound. He wasn't certain, but he thought there might be some new small branches piled on, perhaps red cedar. He tried to look up but could not see much. Light reflected by fast moving snow with occasional glimpses of waving tree tops, if viewed downwind, was all he could make out.

"Jesus, Buck, how long can this last?" Travis hoped not too long. Buck didn't seem to care.

"C'mon, guy, lets get back inside."

Reluctantly, the big dog complied.

Inside, Travis resealed the entrance and rechecked the air passages one more time.

"Don't shake, now," he hoped more than commanded.

He dusted the snow off Buck and himself before entering the tent and closing its flap. He stripped off his outer clothes and arranged them neatly near the foot of the bag. Joshua also turned the girl's pajama tops inside out and laid them on top of his pack. He hoped they would dry, but he couldn't count on it. The four of them were generating a lot of moisture. Grizzly-Grizzle Bear wasn't included.

Joshua looked over Kelly. She was sleeping peacefully. Her breathing was strong and regular. Joshua placed the small gray-brown bear in Kelly's arms.

"Thank you," Joshua said softly.

He cut three one-inch slices from the started sausage log and shared the meat with the dogs. There was nothing else to do but get back in the sack, stay warm, and try to get more rest. If all went well, the next critical decision would not come before the child awoke.

Chapter Twenty-one

"Unbelievable. Absolutely unbelievable. That's the most incredible story I've ever heard. Jesus, look at the time." It was past one-thirty in the morning.

"How much more do you want to hear? I can tell you stories about him for days."

"I want to hear it all, but I've really got to get going."

"You're welcome to stay here for the night."

Maureen could have interpreted this as more than a friendly invitation, and it pleased her to consider it for a moment, but she knew that it wasn't.

"Thanks Kris, but I really have to be going. Judith will be worried."

"Judith?"

"My..... friend."

"Oh, sure, I'm sorry, I didn't mean to..."

"No problem. Listen, I really do want to hear the rest of this story. Can we get together soon? Maybe dinner early next week?"

"Sure, Mo. Give me a call. And thanks for the ear and the help."

The freelance writer left, leaving Kristian alone with her memories and her thoughts. The architect took another Librium and chased it with another Scotch.

Damn, Kristian thought, *I wonder who will be alive early next week.*

It had never been the intention of Joshua Paul Travis to become involved in search-and-rescue. His dream had always been quite simple, really. He had wanted to see the world, so he joined the Navy fresh out of high school. He knocked around Europe and Asia for several years after mustering out overseas. His stint with the Seabees had prepared him well for the various construction jobs he found wherever he went. But Joshua Travis always knew that some day he would return to his home in northern Wisconsin. Then, he would rise early and stoke the fire, put on a pot of coffee and take care of the farm chores. He would come in after chores to bacon sizzling and biscuits baking, wash up, hug his wife, and get ready for work. His work would be outdoors, that went without saying, and it would be of a nature that would allow ample time for hunting in the autumn and for fishing during the spring and summer. There would be a dog or two for hunting and a horse or two for riding and other animals for sustenance. When the time was right, he and his wife would have a family. They would all work hard, but not harried. Be busy but not burdened.

And during that splendid Wisconsin summer of 1968 Joshua's plans seemed pretty much on track. Together, he and Kristian had developed a nice little business tearing down old weathered barns and marketing the siding as decorative lumber. Joshua and his crew were responsible for locating and dismantling the structures. Kristian utilized her artistic talent and architectural training to market the wood. They both took care of the books. Then Joshua got the call.

It is late afternoon on a beautiful August Sunday, just under one year after Kristian's arrival in Wisconsin. They are just back from dinner with some of his family, and she's pleased that she is finally starting to feel comfortable with them, and they seem to be accepting her. Joshua always makes her feel good by telling her how long it took the clan to warm to his free spirited mother, when his dad first brought her home from northern Quebec, but how once they did, she was like a daughter to them all.

There's enough breeze to keep the humidity and the mosquitoes down, and not dreading work on Monday always makes week-ends so much longer. Joshua smiles as he watches her start in on some chores without any prompting from him. Then he goes to answer the phone that has been ringing since they first drove up.

"That was Jon VanStavern," he tells her. "It seems there are some lost kids up around the state game area. He wants us to join the search party. Suggested we bring Jenny-Dog and see if the hound in her knows any-thing about tracking."

"What about the animals?" she asks.

"They'll wait," he tells her. "Unless you don't want to go. Shouldn't take long. Lots of help, plenty of light, and my guess is they didn't wander too far. We should be home before dark."

She smiles because she's happy to be included and because this little adventure will help extend the weekend. He puts Jenny-Dog in the back of the pickup along with some rope and a canteen, and he tells Kris to bring some wine and cheese as he checks to make sure he has bug repellent for them if not the dog.

"No reason we can't have a little picnic down by the lake once we find those kids. It'll be real pretty so long as the bugs don't get too thick," he tells her, happy and excited and confident of the outcome.

And that's the way he was that first time he went out to look for some lost kids. And all the times after that up until Cody.

They got to the boat launch, which was close to where the kids had last been seen and where the search party was gathering. Jon VanStavern explained the situation to them and showed them the beach blanket where the kids had changed out of their swimsuits and the place in the woods where a pocketknife belonging to the boy had been found.

Joshua lets Jenny sniff the knife and the beach things, while Sheriff VanStavern forms a skirmish line to search the area where the knife has been found. Everyone is all set, just waiting for Joshua and Jenny, but

Joshua and Jenny aren't coming. In fact, they are poking around in the opposite direction.

"*Go find 'em girl," Joshua tells Jenny-Dog.*

Everyone is waiting in the woods near where the pocket knife has been found, and Joshua is a little worried that Jenny won't be able to get a scent from the knife or the other things that are wet and have been handled a lot.

"*Let's go, girl. This way," he tells her. But Jenny-Dog will have no part of it. She just keeps barking and spinning and heading in the other direction.*

At first Joshua thinks she is just playing; excited, maybe, about being out by the lake and the woods. But then he thinks how she usually minds pretty well and that maybe, just maybe, she is on to something.

Jon has plenty of people in the search party, so Joshua just tells them to go ahead. They will try their luck over in the other direction.

"*I'll go with you," Kris tells him.*

"*You sure? It's liable to be pretty rugged through there, and it looks like Jenny really wants to haul the mail."*

"*I'm sure," Kristian tells him and off they go.*

The day was warm but dry, and there was enough of a breeze so that you were comfortable, at first, and the bugs were still down. But Kristian was a smoker and had difficulty keeping up. *She is also getting cuts and scratches from the prickly brush that Joshua seems to know how to negotiate naturally.*

Joshua says his senses are keen and clear, just like when he's deer hunting in the fall, but the sights and sounds and smells are different because of the season. Kristian is winded and has a hard time catching her breath. All she can think about is keeping up. There is also a certain tension that adds to the excitement for Joshua and the fear for Kristian, because, as Josh has put it, the outcome is a little more important than whether or not you killed some old buck.

Joshua tries to pace himself and to move methodically through the woods, watching and listening for any movement or sound that Jenny might miss and that might be a clue as to the whereabouts of the kids. But Jenny-Dog doesn't miss much, and Joshua knows that she is on to a lot more than they are. He knows she is following something.

"Look how she keeps checking the air and the ground."

Kristian nods, too winded to speak.

They are moving into the wind, from the northwest for the most part, and they really have to hustle to keep up with Jenny-Dog. Joshua has to keep calling her back when she gets too far out of sight. She is on to something all right. He just hopes it is the kids and that they aren't on some wild goose chase after some animal.

They move quickly through the woods and come out onto an area of tall timothy, wild oats, and pioneer brush that runs along the lake and up onto a high bluff that plateaus into farmland overlooking the lake. The view is beautiful and there are lots of signs of deer. Joshua makes a mental note to come back in the fall, but just now he is a little concerned that Jenny might have been following a deer all along.

He is having trouble watching out for Kris and keeping track of Jenny in the tall grass, and he has to keep calling his dog back, but he can see she is leading them up to the top of the bluff. He thinks maybe the kids have seen the farmland and have decided to cut cross-country to look for a house.

Suddenly, Jenny-Dog pops her head up and stands sniffing the air for a moment. Then her head drops like a stone, and she charges off at ninety degrees from her previous direction, back down the hill, barking all the way.

"Now we'll see," he tells Kristian. "She's found whatever it is she's been tracking."

"Are you sure?" Kristian gasps, her face flushed.

"I'm sure. You okay?"

Kristian nods.

From the top of the bluff, they look down to where Jenny is barking.

She is jumping and spinning and making all sorts of commotion. And there, huddled under a bush, tired and scared and a little scraped up, is the seven-year-old boy with his arm around his five-year-old sister.

The search party was still out when they got back to the boat launch with the kids. Jonathan VanStavern let out a whoop.

"I knew you guys could do it!"

Jon called in the search party. Joshua and Kristian turned the kids over to him to get the first-aid they needed for their cuts and scratches and bug bites. Kristian received some minor first-aid also. Joshua was ready to return to the bluff overlooking the lake. He wanted to relive the adventure, and he thought that spot would be a nice place for a picnic. Kristian just wanted to get home and into a nice tub. She was hot and sore and exhausted. Her muscles ached, and deep in her lungs was a tight tickle that frightened her.

It was Joshua's first rescue. It was Kristian's last.

Chapter Twenty-two

Most people at the lodge slept in. There was not much else to do. The few hearty souls who awoke early generally took one look out the window, went to the bathroom, and returned to the soft, warm luxury of flannel sheets, fluffy down comforters, and heavy woolen blankets. Heat was turned down to sixty-five. Electricity from the generators was routed only to certain designated lights and outlets. The comforting smell of burning firewood filled the air.

By noon on Friday most of the guests had managed to drag themselves to the dining room and to fill themselves with hot coffee, oatmeal, French toast and bacon provided without cost by the hotel. They also gorged themselves on rumors and speculation.

"I hear we got four feet last night."

"I heard twenty-four inches with drifts of four feet."

"Drifts of four feet? Hell, look outside. All the cars are covered, the lift shacks too!"

"How can you tell? Look at it outside. You can't see past the porch."

"Well I'll tell you this much, I never thought I'd be bitching about having too much snow at a ski resort."

"Me neither. Oh well, at least we're warm and cozy. How'd you like to be outside in this stuff?"

The last remark brought an uncomfortable silence to the group as suddenly everyone remembered that there were people outside. Two people at least.

"Anyone hear any news about the little girl?"

People shook their heads. No one said a word.

"Jesus, can you imagine being out in this hell?"

"I don't know. That guy with the dogs looked like he knows what he's doing."

"You don't see him back here, do you? It looks like he didn't know enough."

"Maybe he's holed up somewhere."

"Jeeze, get real. Look at it out there. Why would he hole up if he could get back here?"

"Perhaps he couldn't get back last night."

"You've got that part right."

Jim Beard passed through the serving line.

"Hey Jim, any word on that little girl or that guy who went out to look for her?"

Beard thought about Hanson's advice. He chose his words carefully.

"Nothing definite."

"What does *that* mean?"

"It means we don't know anything definite," Beard snapped.

The guests at the table looked at each other. They decided to let it go. They all knew what it meant all right.

By afternoon, the Martins were awake. The sedatives had worn off. They were exhausted from grief and from tension. They were numb with fear, but not numb enough. No one had awakened them during the night to return their daughter to their arms. She must still be out there! My God, she was gone! She was really, truly gone! The realization overwhelmed them. Diane Martin cried relentlessly. John Martin held her and wept.

"Kelly, Kelly, Kelly," mourned Mrs. Martin.

"I'm sorry, Diane. God I'm so sorry. We should have gone in like you wanted. God, oh God, I'm sorry."

"I just want my Kelly. Why is God doing this to us? I just want my little girl."

Diane Martin also felt guilty. Not only had she acquiesced to her husband's desire for one last run, but it had been she who had suggested Jay Peak in the first place. The Peak had the reputation for the most annual snowfall in the East, and Diane had wanted to ski on powder. She had wanted Kelly to ski on real snow powder. Oh God!

Nancy Grady was also awake. She too was afraid to get out of bed. She snuggled deep under the blankets and held her daughter tight. How would she live with herself if Kelly Martin was not found?

"Sheriff, we've been able to make contact with some HAM radio operators," Beard reported. "We managed to get a weather report from them. I'm afraid this crud is expected to last at least one more day."

"What about that other storm building over the Midwest?"

"They say it's over the Great Lakes now, heading this way. 'Said it was too early to tell how bad it might be. Their best guess projection is that it won't hit before Sunday."

"Great. We'll have one day to dig out."

"If we're lucky. Or maybe it won't hit us at all. Who knows?"

"Yeah, who knows," Hanson muttered. "How is George doing with the guests? Is everything under control?"

"Yeah. Folks are doing pretty well. There's the usual griping because everyone wants to be skiing, but, other than that, people are handling things pretty well."

"Anyone seen the Martins, or Nancy Grady?"

"Not yet. What do you want me to tell them if I do?"

That was a good question. Hanson had to think for a bit.

"Let's stick with the same story I gave Nancy last night."

"Which is?"

"We think we got a broken radio message last night just before the power went out. We're not sure, but we think Travis may be holed up somewhere. We're not sure whether he's with the little girl or not."

"Are you sure this is the right thing to do?" Beard asked.

"Hell no, I'm not sure, but what else can we tell them? If we're all going to be stuck here for a few more days, people got to have some kind of hope. Don't they?"

Beard nodded his acceptance of the plan, if not his enthusiastic support. He looked out the large chalet window.

"Jesus, Sam, look at it out there. It's hard to imagine anyone staying alive for long out there, and she's been gone for more than a day."

Sam Hanson looked outside. It was hard to imagine.

Joshua Travis felt a tug on his shirt sleeve. He looked over at Kelly Martin.

"I'm hungry," Kelly announced. Joshua smiled. The dogs yawned and whined. They were ready to get up.

"You don't say. (Stay down, guys.) Well, should I fix us some oatmeal or hunt us down some bear meat?"

"Oatmeal," Kelly let him know.

"Well, that's probably a good choice seeing as how I don't have my rifle handy. Do you have to go potty?"

Kelly looked around and shook her head, no.

"How do your feet feel?"

"Okay. One of 'em hurts"

"One of them hurts, eh? Which one?"

Kelly got an impish look on her face. She shrugged her shoulders.

"Is it this one?" Joshua touched her left shin. Kelly nodded, yes.

Joshua knew he would have to check it again.

"Are you sure you don't have to go potty?"

Kelly looked around again. She shook her head ambiguously. "Where would I go?" the child asked tentatively.

"You can go right here in this nice warm tent. I'll set up a little potty-rig for you and you can go right here."

"How?"

"Well, what we'll do is take this here 'ol coffee can, that I happened to bring for just such emergencies, and we'll line it with a baggie, and you can go right in there. When you're done, we'll tie up the baggie and fling it outside. How does that sound?"

Apparently, it didn't sound too inviting to the little girl.

"I don't have to go," she decided. Joshua decided not to press it for the moment. He knew kids had strong bladders, and Kelly probably didn't have that much excess fluid in her yet. It was just something he would have to watch. In the meantime, he wanted to check her feet.

Once again, Joshua Travis exposed Kelly Martin's feet. This time he checked the left one first. He lifted her foot to his knee and shined the light across her toes. They were still bruised looking. They didn't look any better than they had before, but they didn't look any worse either. Joshua checked for drainage and odor. He found none. He lightly stroked the child's toes and foot.

"Does that hurt, Kel?"

Kelly shook her head, no. That was a good sign.

"How about here?" He touched her instep.

"No, just the tips of my toes."

Joshua checked Kelly's leg. "How does it feel here?" He touched her leg where the knot had been.

"A little," was the child's reply.

"Good girl." Joshua lightly touched the back of his hand to Kelly's forehead, cheek, and neck. She felt cool, certainly better than before. *Good deal,* he thought to himself. He re-dressed the left foot and checked the right one. It looked good, just as before. He was cautiously optimistic. He decided to keep the girl on acetaminophen to keep down any fever and help minor aches, but he would not give her any more with codeine unless he absolutely had to. He chose not to give her any antibiotics and hoped it was the right choice. He would wait until Kelly had something in her stomach before giving the Tylenol.

"Things are looking good," he announced as he re-dressed the girl's right foot. "Now, how about trying to go potty?"

Kelly shook her head. She didn't want to have any part of that coffee can.

"Come on, honey, I'll help you."

"You have to close your eyes."

Joshua smiled. "Sure, honey. I'll close my eyes. Now take it easy. I'll help you up. Try not to bump your toes."

He lined the can and helped the little girl get her arms through the sleeves of his oversize shirts. Joshua helped Kelly to her feet. She was unsteady. He knelt and held her under her arms.

"Easy does it. One step at a time." They made their way to the side of the tent. Travis did not want the sleeping bag getting wet. The dogs took the opportunity to get up and reposition themselves.

"Easy does it. I'll hold you and you can use the pack for support." Joshua found a packet of tissues that would serve as toilet paper. "That's it. Just squat down here and try to aim for the can."

"Close your eyes. No peeking."

"No peeking. I promise." He held the long shirts above Kelly's waist and was surprised at the amount of urine the little girl evacuated.

"I have to wash my hands."

Joshua hadn't thought about that. He didn't want her using cold snow.

"How about a wet-wipe?" He had some in the first-aid kit. "Will that be okay?"

Kelly nodded it would.

Joshua helped Kelly back to the sleeping bag. He tied the urine filled baggie with a twist-tie and placed the can outside the tent. He rubbed snow on his hands and dried them on the towel. Now for some grub.

"How about some oatmeal?"

"I'm scared," Kelly informed him.

He understood perfectly. He was scared too.

"Now you don't have to be scared, honey. I know my cooking is powerful bad, but I ain't killed anybody yet."

She looked at him with awe. How could anybody be so dumb?

"Not that! I'm scared of the noisy storm."

"Oh, that. For a minute there you had me worried. But you don't have to worry about that ol' storm. Why the harder it blows, the quicker it will blow itself out." He primed and lit the small stove outside the tent door. "Now, how about some cocoa and oatmeal?"

The little girl nodded. Joshua put some snow in a small pot and warmed it over the small but intense flame. He poured off some cocoa and tested it. It was tepid. He decided to warm that also. Unlike before, that would be all right now.

"We'll have this ol' breakfast going in two shakes of a lamb's tail, Miss Kelly. Say, is that what your dad calls you?"

"He calls me Kelly."

"Doesn't he have a nickname for you?"

"Just Kelly," she insisted. Then she confessed, "If I eat my sandwich messy, he calls me Kelly-Jelly."

"Why I can't believe you would ever eat a sandwich messy."

"Sometimes!"

"Well, I'll just call you Kelly. How's that? Or maybe Pumpkin. How do you like that name?"

"You're silly. And you look like Grizzly Adams too."

"Why thank you, ma'am. Grizzly Adams is one of my most

favorite people." The oatmeal was ready. He took the pot off the stove and replaced it with the one with the cocoa in it. He spooned out oatmeal into the empty cocoa cup for the girl and handed her the spoon.

"Give that a try. Careful if it's too hot."

Kelly took nourishment on her own for the first time.

"Mmmm. It's good. It tastes like pancakes." That was the maple sugar.

"Here's some cocoa to wash it down."

"Aren't you going to have any?"

"You eat all you want. I'll have some of this summer sausage." He cut three more one-inch slices from the meat. That just about finished that log. Each dog got one slice and a Milkbone. Joshua ate the last slice. He passed on the Milkbone.

"Well, you did a nice job. Want any more?"

Kelly shook her head, no.

"How about another Hershey bar?"

"I'm not s'posed to eat candy before lunch," the little girl informed him with painful honesty. Joshua looked at his watch. It was after two P.M. Without the watch and its digital readout he would not have known if it was day or night.

"It'll be okay. I'll square it with your folks. How about it?"

Kelly accepted the offer with the wary joy that comes from indulging in forbidden fruit. But Joshua's intent wasn't to tempt the child into parental disobedience. He wanted to get as many calories as he could into the child and the more fat calories the better.

He would have liked her to have eaten some of the summer sausage, with its extremely high fat content, but he did not know if she would like it, and he was afraid it might not sit well on her stomach. His game plan was to have her eat most of the carbohydrates, the cocoa, and the chocolate bars. The dogs and he would subsist on the sausage and snow and whatever little scraps the child might leave that couldn't be stored. Travis wasn't overly concerned about the food supply. Not yet. But there was no reason to be foolhardy. Since he could not predict the duration of the storm, he imposed a rationing regime on food for himself and the dogs. He did some quick calculations in his head and figured they had ample supplies for three days. After that things would get tight. None of this did he tell to the child.

"Well, that was a pretty good breakfast, if I do say so myself. I'm just going to clean up these here pots a little, and then I'm going to take the dogs out and see where things stand. Okay?"

"When are we going home?"

"Well, that's a good question. Just as soon as the storm lets up some, I reckon. That's what I'm going out to check. Judging from the sounds of the wind, we might have to wait it out here a spell. Is that okay?"

Kelly nodded, but Joshua knew that she knew she had no choice. He finished his chores and dressed to take the dogs outside. It was a hassle but it had to be done. He had to keep the air holes clear, and he wanted to gauge the storm from outside. This time he put on his sweatshirt.

Chapter Twenty-three

Kristian could hear the phone ringing, as she had heard it several times earlier. She still didn't feel much like answering it. Why bother? The machine would pick it up. Kristian hadn't felt so lousy since the first trimester of her pregnancy. She was nauseous, her mouth felt like it was lined with cotton, and she was depressed. She had no idea what time it was, and she didn't think to look at her watch. Kristian lay back on the sofa in the den and listened to the voice through the machine

"Hi, Kristian, are you there? It's Jane. Kristian, if you're there, pick up will you? Kris? Are you there? Hello...? Kristian, will you pick up the goddamn phone for Christsake! Jesus, you call me at work and say it's a goddamn emergency, and now you won't even answer your goddamn phone! Well, screw you!" Jane hung up before Kristian was able to answer.

Kristian smiled. Jane never had been one to mince words. She just hoped Jane was home and not calling from out of town after checking her messages. She dialed quickly.

"I knew you were home, you snot. What's the big fucking emergency?"

"How are you doing, Jane?"

"How am I doing? Well, let's see. My company sends me to New York in the middle of the goddamn winter; I have to take a damn train to D.C. to get out because the damn airports in New York are shut down because of a goddamn snowstorm. I haven't slept in two days; my best friend has some kind of an emergency that I don't know anything about and won't answer her phone; and when I finally get to talk to her, all she does is make small talk. Oh, I'm doing just great.... What's up, kiddo?"

"Joshua's out searching for a kid missing in that blizzard in Vermont."

There was an uncharacteristic silence at the other end. Then Jane recovered. "Jesus, Kris, I heard about that kid, but I didn't pay much attention. I just figured it was one of those winter storm stories that happens to somebody else. How did you find out? Was he on TV?"

"I saw the story on the news and had a feeling he might get called. I had Maureen Anderson do a little checking for me, and, sure enough, it was Josh."

"Damn. Well, hell, I wouldn't worry. I don't have to tell *you* that Joshua can take care of himself. What's the big deal? This isn't the first time you've heard about him rescuing some kid."

"I know, but this time it's different. All those other times, I found out after he had gotten back. I knew he was safe. This time he's still out there. At least I think he's still out there. I haven't listened to the news yet. Have you?"

"I don't remember hearing anything about it. How long has he been gone? Do you know?"

"What time is it now?"

"It's eleven-ten."

"Then he's been out almost twenty-four hours. Have you seen that storm? It's horrible."

Jane had not only seen pictures of the storm, she had experienced the edge of it for herself in New York City. She shuddered at the thought of being out in it, but she didn't say anything about it to her friend.

"Look Kris, I'm sure everything will turn out all right. You know Joshua has a charmed life. Nothing really bad ever happens to people like him. But in the meantime, why don't you come on out here and we'll spend the day together. Maybe go to Muir Woods and Mount Tam, or drive up the coast a bit. What do you say? I need to unwind and you need to get your mind off things, so what do you say?"

Kris knew that Jane was wrong about nothing bad ever happening to Joshua. But she was right about her needing to get her mind off things. She wasn't sure that would happen with Jane, but she knew that even if it didn't, Jane would put the best possible spin on things. Kristian wanted to be with her.

"What about Kenny?"

"What about him? He's working. That's what he gets for having a straight job."

Kristian smiled. "I have to shower. I'll be there in an hour."

"I know how you drive, you shit. You'll be here in fifty minutes if the cops don't stop you on the bridge. Just try not to kill yourself on the way over. I'm too tired to deal with that right now."

"I won't. I'll see you in a bit. And thanks."

"Yeah, yeah." Her friend hung up.

Joshua checked the interior dome of their shelter. It looked good. A nice glaze of ice had formed from the heat they had generated. He checked the four air holes, the original two plus the two new ones he had added. *Damn!*

Three of the holes were clogged, even on the leeward side. The fourth was partially blocked. It was fortunate he had caught it in time. Eight hours was definitely too long to wait to clear the air passages. He would not make that mistake again. Joshua opened the holes with the stick and set his watch timer for two hours. Until he knew better, he would check the airways every two hours. Or sooner.

The dogs were whining, especially Buck. They knew it was time to go out. Joshua left them in the tent. He found the field shovel and dug out the shelter entrance. He wasn't surprised to find that he had to dig up, as well as out, to get to open space, even close to the tree. Once outside, Joshua enlarged the clear area near the entrance and called out Buck. Jenny-Dog whined.

Outside, Joshua was amazed by the intensity of the storm. Even in the woods the snowfall was heavy, the wind pure murder. Together they would freeze and choke the life out of a man in short order. Travis looked up but could see the treetops only when he looked downwind, and then only sometimes.

He surveyed the shelter, moving through the deep snow to the windward side. It was covered by at least another foot of snow, more on the side where snow had drifted and piled up. That was good. More strength, up to a point, and more insulation. But he was concerned that the snow would fill the leeward side to the point where he would have trouble keeping the air holes open. He brought Buck inside, dusted him off, and let Jenny out.

"Make it fast." He told her.

She did.

Joshua sealed the passage and checked the air holes one last time before entering the tent. *Damn*, he thought as he entered the warm, humid shelter, *smells like a cross between a kennel and a kitchen.* He didn't worry about it. After a few minutes he would be used to it again. He wondered what it was like for the dogs. Their ability to avoid olfactory fatigue was one of the things that made them so valuable. *Hell, probably smells like a hotel to them.*

"How're you doing, Kelly-Jelly?" he teased. "Ol' Buck didn't try to eat you, did he?"

Kelly shook her head. "He's my friend now," she said with obvious pride.

"That's good. Looks like we're going to have to stay put for a while longer, sweetheart. Is that okay?"

Kelly nodded. She was a good kid. Travis wanted to get her back soon.

Joshua removed his mukluks and struggled out of his snow-pants. He left his woolen trousers on and dug out his moosehide camp moccasins. He removed his down parka but left on his sweater and sweatshirt. If he was going to check the air holes every couple of hours, there was no need for him to keep getting dressed and undressed all the time. Kelly was warm and stable. She no longer needed his body heat in the sleeping bag. He would be comfortable stretched out on the outside of the down filled bag.

"Want anything more to eat?"

Kelly shook her head.

"Are you thirsty?"

"Yes."

"How about a little Gatorade?" Joshua was happy for the chance to get more water in the child.

"When are you going to take me home?"

"That's a good question, honey. Maybe in a few hours. Probably another day at most. It's hard to say. These things don't usually last too long."

"I miss my mommy and my daddy."

"Well, they miss you too." Travis was sure of that. He knew they were going through hell. He hoped they could hold it together.

"Why can't we go home now?"

Joshua decided to be honest with the child. "The snow is too deep and it's very, very cold outside. Most of all, the wind is too strong. We might get lost, or the wind might blow us over. Then we might get buried or freeze to death."

"But we won't freeze to death in here. Right?"

"Darn tootin'. We're all snug as five bugs in a rug, all safe and sound."

"Good."

"Well, what should we do now?"

"Let's tell stories."

"Good idea. Tell me a story."

"No, Joshua, you tell me a story."

"No fair. I told the last story."

"And you tell the next story."

"Are you sure? What kind of a story do you want?"

"A scary story," Kelly demanded.

"A scary story? Aren't you scared enough just being out here?"

Kelly shook her head bravely.

"How about a funny story instead," Joshua suggested.

"A scary story," Kelly insisted. Then she compromised, "a funny, scary story."

As it happened, Joshua had one in mind.

Chapter Twenty-four

Kristian drove a black Porsche 911 Targa. She drove it fast. The roads were wet but the rain had stopped, for the moment. One thing all that Wisconsin winter driving had done was teach her to handle a vehicle on slippery surfaces. Compared to those icy roads, these seemed almost dry.

She cut through the late morning traffic and crossed the bridge before noon. She managed to race through Sausalito without killing anyone. At the exit, Kristian turned onto Rt. 1. She threw the sportscar into the hairpin curves with gusto but not, as Jane had feared, with reckless abandon. The Porsche whined past the cutoff for Muir Woods and sped along the misty coast. Jane had a house at Stinson Beach.

Kristian had expected the drive to rekindle the memories she had spoken of to Maureen. That was one reason she was driving so fast, the other was that she liked to. But to her utter fascination, what stood out most during the drive was how totally different the coast was in the winter. That was a good sign. That was what she needed.

During the ride, she listened to the national news. The blizzard stories were getting old. There was no word on the missing child. She pulled into Jane's drive at 12:30, fifty minutes from the time she had left her door.

"Hello, kiddo. Hanging tough? It's good to see you."

The two women hugged. They had been friends since freshman year in the dorm at Berkeley, then roommates in an apartment on Channing Street when they weren't experimenting with guys. Most of those experiments had been disastrous, and they always knew they could come back to each other, no questions asked, though the answers were usually shared.

Jane had always loved Stinson Beach and Marin County. Her job as top buyer for Magnin paid her handsomely. Kenny, her husband, made a good living also. But it was mostly the generous settlement from her first husband that had paid for the house on the beach.

"I was listening to the radio on the way over. There's still no word."

"I know. I was listening to NPR. But hell, what do they know?"

"Jesus, Jane, I don't know what's happening. I didn't even call into work today."

"You don't have to, remember? You're a partner."

"I know but...."

"Screw work. Come on in. You want a drink? How 'bout some dope?"

Kristian passed. She still felt like hell from last night.

"Shit, you're no damn fun anymore. I suppose you expect me to make you lunch."

Kristian knew she should eat something, but she still had no appetite. "Let's go out."

"Finally something out of your mouth that makes some sense. I'll drive."

"Am I blocking you in?"

"No, we're taking your car. Give me the keys."

Kristian laughed and tossed her the keys. What the hell. The car only cost a small fortune. Jane drove north then turned right, onto the twisting northern leg of road that climbed the hills and led back to Mount Tamalpais and Muir Woods.

Like Kristian, Jane was tall, but, unlike her perfectly propor-
tioned friend, Jane was too lanky and too knobby to be considered
beautiful, or even really pretty. Still, men found her attractive. Jane's
dark eyes and brunette hair were a refreshing change from all the
California blondes. Her glances, like her movements, intimated
availability. Before she married Ken Sloan she was.

Neither woman spoke. A rush of memories flooded them both
as they entered the woods. The redwood and eucalyptus were always
especially aromatic after a rain. These woods, and others like them,
had been their sanctuary during their school years. It was here they
had come to smoke dope and drop acid for the first time. And it had
been here that Kristian had brought Joshua once she decided that
she no longer wanted to beat him but to win him.

"Did you know that John Muir lived in Wisconsin?" Kristian
asked Jane.

"Shut up, I'm driving!"

Kristian smiled. She looked at her best friend. "You're a real
bitch, you know that?"

"That's why you love me. Besides, who gives a rat's ass where
John Muir was from. You just want to talk about Wisconsin. So go
ahead and talk. I'm busy missing trees." Jane loved driving a fast car
that wasn't her own.

"Jane, I don't know what's happening to me. I thought for sure
he was out of my system. I tried to do a damn thorough job of burning bridges. I've accomplished a lot of the goals I set for myself. I
have just about everything I ever dreamed about and then whammo!
This happens, and all I can think about is Joshua. All I care about is
Joshua. Nothing else means anything. Am I nuts or what?"

"Yes. Now shut up and let me drive."

It was starting to snow in Lincoln County, Wisconsin. Jon
VanStavern decided to check things again out at the Travis place.

He knew Josh's neighbors could be counted on, but he wanted to be sure the heat was on so the pipes would not freeze. After he took the left fork at the three-way, he passed the Blazer Pub. Jon noticed Rod Kielor's truck in the lot. The sheriff decided to stop.

"Well, good afternoon, Sheriff. Here for a late lunch?" It was Patrick Finn, the owner, behind the bar.

"No thanks, Patrick. Have you seen Rod around? I see his truck is outside."

"I believe he's in the washroom. Any problem?"

"No, no. I just want to ask him if he can see that Josh Travis's drive is cleared if this snow keeps up." With that, Rod Kielor walked up, shaking the remaining drops of water from his hands.

"Howdy, Jonathan. Did I just hear you take my name in vain?" Rod was an ample man with a ready grin and a willing hand.

"Afraid so, Rod. I was just wondering if you'd mind keeping an eye on Josh's place, and plowing' the drive if need be?"

"No problem. Consider it done. Any word on how Josh is making out?"

"All we know for sure is that he got there. Communications are a mess out there. We don't know if he found the little girl or even if he was able to pick up a trail. Hell, we don't even know for sure if he was able to go out looking. From all reports, things are pretty rough out there."

The hawk like owner and bartender broke in. "Jonathan, you know as well as we do that if there's a child out in that storm then Joshua is out there also. You also know that if there's a whisper of a prayer that the little girl is alive then Joshua and his blessed dogs will find her and bring her home." Joshua was the local hero. He always had been, back to his three sport high school days.

Sheriff VanStavern knew all that. It had been he who had first involved Joshua in finding lost kids. It had been he who had encouraged Joshua to use his God given gifts to help save people lost in the woods. And it had been he who had set up a network of communications and logistics, including the Air National Guard, that could whisk Travis anywhere on the continent on short notice.

Together they had achieved some remarkable results. More than once people, often children, had been saved who probably would have been lost had it not been for Joshua. People had been saved solely because of Joshua's relentless determination and his amazing dogs. Jonathan VanStavern knew well Joshua's skills and talent and determination. It was precisely that stubborn determination that sometimes concerned him, especially after Cody.

"Well, all we can do is hope for the best. A prayer or two probably wouldn't hurt. Rod, I appreciate you looking after the drive. Let me know if you notice any problems, will you?"

"Sure thing, Jonathan. I'll keep a real good eye on the place. Don't you worry."

"Thanks. Well, I'll see you boys, Charlotte, Marion. I'll keep you posted."

"Aye, see that you do, Sheriff, and Jon, just remember, these things are in God's hands, not ours."

VanStavern nodded. It didn't help his feelings of guilt and uselessness. They had accomplished some remarkable feats, to be sure. But Jonathan VanStavern knew that he hadn't done his friend any favor setting him on this course.

Chapter Twenty-five

"Let's see now, I guess it was about nine or ten years ago that this story took place. It was early October and Kris and I were up in northern Quebec. You know where that is?"

Kelly shook her head, no.

"Well, it was way up in Canada, about two hundred and fifty miles from here, near a place called Chicoutimi, and we were visiting my cousin Michel and his wife Odette and their two little girls."

"How old are they?"

"The little girls? Well let's see. They're teenagers today, but back then they weren't much older than you are. Anyway, it was Kris's first time meeting that side of my family, and, all things considered, she held up pretty well even though we did do a lot of talking in French, and at the time Kris's French was a little shaky."

"How come?"

"How come her French was shaky?"

"How come you were talking French?"

"Well, that's what people speak way up in Quebec."

"How come you were talking French *and* how come her French was shaky?"

"Well, because a long time ago, the people who settled in Quebec came from France. But Kristian had never learned much French before we met."

"Why?"

Joshua paused and smiled. He wondered if he would ever get to tell the story. Shoot, he thought, what difference does it make anyway?

"Just never took the time, I guess,"

"Oh." Kelly seemed satisfied.

"Now, where were we?"

"You and Kris were visiting your cousin and talking French."

"Oh yeah. Okay, so we were visiting my cousin and his family, and he and I went out hunting in the morning. I didn't bring any guns to Canada because it was hard getting them into the country, but I knew Michel had a cabinet full to choose from. See, my dad had helped him build the cabinet on one of our family trips back when I was a kid."

"When was that?"

"A long time ago. Anyway, on the way back to the truck we were talking about what a hard worker and good hunter my dad was. Then we talked about what we were up to, and I told him about the barn business and about a rescue Jenny-Dog and I had helped in back in August of that year."

"Did you find a little girl that time?"

"A little boy *and* a little girl. You know, I still get cards from them at Christmas."

Kelly smiled. Joshua continued. "Well, Michel listened intently as I told him how Jenny-Dog and Kris and I tracked down the missing kids. Then he smiled with excitement and he said, 'Je connais un chien on doit voir!' Which means, *I know a dog you have to see!*

"After lunch, we piled into my cousin's VW van to go visit the dog that Michel knew about. The dog belonged to an old bachelor farmer, if belonged is the right word, who lived several miles out on the other side of town. It was a beautiful autumn day, and it was fun going for an outing with the family. The kids had been kept home from school to spend time with their Uncle Joshua and *Aunt Kristian*, and Michel had taken time off from his work for the same reason."

"Where does he work?"

"Who?"

"Your cousin."

"Oh, he works for a construction company." Joshua anticipated the next question. "He builds buildings."

"Oh." Kelly was satisfied.

The old man lives in a run down little place that has a beautiful view, but only if you can look past all the junk and broken machinery that litters what would have been his yard. The old man comes out, followed closely by a pretty, if ungroomed, poodle. But that isn't the dog they have come to see. As Michel and Joshua speak with the farmer, a large reddish tan dog with white on his chest and paws and only one good eye ambles over. The farmer and Michel point him out, and the old man becomes agitated and chases the dog away. He speaks some more to Josh and Michel, and the two cousins begin to crack up. The old farmer doesn't see anything funny.

"The dog's name was *Vas t'en* because the old man was always chasing him away and *vas t'en* means *go away* in French. He must have been six or seven-years-old, and he was blind in one eye from a fight. We guessed him to be a lab/collie mix from his color and conformation. And he was in love with the poodle, even though the old man had spent fifteen hard-to-come-by dollars to have her fixed after the first time *Vas t'en* had gotten to her." Oops, Joshua knew he had made a mistake.

"What do you mean?"

Joshua was caught. He had to think quickly. He told her simply that the farmer did not want the poodle to have any puppies. The child seemed to accept that. Joshua remembered Kristian sniping, *"Typical male,"* and Odette concurring, *"Evidenment."*

"What made Michel want me to see him was that the old man

— 167 —

couldn't lose the dog no matter how hard he tried. He had driven far out in the country and set the dog loose, only to have *Vas t'en* reappear within a day or two. When the man drove into Chicoutimi with his poodle, he could count on the other dog showing up if he stayed in the same place for more than an hour. He even tried bringing the dog to the local pound (though, he explained, it went against his grain; otherwise, he would have just shot the rascal) but somehow *Vas t'en* had escaped and found his way back to the old man and the poodle."

"He shouldn't shoot the rascal," Kelly let him know.

"No, he didn't. Finally, the old man just resigned himself to his fate and started feeding the dog, mainly because he was worried about what the dog would do for food if he didn't.

"I took a shine to the dog right off, because I thought he had character.

"'All the character of a gigolo,' Kris muttered."

"What's that?"

"What's what?"

"A jiggle-o?"

Joshua was stumped for a moment. "Let's see, a gigolo is somebody who wants to play all the time, and never wants to work."

"Oh. I have a cousin who's a jiggle-o. His name is Andrew."

Joshua raised his eyebrow for a second, but he relaxed when Kelly informed him, "He's four." Joshua continued his tale.

"I was interested in this here dog's uncanny ability to orient himself and to follow what must have been pretty weak trails. I thought I might learn some things from him, and so, even though I had my doubts about how trainable he would be, I asked the old man, *'Combien pour prendre le chien?'* which means, *How much to take the dog?*

"The old farmer replied, *'Vingt-cinq, au moins.'* At least twenty-five dollars.

"But I thought twenty-five dollars was a little steep for a questionable mutt that looked to be more trouble than he was worth. I suggested that ten dollars might be fairer, but he insisted on twenty-five, not one cent less.

"Well, we had had a good year, and I figured he needed the money more than we did, so I finally relented, not any too sure that I wanted this darn dog in the first place. Kristian was giving me an evil look, and Odette was going into hysterics.

"And don't you know, just as I dug my wallet out of my back pocket, this old man pulled his purse from his trousers, and we both counted out twenty-five dollars to give to the other! We looked at each other, stunned. Then we all broke up laughing and went inside his shack to seal the deal over a drink."

Kelly didn't get it. Joshua didn't explain. He just smiled to himself, remembering the incident.

"So that was how we acquired *Vas t'en*. Maryam and Marie-Eve, Michel's kids, promptly renamed him *Le Prince Jean-Jacques*, after some storybook character they liked, and we just called him Jake."

Kelly waited. "That's not scary," she complained.

Joshua looked down at her. "Well, just hold onto your horses. I'm coming to the scary part. How about some trail mix, or granola? Or would you like some more cocoa?" Joshua was still trying to get calories into the child.

"No, thank you. I'm not hungry."

"No thank you. I'm not hungry," Kristian told the waiter offering her a menu.

"Don't pay any attention to her. She'll have the cheddar cheese-broccoli soup and a salad. I'll have the same and bring plenty of bread." Jane ordered. They had stopped at the Tamalpais Inn, near Muir Woods. The broccoli-cheese soup was world renowned.

It was raining again and it felt good to be in the dark timbered chalet style restaurant, close, but not too close, to the blazing fire in the fieldstone fireplace. Jane ordered a burgundy. Kristian had hot coffee.

"So what's the deal, Kris? Are you still in love with him? Of course you are. That was a stupid question." Jane always did have a knack for cutting through bullshit. It was one of the reasons she was such a successful buyer for her company.

"I don't know, Jane. I didn't think so."

"Bullshit! You know. You know perfectly well. Look, Kris, it's me you're talking to, remember. I know Joshua. I know what he's like. And I know what you're like when you're with him. It's the only time I've ever seen you really comfortable with a man. And really happy."

"I'm happy now. At least I thought I was. And I wasn't so happy with Joshua the last couple of years, especially after that Wyoming rescue."

Jane reached across the table and took Kristian's hand. She looked into her eyes, like only a best friend can, and told her softly, but plainly, "Kris, you left Joshua because you were afraid you were heading down different paths. He wanted kids and you weren't ready. He got involved in search-and-rescue, maybe too involved, and you got left out, or at least felt you were playing second fiddle to the dogs, which, of course, was bullshit. Mostly, you started to resent the fact that you were living in Joshua's dream, and he wasn't living in yours. After that fire rescue, Kris, Joshua became obsessed. I know that. But face it Kris, he really needed you, and that scared the shit out of you, so you left. Ironic, isn't it, since that's what you always thought you wanted."

"I was scared to death that I would be a widow at the ripe old age of twenty-eight or twenty-nine, possibly with a kid or two, living in the wilds of northern Wisconsin. We've been over this before, Jane. So why am I so fucked up now?"

"Because it's finally dawned on you that Joshua's dream is the only one open to you, at least to both of you, and it may even be too late for that. Do you think I don't know what's been going on for the last four or five years with your furious scramble for success?"

Kristian was silent. She couldn't lie to Jane. Jane knew her too well.

"I really thought I was past that," Kristian explained to her friend.

"Oh yeah, right. That's why the most eligible woman in San Francisco never dates. Or are you like Maureen Anderson? By the way, did she hit on you? Actually, I think you two would make a lovely couple. Drive all the sailors and the homophobes absolutely mad."

"You know about her? Jesus, I had no idea before last night. Christ, I even invited her to stay the night."

"You always were a tease."

"Besides, I date when I have the time and if I feel like it."

"Right. How many guys have you slept with in the last five years?"

Kristian didn't blush. "None of your damn business."

"I rest my case. Listen, I don't give a shit about your sex life, or lack thereof. That *is* none of my business. But just who are you trying to kid, me or you...? Filed any papers recently?"

The waiter arrived with their soup. He nearly spilled it, trying to look down their blouses. Jane unbuttoned her top button to make it easier for him, then told him, "Don't wet yourself, Bucko."

"You never change, do you? That's the same kind of shit you used to pull in college. Remember that time at California Hall with those bikers? Christ, I thought Kenny was going to have a shit fit when he saw you dancing with them."

"Yeah, it was good for him. Never want to be taken for granted. Besides, I can change all right. As a matter of fact, I'm changing right now. You just can't notice it yet."

"What do you mean?" Kristian had a strange feeling she knew

what was coming. She just couldn't believe it.

Jane smiled and nodded. "Yep, almost two months now. You think I should tell Kenny?"

"You shit. How long have you known? Have you really not told Kenny yet?"

"I got the test back two weeks ago. Maybe I'll tell Kenny tonight."

Kristian looked at her long time friend, absolutely astonished. She couldn't tell if Jane was putting her on about not having told her husband, but she wouldn't be surprised. That would be just like Jane. Kenny would be thrilled.

Kristian was curious. "What made you decide?"

She knew that the pregnancy was wanted, if not planned. Jane was not ambivalent about abortion.

"Oh, I don't know," Jane replied. "Tick, tick, I suppose."

Tick, tick indeed, Kristian thought.

Chapter Twenty-six

From *The Beginning, the Hopi people were a Chosen People. The Creator chose the Hopi to work and to populate a magnificent land. The Creator chose the Hopi to draw sustenance from a climate most others would find unendurable. The Creator chose the Hopi to find beauty in the daily rhythms of life and work and love. Above all, The Creator chose the Hopi to be the Keepers of the Flame; to strive for moral perfection.*

By nature and by belief, the Hopi were always a peaceful people. Their kalatakam, their warriors, were meant only for defense. Still, they had many enemies. There were the Tavasuh, who wanted their grain and their women. There were the Castillas, who wanted their minerals and their souls. There were the Congress and the Bureau of Indian Affairs, who wanted everything. Over the years the Hopi faced many trials.

At night during the Times of Trial the elders and the holy people would come together in the kivas. They would smoke tobacco. They would pray.

To allay fear among the children and to strengthen their own faith, the kalatakam would recount legends of heroic deeds. They would tell stories of past trials surmounted.

"Well, ol' Jake was trouble right from the get go. We were camping up at the Mauricie, and we wanted to take Jake and Jenny-Dog in our canoe so we could camp way off by ourselves, but Jake wasn't too steady in the boat so we had to stay put. Then, our first night back in Montreal, visiting some other cousins, Jake got me into trouble with the police because I had parked the truck out on the street, with Jake and Jenny in back, and Jake barked his fool head off every time someone passed by, and it was two o'clock in the morning... Remember that, Jenny-girl?" Joshua scratched his dog behind her ears.

"I always kept Jake on a rope as long as we were traveling because I was afraid that if he got loose anywhere in Canada he would find his way back to his girlfriend. Whoo, boy that farmer would have had a fit. But once we got back to Wisconsin I turned him loose and figured that if he wanted to go back to Quebec, well, I wouldn't be the one to stop him."

"Did he go?"

"No, as a matter of fact, he didn't. Ol' Jake was crazy but he wasn't dumb. He stuck around, sort of, and I started working with him."

"What kind of working?" Kelly asked.

"Well, first I started taking him out hunting with me and Jen, and then I started working with him on finding lost people."

"How did you do that?"

"Well, I'd get my wife or some kids to fuss up the dog and maybe put some cookies or some meat in their pockets. Then, I'd have them go off across the yard and, after a minute or two, I'd have Jake, or whichever dog I was working, run after the person to get a little treat. Then next, I'd have the person do the same thing, but this time I'd have them go around the corner and hide behind the barn."

"Do you have cows in the barn?"

"Sometimes, not usually," Joshua explained patiently.

"What do you have in the barn?"

"We keep our horses in there, and some machinery, you know, tractors and all."

"Oh. What else did you do with Old Jake?"

"Well, each time Jake would find Kris, or whoever was hiding, he'd get a treat and a little fussing, and the next time the person would go out a little farther. Maybe hide in a little harder place to find. I'd have the neighbor kids climb trees and run through the creek and do just about anything you could think of to throw the dog off the trail, just like I did when I was a kid training my first dog to hunt coons. Why before you knew it, ol' Jake and Jenny were finding people lickidy split, no matter how far they went or where they hid."

"How do they know?" Kelly was puzzled.

"How do they know what?" Joshua asked.

"How do they know where to find people?"

"Well, that's a good question. They kind of follow a person's smell," Joshua explained. "Everybody smells just a little bit different, just a little bit special, and dogs have real good sniffers. They can smell things that you and I could never smell, and they can smell things that drift in on the wind. And for dogs, just a little bit of smell can tell them a whole lot."

"What can it tell them?"

"Well, a little smell can tell a dog who, or what, he's looking for. It can tell him if that person is scared or not, or if that person is nice or not...."

"How?"

Joshua thought for a moment. He was well acquainted with canine anatomy. But he knew that this wasn't what Kelly was asking about.

"I can't say for sure, mind you, but my guess is it's kind of like when you smell something special and it reminds you of something else, or brings a picture of something into your mind. Do you know what I mean? Maybe you're a little young."

Kelly concentrated for a moment. "When I smell Christmas trees, I think of Christmas."

"That's the idea. Well, my guess is that dogs can do that with a lot of things, and a whole lot better than people can."

"Why didn't you bring Old Jake to find me?"

Again, Joshua had to reflect. Jake had died, or so Josh believed, some years back. The crazy dog had disappeared one final time, and Joshua just assumed he had either died or been killed. "He went back to his girlfriend in Quebec," he told the child.

"Was he a good finder?"

"A good what?"

"Was he a good finder of lost kids?"

Joshua marveled at Kelly's alertness and inquiring mind.

"Yes he was. He was a very good finder. But there was a problem. He didn't always mind like he should, and he didn't always come when he was called. So I only used him once on a search. After that, I just used him to learn about tracking and for breeding."

"What does that mean?"

"Making puppies."

"Oh... How?"

"Ask your daddy when you see him. Are you going to let me finish this story?"

"Okay."

"Kris and I were real busy because we had a lot of work to catch up on, and we were hoping to have a baby. I still tried to work with the dogs a bit each day, but it was hard to find the time.

"Jake would show up for meals and hunting – usually. He seemed to sense when we were going hunting or were going to work on tracking, and he was a natural at both. I worried about him running deer, but the tail he was after wasn't white. So then I just worried about him getting shot. Not so much by a hunter, as by an irate neighbor with a bitch in season. But somehow he managed to survive, and to this day you can't find a corner in Lincoln County that doesn't have mutts running around that look something like him."

Kelly wasn't sure what all that meant, but she made a special effort not to interrupt.

"Frosty mornings gave me a good chance to see just how the dogs were working. Kris would go hide in the woods, and I'd set Jenny and Jake out after her. You could see her tracks across the pasture and in the fields, and that way I could tell if the dogs were following a ground trail or an airborne scent. It was interesting to see just when they chose the air and when they stuck to the ground. Sometimes, based on the amount or direction of wind, it was hard to figure why they chose which they did. But the one thing I did learn was to let them do it their way because they sure know a heck of a lot more about tracking than I do."

"They're smart."

"Yes they are. We taught the dogs to circle a starting point for a hundred yards, if need be, to pick up a scent. And to split up and work both sides of the creek or the river to find where the trail picked up again. And don't you know, those darn dogs got so's they were competing with each other to be the first on track and to reach Kristian or whoever we were tracking. And we encouraged that because I reckoned it would hone their instincts and might just come in handy some day.

"The dogs were getting pretty sharp. I would give Kris fifteen or twenty minutes to hide, and the dogs would find her in five. Sometimes, after we would get the neighbor kids to hide so's we could track them, we would treat them to cider and doughnuts. Or fresh baked apple pie if we had any."

"Mmmm," Kelly approved.

"Well, by the time mid-November rolled around those two hounds could track a trout in a stream. Then one morning we got another call from Jon VanStavern, the sheriff out our way. It was the first day of deer season, gun season that is, and I was up in my favorite tree blind."

"What's a blind tree?"

"A tree blind? Well, that's kind of like a little tree fort that I sit in sometimes when I'm hunting deer."

"Oh... Do you kill them?"

Joshua wasn't embarrassed at all. He smiled. "I harvest them."

"What does that mean?"

"It means I help feed them all year and then, once or twice a year, when I need meat, I kill one or two of them."

Kelly wasn't sure about all this. She had seen BAMBI. She always believed hunters were bad. Now she was confused. Joshua didn't seem bad. She needed a way to resolve the dilemma.

"Do you miss sometimes?"

Joshua looked at her and smiled. He didn't miss often. When he did, he knew, it was usually worse for the animal than when he didn't. "Sure," he told her. "I miss lots of times. Why if I had a nickel for every deer that got away, I'd be a rich man today."

Kelly felt better. "What happened with the sheriff?"

The tent fluttered and breathed with changes in air pressure. Even sheltered as they were, the sounds of the storm were invasive; the constant jet roar of super chilled air; the punctuated popping of frozen wood; the crash of a nearby widowmaker. Joshua looked around and knew enough to be frightened. Then he looked at Kelly, smiled, and related the story.

Chapter Twenty-seven

Jonathan VanStavern hesitated to ask Joshua to get involved again, but Tom Royce, down in Sauk County, was an old friend, and it sounded like the situation might be serious. A university family from Madison was camping down near Lake Delton with their four-year-old daughter and their two-year-old son. The father had gone to get some fire wood, thinking the boy was with the mother and daughter. The mother thought the boy had gone with his dad. The truth was that the boy had gone off by himself.

Jon swallowed hard when Kristian answered the phone, then he went ahead and asked, "Kris, we might have a life or death situation here. Little boy's only two. He won't last long."

Kristian did not hesitate. "Josh is out hunting, Jon. You make whatever arrangements you need to, and I'll find him as quickly as I can."

VanStavern was relieved and went about lining up a small plane that could fly Joshua and his dogs down to the Dells. Then he headed out to their place.

Kris hung up the phone. Joshua was still in the woods. He's probably up in the blind he built at the edge of the cornfield, but if he's not he could be anywhere.

Jon sounded nervous, not like in August, and he had told her that time could be crucial to this kid lost way down in the Dells. The day is cold, this kid is only two-and-a-half-years-old, and there are lots of itchy hunters out in the woods.

At first she is unsure what best to do. If Josh isn't in his cornfield blind, it could take her all day to find him even though she knows he probably isn't too far. She thinks about tying a rope on to Jenny and trying to have her track him, but then she thinks it will save time to send Jenny out alone, while she heads up to the blind.

Kristian wraps a note in a scarf that she ties around Jenny's neck and tells her to go find Joshua. Josh had told Jenny-Dog to stay put, but she takes off like a shot towards the woods. Kristian now knows she probably won't find Joshua up at the field blind. She goes there just to be certain.

Joshua is not in the field. As Kristian starts trotting back down towards the house, a terrible, sinking feeling wells up deep in her stomach. She has forgotten to put any orange on herself or a bell on Jenny.

"I had gotten to the blind by the field too late to see any deer, so I moved to the tree blind in the woods and sat a spell. It was cold for November. Even with the blue sky and the sun out, the ground was frozen and there was still a hard frost down after nine. Everything was gray and brown and tan, except for the sky and the frost, and the deer were invisible, except when they moved."

"How do they get invisible?"

"They're just real hard to see because they're colored just like the trees and bushes. It's called camouflage."

"Oh."

"I had been sitting in the tree well over an hour, trying not to move and to use my ears as much as my eyes. There was a light breeze from the northwest, so it surprised me a little to hear something come from the southeast. I carefully shifted around and braced my left foot against a lower branch. I had a 308 Ruger with me, that's a rifle, that I brought to my shoulder, but all I could see were a couple of squirrels in the nearby oaks. I left the safety on. Then I saw a little movement in the brush at the edge of the woods. Whatever was coming was moving fairly quickly. That surprised me too, see, because I hadn't heard any shots and, whatever it was, it wasn't making noise like a deer and it seemed a little small. I figured it might be a small doe or a fawn. I lined up my sights, but I held my fire."

"You shouldn't shoot because it's Jenny-Dog!"

"That's right. And lucky it was that I didn't shoot because coming outta the bush, and making for me lickidy-split and a barking as she ran, was Jenny-Dog."

"See! I told you."

"You're right. At first I was ticked off... you know, mad. I figured she hadn't stayed home like I'd told her to and was just out for a good time. That fool dog, I thought. She's gonna get herself shot by some dam...I mean darn hunter, if she pulls stunts like this too often. Then I saw Kristian's green and gold scarf wrapped around Jenny's neck and I got worried, so I unloaded my rifle and climbed down out of the tree."

"She's not a fool dog. She's a good dog. She's just like Lassie."

"Better." He reached over and stroked Jenny-Dog along the neck.

"There was a piece of tape around the scarf and on it was written, *note inside*. I took the scarf off Jenny and opened it up to find the note. It was a folded piece of paper that just said, *Kid lost – Jon needs help – Emergency!*"

"Just like me!"

"Just like you. Well, I eased my rifle sling over my arm and up onto my shoulder, and I told Jenny to stay close to me. And as we headed back to the house, I kind of wondered just what was going on."

Kelly nodded, entranced. Her mouth was open, her eyes and ears were wide.

The sheriff drives up just as the man and the dog are clearing the woods. Joshua breaks into an easy jog as he gets into the open, but he is careful. This is no time to twist an ankle. Kristian goes out to meet them, expecting Joshua to chide her for forgetting to put the bell on the dog, but he doesn't. He just tells her it was good thinking, sending Jenny out after him, as he pushes into the den to put up his rifle and grab the rescue pack he has prepared. Kristian notices that he doesn't forget to pack the orange coats and the bells they have made for the dogs.

"Jon met me as I came out of the house. He took my pack and placed it in the opened trunk of the car. I told Jenny to go with him and get in the car, and, sure enough, she did it like she knew what I was talking about. Then I went over to the tack room to get the harnesses and line I had made, and, after that, I whistled for Jake and put a leash on him. I put him in the back with Jenny, and I climbed into the front with Jon. And as we drove down the drive and onto the road, I felt bad because I hadn't even said good-bye to Kris."

"Why did you forget to say good-bye to Kris?"

"Well, I was in a hurry and I just didn't think."

"You should have said good-bye."

"Yes, I should have."

"Then what happened?" Kelly prodded.

Joshua continued.

The lights are flashing and the siren is blaring as they speed towards Peter Haennicke's field, where a small plane is prepped and waiting. Jon has to shout to be heard as he fills Joshua in on the situation down in the Dells.

"Maybe it's nothing and, then again, maybe it's something. But when my old buddy from Sauk County spelled it out to me and asked for my help, I was hard pressed to turn him down. Especially since the reason Tom called in the first place was because I had told him the story of your successful search back in August."

VanStavern fills Joshua in, as best he can, on the way over to Haennicke's. The family was camping at the Mirror Lake campground when the boy wandered off. After a frantic half-hour of looking, the mother and daughter went to the ranger office to get some help.

Nobody thinks the child can be too far, and a search party is being or-

ganized. The sheriff keeps in radio contact through his office with Royce's office, hoping the kid will turn up. But he doesn't. The real problem is that the parents aren't real outdoorsmen. They didn't appreciate the danger of hypothermia in November and, of course, they didn't realize that gun season had just opened. None of them were wearing orange or even any red, and even though Royce's men and the game wardens have tried to warn the hunters in the area to be on the lookout for a little kid, it is impossible to get to all of them. All in all, this weekend just isn't a good time for a bunch of tenderfeet to be poking around in a hunting area.

Joshua nods and Jon knows he understands. So does Peter Haennicke, who has his plane all checked out and fired up, ready to go. VanStavern shakes Josh's hand as Joshua loads the dogs and climbs on board.

"Thanks, Josh," he yells to him, "and good luck!"

"No sweat, Jon" he calls back. "They'll probably find him by the time we get there. Either way, when I get back you'll owe me a beer."

"You're on," the sheriff promises.

Jonathan VanStavern watches them taxi down the field, turn into the wind, and take off. As he watches the plane rise, he says a little prayer.

"The sky was clear and blue as we flew over the patchwork of gray-brown woods and tan fields. The river and streams looked like blued gun steel, and there was still a light frost.

"We headed due south, straight over Wausau and just west of Stevens Point, and I couldn't get over how many deer we scared up, flying low over the brush and especially in any cornfields that hadn't been cut. We even saw a couple of fox, south of 73, and I was sure enjoying the ride. I guess I wasn't too concerned about the little boy, reckoning he would probably be found by the time we got there. Still, I put the orange coats and bells on the dogs while we were in the air. No sense taking extra time on the ground, I figured.

"But even though it took us an hour to fly down to the Dells, and another fifteen minutes in a squad car getting to the camp-site, the little boy was still missing. And with all those people tramping around, a couple even with dogs, I grew concerned, and I wondered just how hard it would be for my guys to get a scent, or if they would get a scent at all. And I sure wanted to find that kid before night fall because asking a two-year-old kid to survive a cold November night alone in the woods was asking a lot."

"What does 'vive mean?"

"Survive? It means to stay alive."

"We survived a night alone in the woods."

"We sure did. But we weren't alone, were we? We had the dogs, and Mr. Grizzle, and we had each other. This little boy was all alone."

Kelly had to think about that. Tentatively, she asked the dreaded question. "Was he dead? I don't think he was dead. I think you found him 'live, maybe he was hurt a little."

"See. I told you this was a scary story. You sure you want me to go on?"

Kelly wasn't sure at all. "Just tell me if he was okay."

"Sorry. You have to listen to the whole story to find out. Do you want me to continue?"

"Okay, but stop if he was dead."

Joshua smiled and continued.

He's introduced to the sheriff and the little boy's parents, and they walk over to the tent in which the family has been camping. He asks the sheriff and the DNR people to clear the area of all the people that have gathered, especially the ones with the dogs. Jake is a lover, but he can also be a fighter, and that is just one more hassle that he does not need.

The area is cleared, and he takes some objects to give the dogs the scent. Then he turns them loose.

"My game plan was to let both dogs look for the trail but then to harness up Jake and let him follow Jenny-Dog, who would be running loose. I still didn't trust Jake enough to let him take the lead, especially with other dogs in the area.

"We used a soiled diaper and a small blanket to take a scent. The boy had used the same sleeping bag as the mother, but he liked his own security blanket. I would have liked a toy animal, but it looked like the boy had taken the only one he liked with him."

"Like Grizzle."

"That's right, like Grizzle. Well, I set the dogs loose to find the trail, and in a matter of minutes it looked like they had it. But that was my first mistake. I should have kept Jake on a rope.

"I put on my pack and called Jake back to me, but he didn't come. I called him again, trying not to lose my cool, but that dang dog acted like he was deaf as he trotted off into the woods, sniffing and a peeing as he went. Damn, I thought to myself, who trained that mutt anyway?"

"It was you, Joshua! You trained that mutt! You shouldn't say *that* word." Kelly scolded with glee.

"I'm afraid that's true, and I have to own up to it. The problem was that I just did not trust Jake. In practice he had always been right on the mark. But for all I knew, he might have picked up the scent of some coon or some bitch in season, and if he had and if Jenny followed him, we would all be up a creek – especially the kid."

"What's a bitchin season?"

"Well, a bitch, that's a female dog. And when boy dogs find her real pretty, we say she's in season."

"Was Jake a boy dog?"

"He sure was. One hundred percent boy dog."

He harnesses up Jenny-Dog and tells her to, "find the boy. Don't worry about Jake, ol' girl. Just find the little boy." But Jenny doesn't even sniff the ground. She just takes off after Jake. Joshua can do nothing but follow. And he's worried.

"But I didn't need to be. Jenny took me out of the campsite, to an open field of uncut timothy and clover. We followed a narrow trail that I figured to be Jake because I didn't see any deer marks. I hoped it was the boy's trail too.

"On the other side of the field was another patch of brush and woods, mostly white pine and maples with some paper birch and willow that looked to surround a marshy pond. The woods were guarded by a lot of staghorn sumac, poison ivy, and wild berry thickets.

"Jenny took me along the perimeter of the brush and woods for about twenty yards, and then she tried to dive underneath some raspberry vines and make her way towards the pond. I had to have her hold up while I carefully made my way past the thorny brush.

"We picked our way down towards the pond, and I heard Jake barking and splashing in the water. Then I made my second mistake. I imagined the worst and nearly panicked, catching my forehead on a low pine bough in the process. And when I got to the water's edge, I couldn't believe what I saw!"

Kelly was breathless, her eyes as big as saucers.

The little boy is standing on the muddy bank, happy as can be, throwing a stick maybe a foot or two into the near frozen water. And every time he throws the stick, old one eye Jake wades into the muck and wet to retrieve it and drop it at the boy's feet. Jake is barking and wagging his tail and jumping up and down excitedly, hoping for another throw!

"Yea! See, I told you the boy would be all right. I told you. That was a good story."

Joshua scratched Jenny-Dog again. She moaned with delight. He gave Buck a pat on the head just to be fair.

"How do your feet feel?"

"Okay, I guess. It doesn't hurt."

"I'm going to check on our air holes, and then we'll eat a little something. Do you have to go potty?"

"No, I don't have to."

"Okay, sweetheart. You're doing great. Just sit tight and I'll be back before you can say, Jack Robinson."

The dogs got excited and jumped up as Joshua moved towards the tent flap.

"Sorry, guys, not this time. You guys stay put."

Jenny-Dog complied immediately, as she always did. Buck stood his ground for a moment and then went into a long, deep stretch. He finally went down, in his alert position, as if it had been something he had been meaning to do anyway and had chosen on his own accord. Joshua left the tent.

Chapter Twenty-eight

Kristian and Jane walked through the drizzling forest, taking in its fragrance and its memories. The sweet, spicy aroma from the fallen redwood needles and eucalyptus leaves was evocative of things past. Each woman experienced flashbacks and instances of *déja vu*. They walked together, silently, occasionally exchanging glances and troubled smiles.

"What made you decide to have a baby?" Kristian asked her friend.

"Who says I decided. Maybe it was an accident."

"I know you. You decided. Kenny is going to be so excited. I can't wait for you to tell him."

"He's wanted kids since we got married. I don't know, Kris. I have a good job and a lot of material things. Christ, considering the way we were in college and some of the stunts we pulled... well, that I pulled anyway, things have really turned out incredibly well, wouldn't you say?"

Kristian knew what Jane was talking about. It was true for both of them.

"But somehow it just isn't enough, is it? Do you know what I mean? Of course you do. Hell, that's what this is really all about, right? I mean, there comes a point when acquiring more things and going to cool places just doesn't do it anymore. At the very least, you need to have someone to share things with. But I need something else too. Maybe I need to have something I can leave my mark on and leave behind, something to show that I was here."

Kristian was seeing a side of Jane that was rarely exposed. She listened to her friend, knowing exactly what she meant.

"You have your houses and your buildings and all those award winning designs. I don't know if it's enough – I doubt that it is – but at least that's something. But what the hell do I have? A bargain priced spring line-up and a goddamn house on a beach that will probably get washed away by some storm."

"You have Kenny."

"Yes, I do. God, sometimes I don't know why he puts up with me. But you know, Kris, what I want more than anything else? I want to have a family. A family like Kenny has. Not one like I had, or didn't have."

Kristian understood Jane more than she cared to admit. They had both come from broken homes. She smiled when she thought about her friend raising a child, or children. Jane's kids would be real pistols. That went without saying. But Jane would be a good mother as long as she stayed away from drugs. Kenny would see to that.

"What about you, hot shot? Don't you think that's what this is all about? Are you finally realizing that there's more to life than fancy buildings and fast cars? You know, I never told you this, but I really envied you living out in Wisconsin on that farm in the woods with Joshua. I really thought you had it made. I understand why you left, but I always thought it was a mistake. You won your game, kiddo, but you lost the prize."

Joshua cleared the two-inch air vents. There were four of them now, all on the leeward side of the shelter. Even after only one hour they had started to plug, so fierce was the storm. He looked over the interior of the shelter. He wasn't too sure about the strength of the sugar maple that formed one of the basic structural supports. He knew they rotted quickly. The fresh green spruce spar that he had seen on the outside gave him some comfort, but not much. The vines were mostly involved with the maple and the hemlock.

The weather outside was relentless. The candlelight flickered but the protected flame never went out. The tent breathed with the changes in air pressure inside and outside the shelter. Those pressure changes also caused fissures in the glaze that had formed on the *wickiup* ceiling and the fly. Joshua caught his breath each time a piece of ice or snow fell. *How long can this go on*, he wondered. *How long will our luck hold?* He tried the walkie-talkie once again, just on general principle. It was no use.

"How about some grub?" he asked as he returned to the tent. The dogs were ready.

"I'm not hungry."

"I know, honey. Just try to eat something. It helps keep you warm."

"Can I have another candy bar?"

"Sure." Joshua handed Kelly the chocolate and cut meat for himself and the dogs from the second length of sausage. "How about something to drink?"

"Gatorade."

"Okee-doke." He poured some liquid into a cup and gave it to the girl.

"I'm tired of this old tent. I want to go home."

"Me too. But my guess is we're going to have to stay one more night out here. Think we can handle that?"

"What are we going to do?"

That was a good question. The fact that Kelly was bored was a good sign. "Well, we can sing some songs and tell some stories. We can play some games like twenty questions. Do you know that one?"

"I don't like that game."

"Well, how about a song. Do you know any songs? Why don't you teach me a song?" Joshua knew he had to occupy the child's mind. They were in for a long night. He hoped she would sleep through at least part of it. He knew he wouldn't be able to. He had to keep vigil over the air holes.

"I know the I'm Gonna Tell song."

"You don't say. How does it go?"

Kelly sang the song. "I'm gonna tell. I'm gonna tell. I'm gonna tell on you. I'm gonna tell. I'm gonna tell. I'm gonna tell on you. I'm gonna tell, I'm gonna tell... that's all I know."

"That's a good song. Do you know any others?" Kelly shook her head. She was embarrassed that she did not know all the words. Joshua took the lead.

"Well, I know lots of songs. How about if I teach you some songs?"

"Okay."

"Do you want to learn French songs or English songs?"

"French songs *and* English songs."

"Okay, I'll teach you some French songs first. Then when you see your mommy and daddy, you can surprise them with your French songs. How does that sound?"

The thought of seeing her parents again and surprising them with a French song sounded grand. It was too wonderful to imagine.

For Kelly's parents, at that moment, the thought of ever seeing their little girl alive again was too much to imagine. But, thanks to Sam Hanson, they still hoped.

When George Hoffman brought a tray of food to the Martins, he informed them that Sam Hanson had gotten a broken message from that Mr. Travis who was out looking for their little girl. George had no idea the story had been fabricated. Like the Martins, Hoffman needed hope too. Besides a genuine concern for the child, it had been his employee who had permitted the Martins' child to wander off. Mr. Martin wasn't an attorney, thank God, but sooner or later his mind would turn to lawsuit. George Hoffman wanted them to know that everything possible was being done.

The Martins dressed immediately and hurried downstairs. The main power and telephones were still out. The emergency lights and cool temperature presented a somber atmosphere that permeated the lodge. Andy Johnson was taking his turn at the radio. Like Jim Beard, he had been instructed to be as ambiguously positive as he could.

"We heard you got a message from that tracker," Mr. Martin began.

"It wasn't me. It was Sheriff Hanson, I believe. And that was last night. We haven't heard anything since."

"What did he say?"

"From what I was told, the message was pretty broken. It was difficult to understand. We think maybe he's holed up somewhere, waiting out the storm."

"What about Kelly?" Mrs. Martin had to know.

"We don't know. We don't know whether he's with her or whether he's holed up by himself."

"But he may have found her!?" Mr. Martin became intense.

"We just don't know. I'm sorry." Andy Johnson was very uncomfortable. Lying did not come easy to him, and he did not believe either the man or the child was still alive.

"Why else would he hole up? He must have found her! Why else would he stay out when he could come back here if he didn't find her?" Mr. Martin was excited, almost frantic. Sheriff Hanson walked over.

"Mr. Martin, as I explained to Andy here, the message was pretty garbled. We just don't know what's going on, and we haven't had any contact since last night. That may mean nothing. He would have to have the radio turned on to receive us, and the batteries go pretty fast on those outfits, especially in the cold. We're hoping for the best, but you have to understand, we just don't know what the situation is for sure."

Sam Hanson wondered if he was doing these people a favor by raising their hopes. Like Andy Johnson, lying went against his nature, but hell, what else could he do? For John Martin and his wife, there was no doubt. Their daughter had to be alive. The alternative was unthinkable.

"I want to man the radio," John Martin announced.

Deputy Johnson looked at the sheriff. Hanson nodded.

"Show him how to work it, Andy."

From that moment on, for the next twenty-four hours, John Martin sat by the radio equipment trying vainly to contact the man whom he believed was keeping his daughter alive.

That man was trying to establish a routine. It had been roughly twenty-four hours since he first found the child. With the exception of the fire rescue in Wyoming, it had been the longest twenty-four hours of his life. Three things made it particularly difficult. First, he had to clear the air holes every two hours or else they could suffocate. That meant he could sleep no more than a couple of hours at a time, and then only lightly. Second, there was no way of telling how long the storm would last. He prayed he was rationing the food adequately. Finally, being trapped in a situation where their survival was in many ways beyond his control created an unrelenting fear and constant tension that was almost unbearable. Neither the fear nor the tension was new to him. They accompanied him on every rescue. He should have been used to them. He just wasn't.

Every four hours Travis would leave the shelter to check the condition of the structure and the strength of the storm. He would examine the girl's feet every four hours also, if she was awake. Joshua was concerned. The bruised area appeared darker and larger, but perhaps it was his imagination or the light.

"Kelly, do you know if you're allergic to any drugs." He knew it was a silly question to ask a six-year-old kid. Kelly just shrugged.

"Have you ever been really, really sick and the doctor had to give you some special medicine, or a shot, to make you better?"

Kelly shook her head, no. Then she remembered, "Once, when I was at Montessori pre-school, I got a real bad earache. Mommy took me to the doctor, and she gave me a shot. I cried. I don't like shots."

"How did you feel after the shot?"

"It hurt," Kelly told him. She left no doubt that she was the aggrieved party.

"What hurt?"

"My Bottom!"

"Oh. How did your earache feel?"

"It went away."

"And everything was okay after that? You didn't get more sick before you got better, did you?"

"Everything was okay."

Joshua couldn't be certain. It sounded like Kelly didn't have a problem with antibiotics, at least some antibiotics. She didn't wear any medical alert pins or bracelets, but he knew that might not mean anything, especially with a young child. Still, he hesitated to start her on anything if he did not really have to. He had Ampicillin in his kit, 250mg. capsules, and Erythromycin wafers. Joshua decided to wait four more hours. Then he would decide.

Every eight hours they would eat and the dogs would be let out. Toileting was on an as needed basis, but Joshua had to be careful that the child did not have an accident.

One, and only one, tin-can candle lantern burned continuously, providing flickering comfort and illumination. Joshua knew from experience that each candle would last thirty-six to forty-eight hours. That added up to three to four days of light plus a couple of hours from his battery powered lights. He didn't think the storm would last that long. If it did, they would have serious problems. It would be difficult to clear the air holes in the dark. Food would be running out. And toileting, for the child at least, would be messy.

On the bright side, the shelter seemed to be holding. Their three tiered system, tent, fly, and shelter was doing a remarkable job of keeping the heat generated by their bodies and the small fires in, and the storm out. So efficient was their set-up that Joshua was able to place snow in a container and melt it just by having it in the tent with them, providing a ready water supply. One thing that concerned Travis was the amount of snow building on the top of the shelter. From his barn experience, Joshua knew well what excessive snow build up could do to roofs of structures. If the shelter collapsed, they would be finished. On the other hand, it was that very snow that insulated them from the killing wind and sub-zero temperatures outside. Joshua decided he would try to skim off any snow more than two feet if he could do it safely.

"Is it *ever* going to stop snowing?" Kelly asked.

"Oh sure, it could stop snowing any time now. Probably in a few hours."

"Why is it always snowing? I don't like the snow any more."

Joshua knew exactly how the little girl felt.

"You know, the Indians out my way have a story about that. Want to hear it?"

Kelly did.

"The Indians say that a long, long time ago there were only long summers and short, mild winters. The people were very happy in the spring and the summer and the fall, but they grumbled all winter long. They didn't know how good they had it. So Winter decided to teach the people a lesson. He turned the world very, very cold."

"Like now."

"Yep, just like now. Old Winter turned the world so cold that everything froze. The lakes froze. The streams froze. Even the rivers froze, it was so cold. Old Winter turned everything so cold that one night the very moon itself froze. And do you know what happened when the moon froze?"

Kelly shook her head.

"It shattered! There it had been, up in the sky, big and round and yellow. And then it shattered all to pieces, and the pieces fell to earth, and the Indians could not see the moon any more. For eight days and eight nights the pieces of the moon fell to earth. That was the first time the Indians had ever seen snow. And when the pieces of the moon stopped falling and the snow stopped coming down, the Indians looked up into the clear black sky and, sure enough, where there once had been a full, round moon, now there was only a sliver of the moon left. The Indians call that time the Time of the Frozen Moon. They say that's why we have phases of the moon, and also why we have big snow storms: To teach us not to grumble."

Kelly wasn't sure how she felt about that story. She wanted to grumble, but now she was careful. "I hope it doesn't snow for eight days and eight nights."

So did Joshua.

Chapter Twenty-nine

"Margaret, I'm going over to Joshua's place to check on things," Jon VanStavern let his wife know. "It's snowing pretty hard now, and I just want to make sure there are no problems."

Margaret VanStavern knew that as far as Joshua Travis was concerned it was an unnecessary gesture. The Nelsons and Rod Kielor would take care of things just fine. Margaret also knew that for her husband it was a very necessary gesture. Jon could never relax when his friend was out on a rescue mission.

The two families had been friends as far back as anyone could remember, always a half generation apart. Joshua's father had been like another older brother to Jon. In fact, they had been closer than Jon was with his real brothers. Likewise, Jon had been the closest thing to an older brother Joshua had ever known.

Normally Margaret would not interfere. She knew that Jon felt responsible for some of the things that had happened to Joshua over the years. He felt especially badly about Kristian leaving. He believed that if Joshua had not gotten involved in training dogs and rescuing kids then Josh and Kristian would not have had some of the problems that they had had. At the very least, they might have had a better chance of working them out. Margaret VanStavern knew that that was all hogwash. Still, normally she would not interfere.

But circumstances this night were not normal. Margaret knew

that Joshua's life was in danger. She worried about Joshua. And she worried about her husband, about how he would respond if the worst happened.

Margaret VanStavern took her husband by the hand. "Jonathan, I know how you feel. And if it helps for you to keep an eye on Josh's place, that's fine. Just remember that Joshua Travis makes his own decisions, no one else. He's as independent as any man I've ever met, just like his father was. Joshua chose to join the Seabees when he graduated from high school even though everybody in the county wanted him to accept that scholarship to Madison. He chose to ramble around the world for four or five years after he finished his service in the Navy, and he chose to come back home when he was good and ready. Joshua Paul Travis chose to go to Vermont, Jonathan. Nobody forced him. Nobody could have forced him. Not even you, dear."

"I asked him, Margaret. He's never turned me down, Margaret, not once."

"That's not so, Jonathan. Sam Hanson asked him, not you."

"Same thing."

"He doesn't go out on manhunts with you, does he, dear? You asked him once and he said no. You accepted that and you never asked him again."

"That's different."

"Yes, that is different," Margaret explained patiently. "Joshua does not believe he and his dogs were put on this earth to track down criminals. He does, however, believe it is his job or his duty or his responsibility, divinely called or not, to find lost kids."

"I'm the one who got him started."

"Yes, you are the one who got him started, and you help him to continue. I believe Joshua appreciates all that you have done and all that you do."

"Even if it cost him his marriage?"

"Kristian did what she felt she needed to do, and Joshua does what he feels he needs to do. Both of them love you. You know that."

Jonathan VanStavern knew, in his heart, his wife was right. He was a lucky man. After thirty years of marriage, he still loved his wife very much. He hugged her.

"I won't be gone long. I just want to make sure all the barn doors are closed and that the animals are all right." He pulled on his green wool Ranger's jacket and his leather gloves as he headed out the door. "Looks like it's really comin' down."

Ken Sloan had been home for a few hours when his wife and Kristian returned to the house at Stinson Beach. He gave his wife a quick kiss and Kristian a big hug.

"Well, hello stranger. I was wondering who it was my wife ran off with this time."

"Hi, Kenny. It's good to see you."

"Come on in. I've got a pot of my infamous chili going and a six pack of beer that needs polishing off."

It was still drizzling out and the wet, salt wind was cold. The hot chili and beer sounded pretty good. "I've got to get going," Kris told him.

"Bullshit," Jane interjected. "You just think I want to be alone when I tell him. Christ, that's the last thing I want. Besides, you said you wanted to see the look on his face."

"Tell me what? What are you two wenches planning? Don't tell me. You're running off with each other. I knew it! I knew as soon as I got home early and didn't find my wife faithfully scrubbing the floors, like she always does, that she had found somebody else. Alas, what can I do but wish you both well and bid you, *Adieu.*

"I get to keep the house," he added.

"In your dreams, buster," Jane retorted as they made their way indoors. The friendly aroma of bubbling chili filled the beach house.

Inside, the air was warm and humid. The windows were partially fogged from the steam. Looking out, you could see the surf and the ocean. Mist and fog obscured distant views.

It was warm and cozy inside, eating hot chili and warm Italian bread. The cold beer was just the right touch. Kenny Sloan bubbled over more than the chili as he digested the incredible news he received from his wife. He never really thought it would happen. Ken Sloan was a saint, Kristian knew, to put up with all the crap Jane had pulled. A bonafide, personable saint with an even disposition and a great sense of humor. Kristian was happy for them.

"So what brings you out this way, Kris? Gosh, it's been ages since we've seen you, between your work and our jobs." He got up to clear the dishes.

"Joshua's out on a rescue mission, and Kristian's afraid she'll never get to see *her own true love once more*," Jane explained parodying the prose of the sixties folk-songs they all used to listen to.

"My God, that's right!" Kenny exclaimed with sudden recognition. "Out in Vermont, that little girl. I remember when I heard it on the news I thought, they need Josh Travis and his dogs. You mean to say he's really out there? Is that the one?"

"He's there," Kristian confirmed.

"Oh Kris, I'm sorry." Kenny was truly sympathetic. Jane was not.

"Why the hell are you sorry? You both know that Joshua is the only chance in the world that little girl has. Think about *her* for the love of God. Think about her parents! God, what they must be going through. And stop talking about Joshua like he's dead, for christsake. I need some cheesecake."

Jane got up and went to the refrigerator. Kristian started a pot of coffee. She wondered how Jane could be so upbeat, so optimistic. Perhaps she hadn't seen pictures of the storm.

"You know, Jane, you're going to feel like shit if you're wrong," Kris told her.

"We all are." Jane answered. "But I'll be damned if I'm going to mope around grieving before I know that anybody's dead. Besides, that's not the problem."

"It's not?" Kristian raised her eyebrows. "And the real problem would be.....?" Kenny was wise enough to stay out of it.

"The real problem is: Just what are you going to do when Joshua comes marching out of the snow, with or without the kid? Think about that one, kiddo. Let's have dessert in the living room."

Kristian was dumbfounded. She was speechless. Was Jane right? She was right about almost everything else. The only part Jane had wrong was the part about Joshua marching out of the snow, with or without the kid. Kristian knew that Joshua would not come out of the snow without the kid.

Chapter Thirty

"What do you say, Pumpkin? Are you about ready to get some sleep?" Joshua followed his routine with practiced self-discipline. Conditions had not changed, with the possible exception of Kelly's toes. Still, he was reluctant to start the child on antibiotics. He wasn't equipped to deal with an allergic reaction to the drugs. He had some Benadryl in his first-aid kit, but he did not know if that would be enough if there was a problem. The bruised area seemed larger, but there was still no exudate or odor. Four more hours, he decided.

"Play another song on your harmonica," Kelly demanded.

"Another song, huh? Got any in mind?"

Kelly shook her head. "A good song," Kelly expected.

"A good song, huh? Hmm, let me think. I know. I know just the right song," Joshua announced, inspired. The song was "Tonight I'll be Staying Here with You" from Dylan's *Nashville Skyline* album. Joshua had given the album to his wife years ago on her twenty-sixth birthday, not long after she lost the baby. He began the song's introduction with his harmonica. Then he softly sang the first verse.

Buck howled during the instrumental. Kelly smiled with delight.

"Sing the chocolate song," Kelly pleaded when Joshua was done.

"The chocolate song?"

"You know, the one where mama is baking the cake and papa is making chocolate." Kelly liked that song. It gave her a warm feeling inside.

"If I sing that one, will you try to go to sleep?"

Kelly promised.

Joshua smiled and sang the song softly. His calm voice belied the fear and tension he fought. For the moment they were safe, but that could change with a gust of wind or a toxin-producing bacterium.

What a neat kid. I'll bet her parents are real proud of her. And smart! Why she's as smart as a whip. He had inadvertently switched the roles of the parents in the song. Kelly had caught it right away.

"No, no! Mama is baking the cake. Papa is making the chocolate!" she corrected.

What a wonderful child. Her parents are very, very lucky. After three repetitions of the song, two in French, one in English, Kelly was asleep.

Joshua lay back and tried to relax as much as possible. He smiled as he thought back to old Jake and the rescue in the Dells. He had always felt good about that rescue and its aftermath. He had learned a lot, and it warmed him to think about it now. But, if the truth be told, it was that rescue, even more than the first, that had set him on his chosen course with all its ramifications, intended or otherwise.

Kris is waiting for him with the pickup at Haennicke's field. Jon VanStavern is there too, but Joshua does not want him to have to transport them. Jake is still wet and stinks to high heaven even though Josh had rinsed the muck off him at a hand pump back at the campsite. He feels badly about Peter's plane.

Kristian runs up and kisses him. Jon shakes his hand and clasps his shoulder. Then the sheriff shakes Peter's hand. VanStavern insists on buying lunch for everybody. That sounds good to Joshua. He hasn't eaten anything since five that morning.

They load the dogs into the truck and follow Jon and Peter, in the squad car, to the Blazer.

D.M. GREENWALD

They sit at the bar, Josh and Kris in the middle, Jon on the left, Peter on the right. The charcoal grill is sizzling. The draft beer is fresh. Jon orders burgers and roast beef sandwiches, on hard rolls, and beer all around. The ranch fries come with it. Kris orders a Bloody Mary. She likes the way they make it, with lots of Tabasco and Worcestershire and pepper and a stalk of celery and wedge of pickle to boot. Jon orders a shot of C.C. for Josh and asks Peter what he wants.

They raise their glasses and toast each other and the dogs. And when Patrick finds out what has happened, the drinks are on the house.

Jonathan is interested in all the details, but Joshua is hungry and wants to eat. When he is asked what happened, he just shrugs his shoulders and says, No big deal. The kid wandered off and the dogs found him. It is up to Peter to provide most of the information, like how worried everyone there was, or how there weren't any tracks to start with, but less than five minutes after their arrival Josh and the dogs were hot on the trail.

Haennicke tells them about Jake in the muck and how black his legs and belly were before Josh rinsed him off. He doesn't have to tell them how bad Jake smelled, they know that first hand, but he does. Apparently it has made a lasting impression on Peter and, quite possibly, on his plane.

It was nice and warm and cheery that afternoon in that pub, Joshua remembers. *There is a fire in the fireplace and a football game on the TV and he is happy being there next to Kristian. Joshua is proud of the way they have handled things, from the time Kris first got Jon's phone call to the time he called her when it was over, telling her that everything was all right and asking her to pick him up at the plane. He also remembered that when Pat set up another round, he did not refuse even though it had turned into a beautiful day outside. Kristian wonders if everything is really okay.*

They killed a good two hours in the bar that day, drinking and talking and getting slapped on the back. *When they finally leave for home, he asks Kristian to drive. He is feeling the booze and getting tired. It isn't just that he has been working hard, or that he was up early and has*

— 204 —

been active all day. There is something more. This time there is a tightness in his gut that he can not shake. A tightness that comes from the realization that he really has been involved in a life-and-death situation. And that things can go wrong.

It had been different, the first time, back in August. It had been a game then. The kids were older. There hadn't been too much real danger, and, basically, he had been just one of the crowd. The responsibility hadn't been all his.

This time the searchers had had plenty of time to find this kid if they were going to. And if the kid had stayed out all night, or headed towards the nearby river with its sandstone cliffs, or even just fallen into the water much before he was found, he would have died.

There was no question about it. I was lucky both times, he thinks.

They reach home and he snaps out of it. Kristian helps him get his gear from the back of the truck. As they grab for his duffel, he takes her by the wrist and tells her how great she was today.

"Yeah," *she says,* "like I really did a lot," *but she's pleased with how she handled herself, and she's pleased that he's noticed. Then she looks at him and asks if everything is all right.*

"Sure," *he responds.* "It's just that things were a lot closer this time than I thought they would be. And ol' Jake didn't mind like he should have."

"Does he ever?" *she asks and he smiles.*

"I know just what you need," *she suggests.* "A warm bath and a hot woman." *And he's tempted.*

But there is work to be done, so he takes a rain check and tells her, "There's someone around here needs a bath a helluva lot worse than I do," *and he eyes Jake, slinking away towards the barn.*

Kristian's offer sure was tempting, he remembers warmly as he lay in the flickering golden light of the candle, listening to the storm, watching the tent walls breathe and shudder. *But the day is moving on and he has things he needs to get done, and he wants to put in another hour or two in the woods before dark to try and get his buck. He figures to take Kris up on her little proposition after chores that night. Right then, Joshua wants to get to work with Jake a bit and find out for himself whether you can teach an old dog new tricks. He reckons the first thing he has to do is get Jake smelling at least a few shades better than week old road kill.*

He walks over towards the barn to where Jake is lying in the sun. He kneels down, scratches the dog behind the ears, and slips a rope on him. He tells Jake, "C'mon, buddy," and starts heading for the hose. The dog follows along, warily. He does not know what's in store for him, but he doubts that it's good.

It's funny, he thinks, how a dog will go charging through brush and bramble to go crashing through thin ice and thirty-two degree water for the pleasure of retrieving a dead bird, or even a practice dummy. And that same damn dog will act like the most wretched, most put upon creature on earth if the water should happen to come out of a tap and maybe have a little soap mixed in.

He's no longer miffed that the dog did not come to him at the start of the search when he called him. Hell, the dog knew what he was doing, and you can't argue with that. Still, it would be nice to have ol' Jake maybe a tad less independent.

He thinks back to the old French-Canadian farmer in Chicoutimi and he's not optimistic.

The trick would be to get Jake to mind better without killing his spirit, or him, in the process. Joshua finishes hosing him off after soaping him down. Then he rubs him with a towel. Jake doesn't mind that.

Joshua ties him in the tack room to dry off and builds a fire in the wood stove there to keep him warm while he is drying. He doesn't want him out rolling around in God knows what after all it took to get him clean. Then Josh gives Jake and Jenny a couple of Milkbones for a treat.

He walks to the house to get his rifle and go back out to the woods. Kristian is in the den, working on some plans at the drawing table. She's wearing faded jeans and a white cashmere sweater, and he can see just a little of her bare back, above the waist, as she leans over her work. Damn, he thinks to himself, but she is one beautiful woman.

He goes over to the table to see what Kris is working on. He notices that she smells good, all fresh and clean, like she's just bathed with herbal bath oils. He looks out the window and sees that the sun is setting. If he's going to get out in the woods, he had best do it now.

He puts his hand on her shoulder and asks if her earlier offer still stands. She turns her head to look up at him and smiles. She gets up and goes to draw water for another bath.

What the hell, he thinks, my buck will be there in the morning.

Joshua smiled as he fell asleep. In an hour and ten minutes he would have to clear the air holes again.

Chapter Thirty-one

Everything was okay out at the Travis homestead. The dark ce- dar-sided Quebecois style house and the red painted barn were both buttoned up tight. The electricity and the heat were both on. All that Jonathan VanStavern accomplished was to stir up the dogs which stirred up the horses.

It was now snowing hard in Lincoln County, Wisconsin. The wind was blowing and the roads were getting bad. Still, Sheriff VanStavern was not surprised to see the parking lot at the Blazer Pub filled with cars and pickups. After all, it was Friday night, snow or no snow. He decided to stop. He wasn't looking to drink, but he knew it wouldn't hurt on a night like this to shake a few hands, slap a few backs, and gently, but firmly, remind people to take it easy. "... what with the slippery roads and the snow. I'm not looking to get called out at three A.M. to dig anyone out of a drift."

"Don't worry, Jon. By three A.M., we'll have enough antifreeze in us to last until spring."

"That's what I'm afraid of, Jack. How's Mary?"

"Don't get me started. Say, Jon, anything new on Josh Travis?"

"I called the Vermont State Police a couple of hours ago. They still don't have any word. The phones are out at the rescue site, travel is virtually impossible, and radio contact is sporadic. They know he got in, and they know he went out. That's all they know."

"He's in our prayers, Jon."

"I know that, Gus. I'm sure he knows that too."

"Say Pat, why don't we get out those old game films? You know, the ones with Joshua in them," Gus Harley suggested.

"Which ones would you like? We've got the '54 and '55 championship games and the 1953 Geneva game. What be your pleasure?"

Jon nodded to Gus and to Patrick. Watching the games was a good idea. It would give people the camaraderie they were looking for on a night like this and hopefully cut down on the alcohol consumption. People tended to nurse beers when they watched the games rather than drink hard liquor.

"That '53 game was the one where Josh got hurt, wasn't it? We don't want to see that. Show the championship game."

"Yeah, show that game when we first won the championship."

"No, no. Show the '55 game. Josh was prime that game, and we creamed those big city boys, black boys and all."

Of the two games, the nineteen fifty-four championship game was actually the more interesting, at least from a competitive standpoint. Joshua had started at tight end since his sophomore year, and in nineteen fifty-four, as a junior, he was a leader of the team. His size, his skill, and his concentration and determination enabled Joshua Travis to play at a level rarely seen in high school football.

The state championship was held at the University of Wisconsin stadium in Madison. The Merrill Blue Jays were playing the Thomas Jefferson Minutemen from Milwaukee. For the rural and small town boys from Lincoln County, it was the first time they played against a team with a significant number of black players, colored boys they had called them back then. The game was also important because there were a significant number of scouts from major colleges. They were especially interested in Joshua.

"God, remember how all those college guys tried to get Josh to commit after that game?"

"I heard there was even a member of the Packers organization down there."

"That was just a rumor."

"Maybe, but I know for a fact there were Packers people at the '55 game."

Nobody disputed that.

The Merrill boys weren't used to the speed and agility of the Milwaukee team. The Jays air attack was shut down, except for quick passes over the middle to Joshua and the other end. But the Merrill boys were tough, and they had a lot of heart. They ground out yardage behind their big linemen and used the double-coverage on Joshua to open holes in the secondary. Quick scoring pass plays by Jefferson were answered with long, time consuming drives by Merrill.

The winning touchdown was scored by Herk Lattimore, for Merrill, after left guard Donnie Gussick opened a wide hole and Joshua Travis took down the linebacker with a devastating block.

"I'll tell you what now," Patrick announced. "We'll show the '54 game tonight, and you can all come back tomorrow night and we'll watch the '55 game. Does that suit everybody?"

The guaranteed excuse to come back was a winning ticket.

"Now before we begin, what say we all take a moment and say a little prayer for Joshua and the wee child he's out about rescuin'."

The warm, dimly lit bar, with a fire in the fieldstone hearth, fell silent.

"Have you two had enough fun for one night?" Kristian asked her tormentors. All evening long she had endured the loving taunting and teasing gamely served up by Kenny and Jane Sloan. They were ruthless, but it was why she had come. She knew they would help her put things in perspective.

Kristian had not required much coaxing to agree to stay the night. The intermittent rain and dark, slick roads made her decision easy. She also knew she did not want to spend another night like the last one. No matter how hard she tried, Kristian could not be as optimistic about the outcome of the rescue as Jane was. If the news in the morning was bad, she did not want to be alone.

"Hey Kris, when you go back to Wisconsin, can we have your townhouse?"

"Can you afford it?"

"Oh, we aren't offering to buy it. We'll just keep it for you for five or six years until you decide to come back again. Of course we'll use it once in a while to make certain everything is okay. Do you mind if I paint the bedroom?"

"Hell yes I mind if you paint. You might have your bosses buffaloed, but I know you're colorblind. Or is it just that your taste sucks?"

"That's low."

"Besides, who says I'm going back to Wisconsin?"

"Oh, give me a break. Kenny, where's that Linda Ronstadt album?"

"Which one?"

"I think it's the *Heart Like a Wheel* one. Let me look.... Here it is. Now, which track is it?" Jane placed the record on the turntable and cued the needle to the Hank Williams classic, "I Can't Help It (If I'm Still In Love With You)". The music began, followed by Ronstadt's earthy voice.

Jane and Kenny joined in on the refrain:

"You guys are shameless," Kristian reddened and laughed. They didn't let up. The next time the refrain came up they were both in her face.

Kristian just shook her head, resigned to her fate. Jane and Ken were encouraged. They joined in the verses, exaggerating the feeling and expression.

After the final refrain, Kristian yielded. "Okay, okay, I get the message."

"Good. Now maybe we can get some sleep. You know where things are, right?"

"I know. Thanks guys."

"Fuck you."

Kristian just shook her head, smiling. She sat alone in the living room, reclining in a futon, overlooking the ocean. It was only yards from the public beach that she and Joshua had frequented that summer they had first met. Now it was cold and dark and dangerous. God, she hoped Jane was right about Joshua marching out of the snow. But she knew that her anxiety was rooted in more than her own ego as Jane had implied. The simple fact was that Joshua was unlike any man she had ever known. The thought of him not being alive was unbearable.

Kristian put her feet up on the ottoman and lay back. She listened to the water lapping the shore, barely audible through the closed windows and dripping rain, and thought about her life with Joshua. From the start, it had been like a dream. That beautiful summer of courtship in 1967. It could have been a ritual described in Leopold's journal. She thought it would never end.

She had been wrong.

Chapter Thirty-two

The snow plows pushed through the increasing snowfall in Merrill and in Lincoln County, Wisconsin. The new storm was moving east. The Blazer Pub was dark and empty. Most of the county was buttoned down tight.

A downstairs light was still on at the VanStavern homestead. An upstairs light winked on.

"Jonathan, come to bed. There's nothing more you can do."

"In a minute, dear. I'm on the phone."

He continued his telephone conversation in his den. "So you still haven't had any contact with the ski lodge since last night."

"That's right, Sheriff. Phones are out in that part of the state, power too probably. Radio contact is always iffy because of the mountains, and the storm hasn't helped. We have had sporadic contact with some HAMs who made contact a while ago. All we know is that everyone at the lodge itself is safe. The situation seems under control, so far. They didn't know anything about the little girl or your man. Sorry."

"I appreciate your info, Captain. Please give me a call if you hear anything new, will you? Call anytime, day or night. Here's my home phone number...."

"Will do, Sheriff. Say, I hear you got a bit of a storm out that way yourself. How much have you got?"

"We've had eight inches already and it's still coming down. It's not as bad as what you've got."

"I just hope it stays out in your neck of the woods. At least give us a chance to dig out of this one."

Jonathan VanStavern hoped so too as he climbed the stairs up to his wife.

Things were quiet at Jay Peak. Most people were sleeping. There wasn't much else to do. Things grew more somber with each passing hour. Fewer and fewer people expected to see the missing parties alive. John Martin still manned the radio in the office extension. Every ten minutes he broadcast a searching call. Every ten minutes he was disappointed.

At first, Sam Hanson wondered if he had done the right thing, making up the story about radio contact. Given the circumstances, he decided that he had. At least it kept hope alive for the Martins. Without that they would have lost it entirely, and who could blame them?

Hanson stared out the large window. All he could see was snow whipping around furiously in the dark. He weighed what he could he have done differently. He had gotten someone on the scene as soon as possible. He had taken charge of the situation himself. He had gotten Leah up there and forced him to go out. Had that been a mistake? Had that made it more difficult for Travis and his dogs? Or should he have pushed Leah to stay out longer, to look harder? After all, Travis and his dogs found a trail to follow, didn't they? Maybe if Leah had found that trail they would have the little girl back, even if she was dead. At least then he would not have sent another man out into that night.

Jim Beard was up also. He looked in on Mr. Martin and then strolled over to the window where Sam Hanson was standing. Along the way he picked up two coffees from the buffet table. He seemed to sense what Hanson was thinking. He had gone through his own set of *what ifs*.

"He knew the risk, Sam. You didn't make him go out." Beard handed him the coffee.

"I'm the one that called him. He wouldn't be out there if it wasn't for me."

"You were just doing your job, Sam. You wanted to give it your best shot. We all did. There's nothing more you could have done. Believe me, I've been going over it in my mind too. We did all we could do."

"Then why are we up at three A.M.? And why do we feel so damn guilty?"

Jim Beard didn't have an answer to that.

Joshua Travis last cleared the air vents for his shelter at three A.M. Now he was outside carefully removing excess snow from the mound. It was difficult, treacherous work. He guessed there to be at least three to four feet of snow covering the limb and vine wickiup. The drifts on the windward side were deeper. He considered more than two feet of snow superfluous. More than three feet was dangerous. There was no way to judge how much the structure could support, and snow was still coming down.

Travis used his trenching tool to scrape away snow from the areas he could safely reach. He took care not to scrape too deep or to disturb the supporting branches or vines. It was cold, chancy work. Small branches and twigs fell from on high. Usually he did not hear them until they hit. Sometimes not even then.

There, he hoped, *that will have to do it for now.*

Joshua was relieved to get back into the relative warmth and safety of the shelter. He inspected the interior one last time and cleared the air ways again for good measure. His lantern batteries were beginning to fail. He had only one extra set. From now on he would try to confine most of his outside activity to daylight hours. He tried not to wake up Kelly when he re-entered the tent. It was four A.M.

Something smelled foul as he entered the tent. Joshua looked suspiciously at the dogs curled up on either side of the sleeping bag. Perhaps all that summer sausage had made them gassy. He took off his parka and undid his mukluks. The odor was faint but putrid. Joshua struggled out of his overalls. He lay back on the sleeping bag, next to the sleeping child, and covered himself with his jacket. *What was that rancid smell?* He couldn't get it out of his mind. He sat up and rolled towards the dogs, first Buck and then Jenny.

Joshua tried to imitate his dogs in tracking down the mysterious odor. He sniffed his dogs from head to toe. *Where do I know that odor from?* There was something familiar about it. It reminded him of something that had to do with dogs, he was certain, but he could not quite place it. There was something about it he associated with fear, but what was it? Perhaps one of the dogs had a problem with its anal glands. Sometimes when dogs were attacked or afraid they let loose with a discharge from those glands that could put a skunk to shame. But that wasn't it. *What is it?* There was something very troubling about it.

Search as he might, Joshua could find no evidence that the foul odor came from the dogs despite his nagging association. *Could it be the child? Oh, Jesus!*

Joshua gently unzipped the sleeping bag from around the sleeping child. Sure enough, the odor was frighteningly more pronounced. Perhaps the child had messed herself. That would be annoying but manageable. Then he remembered with what he associated the odor. Fear pierced him like a dagger.

When he was a boy, he had had a dog named Prince. The two of them had been inseparable. They hiked, swam, played, hunted and slept together. When Joshua was sixteen and Prince was fourteen, the dog developed a tumor in his mouth. Two weeks later Prince died in his arms. The foul odor that emanated from Kelly reminded him of that tumor.

Joshua fought to stay calm. He lightly brushed the back of his hand across the girl's cheek and forehead. Not too bad, he thought, certainly not pronounced fever. That sign was inconclusive, he knew, but it was better than the alternative. He opened the bag further. Kelly woke up.

"How are you feeling, sweetheart?"

Kelly stretched but did not answer. The stretch was another good sign. So was the fact that Kelly wasn't crying. She did not appear to be in undue pain.

"Does your foot hurt, honey?"

Kelly shook her head, no. "Is it morning?"

Joshua smiled. That was an encouraging question.

"Yes it is, sweetheart." It wasn't quite a lie. "How do you feel?"

"Okay. I have to go potty."

"Okee dokee. Do you think you can hold it for a minute? I just want to check your feet. Do your feet hurt?"

"No."

"No, you can't hold it, or no your feet don't hurt?"

"I can hold it."

"How about your feet?" Joshua had already begun undressing the left foot.

"That one hurts a little."

Joshua worked quickly and carefully. Even before he had all the gauze off, he knew what he would find. He had to switch lanterns. The batteries in the one were shot. As he removed the final level of gauze he saw the source of the odor. A brown, serous, foul smelling exudate oozed from her injured toes.

Damn. Should have put her on antibiotics.

Joshua knew there were two possibilities, cellulitis or myonecrosis – gas gangrene. He also knew he was not competent to make an accurate diagnosis, but he had no choice. Now, more than ever, the girl's life was dependent on the decisions he would make over the next few hours. He had already made one serious mistake. He could not afford another.

"How're you doing, Kel?"

"Okay," the child responded. That was good. Kelly was alert and not screaming in pain. All signs pointed to cellulitis.

Joshua painted the child's toes with Betadine and dressed them in gauze once again. He covered the foot with the sock and opened the container holding the erythromycin. He consulted Lieberman's crib sheet. For kids, it said 30 to 50 mg/kg/day/3. Double for severe infection.

"Kelly, do you know how much you weigh?"

Kelly did not know. Joshua did some rough estimating and some quick calculations. He decided on 2000 mg/day. He carried 200 mg wafers. They were cherry flavored. That would help. He counted out four wafers and handed them to the girl.

"Here, sweetie. Eat these, will you?"

"What's that?"

"It's sort of medicine, but it tastes like candy."

"Ugh. It tastes like vitamins," Kelly complained.

"Eat them all up, honey. They'll make you feel better."

"I feel okay now. I just want to go home. And I have to go potty!"

Joshua helped the little girl go to the bathroom. He watched for any reaction to the antibiotics. No need to panic, he thought. It looked to be cellulitis. That wasn't good, but the toxins produced by the crepitis causing bacteria were neither as strong nor as fast spreading as the ones produced by gas gangrene. There was a slight chance the cellulitis would degenerate to myonecrosis, but Joshua had read that those instances were unusual, at least under normal circumstances. He hoped the antibiotics would take care of that. He wished he had started them sooner.

No, there was no need to panic, but Joshua Travis decided that as soon as it was light out he would re-evaluate their situation. If at all possible, he would get Kelly back to the lodge that day.

Sam Hanson returned to the big armchair near the fire and finally allowed himself some sleep. Jim Beard placed a pillow under John Martin's head. Martin had finally fallen asleep in the chair by the radio, his head on the table by the microphone. Diane Martin slept in a sleeping bag at his feet. Aside from Jim Beard, only Barry Steiner, the reporter, was still awake. He was working on his story, perfecting three different possible endings. He checked the phones almost as often as John Martin checked the radio, with the same result.

In Lincoln County, Wisconsin, Jon VanStavern lay wide awake next to his comforting wife. She had been right, of course. She usually was. But maybe if Josh hadn't gotten so involved with dogs and rescue work, he would have been more in tune to Kristian's needs and dreams. Perhaps Margaret was right. Perhaps Kris had her own path to follow, and it would not have made any difference. But one thing Jonathan VanStavern knew for certain: If he hadn't gotten his friend involved with tracking dogs, Joshua would not have gone through that hell in Wyoming five years ago, before Kristian left. And he wouldn't be out in a killer storm in Vermont that very night.

Kristian slept fitfully on the futon in Jane's living room. All the tension and alcohol and Librium of the past two days had finally caught up with her. She felt safe there, with Jane and Kenny, but even in her sleep she knew things would not continue the way they had.

High on the mesa in Arizona, the old grandmother also sleeps fitfully. At times she appears to be crying. Still, her Vision does not end. It goes on forever. It must end soon, her attendant daughter prays. It must end soon.

Chapter Thirty-three

"It is enough, Taknokwunu. You must stop now or they will die."

"It is not finished, Gogyeng Sowuhti. Do not interfere."

"You must not kill the Son of Light."

"The Son of Light and the wolf dog may go if they choose. White Wind and the child must remain."

"You demand too much, Taknokwunu."

"Be gone, Gogyeng Sowuhti, or you will die also!"

Joshua knew he would have to wait until six-thirty A.M., or thereabouts, before venturing out. In the meantime, he prepared to evacuate the child. First, he cooked oatmeal and warmed the last of the cocoa for Kelly. He and the dogs started in on the third summer sausage. He also ate some granola and trail mix, and he gave the child a candy bar, two if she wanted. Joshua knew from the sounds outside and the movement of the tent that the storm was not over. If they left the campsite, they would need lots of energy.

Joshua considered the best way to move Kelly. She was light and he was strong, but carrying her in his arms was out of the question. He figured he had two possibilities. He could jury-rig a makeshift travois, using his pack frame, the tent fly and possibly some tent poles and drag Kelly back. Or he could modify his backpack and carry her out. He opted for the latter.

His backpack was by Jansport. It had two main compartments

and an external frame with additional outside pockets for storage and outside frame space for sleeping bag and tent. Normally the compartmentalization was an asset, enabling him to have quick and easy access to the things he needed. Now it was a liability. Joshua wanted one large compartment. Large enough to hold a little girl wrapped in a sleeping bag.

Travis emptied the contents of the pack onto the space blanket and organized them neatly. He took his finely honed lock-back knife and removed the top cover of the pack. He unbolted and removed the aluminum "C" frame tube that gave the top of the pack its shape. Then he adroitly cut through the partitions separating the backpack compartments. Joshua took great care not to cut too near to seams or zippers. If necessary, he could reinforce the now single compartment sack with adhesive tape and rope. He would probably have to modify the sleeping bag also, but he wanted to wait until he was sure they were leaving to do that. Joshua checked his watch.

"Kelly, I have to go outside again. I may be gone for a little bit, but I shouldn't be gone for too long. Jenny-Dog will stay with you. Okay?" The dogs got up with anticipation and excitement.

"What about Buck?"

"He's going to come with me. Down, Jenny. You've got to stay here. You want another candy bar before I go?"

Kelly shook her head, no.

"Okay, you sit tight. Stay in the sleeping bag, okay? Promise?"

"I promise."

"Good. I'm going to see if things have settled down enough for us to make it home."

"Yeaaa!" Kelly approved.

Joshua grabbed his snowshoes and excavated the shelter entrance. His optimism faded as soon as he dug through the passageway. The snow was deep and still coming down fast and furious. The trees afforded some protection from the vicious wind, but the frenzied whipping about of the tree crowns betrayed the true ferocity of the storm.

"C'mon, Buck, this way." Joshua checked his compass and oriented himself by the shelter and the wind. Even in the woods, the snow was to his hips. He had to trudge through the snow between the trees and the heavy brush. Buck had it worse, following in his master's footsteps, occasionally deviating to try alternative routes over downed trees and fallen limbs. It took a full fifteen minutes just to break track to the clearing that was the cross-country trail. The wind nearly knocked him over. The snow drifts were up to his chest. And this area was still protected.

"Hold up, Buck!" Joshua had to shout to be heard above the wind. He turned his back to the relentless storm and thought about putting on his snowshoes and testing the conditions in the open. Before he did, he reviewed his three options: He and Buck could go back for the child and then try to make it in. He would have to leave Jenny-Dog at the camp. She wouldn't like that, but he doubted she could make it through the deep snow and into the wind. Even Buck would have a hard time. But Joshua didn't like the odds. Kelly was in better shape than she had been before, but she wouldn't last long if they got lost or went down. Neither would he with all the gear left in the shelter.

Joshua considered putting on his snowshoes and going for help. Again, he thought the risks were too great. Even if he could make it, which was far from certain, Kelly would be alone for hours. She would be scared. If she needed first-aid, there would be no one to help her. Most importantly, the air holes would clog with the blowing and drifting snow. It would be difficult to relocate the shelter even if he made some kind of landmarks. They would be dependent on Buck, and who knew what kind of shape he would be in? By the time he returned with a rescue team Kelly could be dead.

The final option was to wait out the storm. He wondered how long the storm could last, worst case scenario. As a kid, Joshua had read about horrendous storms on the Great Plains that had lasted a week or more, but those had mostly been in the early eighteen-hundreds. Had there been any winter storms of that magnitude lately? How long could they hold out? They had already gone through more than half the food he had brought. Joshua looked down at Buck. That would be a hell of a way to go, but he knew that food would not be a problem. He thought about Kelly's toes. Joshua wasn't happy with option number three either. Unfortunately, it was the only one that made any sense. So long as Kelly demonstrated no clear evidence of gangrene, staying put was the rational choice.

Kelly would not be happy.

"C'mon, Buck. Let's get back to Kelly and Jenny-Dog!"

Buck took the lead back. Joshua noticed a newly fallen limb they had to circumvent to return. Even Buck, the great dog born and bred for a winter storm, was happy to get back to shelter. Once he had dug through the sealed entrance and entered the shelter, Joshua could hear Kelly talking to Jenny-Dog and herself. Joshua was frightened. Incoherent speech and babbling was a symptom of advanced gangrene.

"You're a good doggie, and Buck is a good doggie, and soon the wind will stop, and the snow will go away, and we'll see mommy and daddy and Andrew and Barbie and....."

Joshua's fear eased. He realized that Kelly was talking to Jenny to keep their spirits up and her own fear down. As long as he was there, Joshua cleared the air holes once more. He pulled off his ski mask, brushed the snow from Buck and his own clothes and removed his parka as he prepared to enter the tent.

"Is it time to go home now?" Kelly asked before Joshua could say anything.

"Ah, I'm afraid we're going to have to stay put a little while longer. How's your foot."

"Waah!" Kelly replied. It wasn't a cry, just a noise she made to express disappointment.

"How's you're foot, Kel?" Joshua asked again.

"It hurts a little and it's pumping."

"Pumping?"

"Not pumping, beating." Kelly searched for the right word. "It's beating. Like my heart."

Throbbing was what Joshua guessed Kelly meant. That wasn't unexpected. It was consistent with cellulitis.

"Want anything else to eat?" Joshua hesitated to make the offer. If the storm lasted much longer, he would have to cut the girl's rations as well as his and the dogs'. He was relieved when Kelly shook her head.

"Well, we might as well get some more shut-eye," he told her as he removed his mukluks and overalls.

"You said we could go home," Kelly reminded him.

Joshua hesitated. "We will. Just as soon as the storm lets up."

"That's what you always say."

Joshua didn't have a good answer. He wondered if he was being overly pessimistic about their chances for making it back, or overly optimistic about the condition of Kelly's foot. Was he being too cautious because he did not want to leave Jenny behind? Joshua listened to the wind outside. He didn't have a good answer.

"Just as soon as the storm lets up. You'll see. It shouldn't be too long now. Why don't you go back to sleep and I'll listen to the storm. As soon as it lets up, I'll wake you."

Kelly wasn't happy, but what could she do? She turned over on her side, away from Joshua, facing Jenny-Dog. Jenny-Dog could see she was crying.

Joshua lay back, on the outside of the sleeping bag. He covered himself with his parka. He was still chilled from being out. Then he remembered something and sat up. Joshua reached over and lit and hung the second tin-can candle. The first one was almost finished. He did not want to be without light.

Joshua lay back and listened to the storm and the trees. *Damn,* he thought, *how long can this blasted weather continue?* Anything was possible. He went over his decision to stay put. Was it right? What would he do when the food ran out? Would he really be able to do what was necessary to survive? Joshua looked over at Jenny-Dog and Buck. It wouldn't be easy. He would have to use his ax and his knife. That would be messy. How would he decide at what point it was necessary? Would he choose Buck, the larger of the two, or Jenny-Dog, his long time friend who had found the child, but who was now getting old?

Damn, he told himself. *You gotta stop thinking this way.*

But he did not stop thinking that way. He knew he had to prepare himself, mentally and spiritually.

Joshua lay back and listened to the storm and the trees. Maybe it will pass through soon, he told himself.

Then he closed his eyes and prayed.

Chapter Thirty-four

Ken Sloan started breakfast after his morning run. He tried not to awaken Kristian, who had finally fallen asleep on the futon in the living room. Jane was still in bed listening to the news on NPR and surfing the channels of her TV. If there were any new developments, she wanted to be aware of them.

There weren't. The storm in New England was still making headlines due to its length and severity, but, other than pictures of people struggling in the cities or making do in the suburbs, most information centered around statistics connected to the weather and the problems they were creating in general.

"Boston has reported over thirty-six inches of snowfall since the storm began. Burlington, Vermont is now reporting more than four feet of snow with drifts over twenty feet not uncommon. So far, more than a sixteen deaths have been attributed directly to the storm. Another ten people have died of heart attacks, and at least seven people are missing. Schools, of course, were closed yesterday, and officials tell us that even if the snow were to stop right now, it is doubtful that they could reopen before Tuesday or Wednesday."

"And why is that, Harry?"

"Well, Peter, in addition to the problems associated with digging out and opening the roads, officials aren't certain what condition the buildings are in. Many of the schools may have broken pipes and water damage,

and there is a lot of concern about the safety of the buildings due to excessive snow build up on the roofs."

"I see. And does the snow look to be slowing down, Harry?"

"Not as far as anyone here can tell, Peter. Snow is still falling at a rate of one to two inches per hour, and the winds continue unabated at gale strength."

"Okay. Well, thank you for that report. You'd better go inside and warm up."

"You don't have to ask me twice, Peter. We'll keep you posted."

"Anything new?" Kenny asked.

"Not about Joshua. There may be a second storm moving into the area."

"The same area? Jesus! Are you going to tell Kris?"

Jane had to think for a moment. She reflected on what Kris had said last night about her feeling like shit if she was wrong.

"Kris will find out soon enough. What's the weather like here?"

"It's February," Kenny replied. Jane knew what that meant. Then he added, "but there are some breaks in the clouds. Maybe it will clear off a little."

That would be nice, Jane thought.

Kristian was up. She lay on the futon, looking out at the beach and the surf, pondering what the day might bring. She had made the right decision, coming to Jane. Jane had forced her to recognize matters she had deeply buried. Now she would have to address them. The only question was, how?

"Well, don't you look ravishing," Jane mocked from across the breakfast table as Kristian sought out the coffeepot. "Do you think I can trust my husband to control himself once he is smitten with such beauty in the morning?"

"Shut up," Kris told her friend. "Any news?"

"No. It's just more of the same."

Kristian nodded.

"Kenny says it may clear up for a change. Let's take a ride down to Santa Cruz or Monterey. Whaddaya say, Kenny?" she called into the bathroom.

"Fine with me," Kenny called back.

"I've got to go into the office for a while. There's some work I have to get done."

Jane looked at her. "Are you sure?"

"Yes. Don't worry, I'm okay."

"Okay, but you're taking us out to dinner tonight. After all, we did feed you chili and beer. You owe us big time. Tarantino's should do. Maybe we'll stay over at your place tonight, just to make sure we want it."

"Fair enough. What's for breakfast?"

"Kenny was making French toast and bacon before he decided to take care of his manly needs. I guess it's up to his poor pregnant wife to finish the job, as always. I swear that man is more trouble than he's worth."

Kristian smiled at her friend from behind her coffee cup. "You're so full of shit."

Jane got up and cut a fart.

It was well past ten when Kristian left her friends at the beach and headed back to the city. She really did need to go into the office. She had a meeting with important clients scheduled for Monday, and she hadn't finished the preliminary sketches she had promised. The clients had insisted on a feature that just did not work aesthetically, and Kristian had been having difficulty resolving the conflict. The solution came to her last night as she lay on the futon thinking about Joshua and the past. Now she wanted to get the ideas on paper while they were still fresh in her mind. *Funny how those things happened.*

Kristian did not mind going in to the office on Saturday. With any luck, it would be deserted and she would not have any distractions. That was what she needed, to focus her attention on something other than Joshua and the storm. But as she approached the freeway, Kristian downshifted abruptly, pulled off the road and stopped on the shoulder. She thought of something for an instant and came to another conclusion. Instead of turning south on 101 and heading back to Sausalito and the city, Kristian turned north and sped towards San Rafael and the bridge to Richmond.

Am I nuts? Kristian wondered, as she raced her Porsche across the long, gently arching bridge. *Do I really have the guts to go through with this? And to what purpose? I must be nuts. Certifiably mad. Stark raving crazy.* She exited at Richmond and took 80 south towards El Cerito and Berkeley.

In Berkeley, she found a parking space just a few blocks from the courtyard that contained the Bijoux, the small theater on the north side of campus she was going to. Things had not changed much on this side of campus since she had attended. The Great American Pie shop was gone, but the ice cream parlor next door was still there. So was the trellised courtyard pizza place. Kristian hurried to the ticket window and quickly purchased a ticket. That was the easy part. The hard part would be going in.

The first showing was scheduled to begin at 12:30. Kristian checked her watch: 11:45. She decided to walk up the long hill to the Rose Gardens and reconsider her impulsive decision. The day had cleared off nicely. There were still many heavy clouds in the sky, but there was neither fog nor smog and the view of the bay from the Gardens was wonderful. *What the hell am I trying to prove?*

At 12:10, Kristian reluctantly left the gardens and found her way back to the theater. In the darkened room, she was one of only a handful of people in the audience for the first matinee. She knew that by evening, on a Saturday night, the small theater would be crowded. That was what had encouraged the theater owners to do what they did. Every weekend, with rare exception, for the last dozen years, they showed the same classic movie by French master Claude Lelouch, *Un homme et Une Femme*, A Man and A Woman. They knew they would never run out of the endless lovers and would be lovers searching for the inspiration that would elevate or renew their relationships. That wasn't what Kristian was searching for. She was looking for more.

The theater darkened and the familiar sound of the harbour horn was heard. Kristian was surprised how much she envied the mother reading *Le Petit Chaperon rouge* to her daughter. The familiar, haunting strains of the organ began. She was mesmerized by the boat passing through the initial credits.

Certain scenes and lines struck a chord deep within her being. Kristian was amazed at how much she could empathize with the main character's wife. Before, she had always considered her to be a throw-away character. Now she was real.

The dog in the beach scene reminded her of Jenny-Dog, without doubt, at least when viewed from a distance. Kristian almost lost it during the love scene, with its color flashbacks. She knew exactly what Anne was going through. It wasn't until the movie was over that she realized that she had watched the entire movie in French without the need for subtitles.

One hour and five minutes later Kristian emerged from the theater visibly shaken. Whether the experience would be cathartic remained to be seen. Kristian knew she could not drive. She walked south, down to the campus. The lush grass and fragrant eucalyptus calmed her. She sat on a damp bench and smoked a cigarette. After a second Winston, Kris regained her composure and returned to her car. The afternoon was moving on, and she had to get back to the city. Jane and Kenny would be coming in at 5:30, and she still had to get cleaned up and changed. There were also those sketches she should at least start.

As she got back onto 80 and drove in the direction of the Bay Bridge, the line from the movie rang through her head. *If I had another chance....what would I do?*

As soon as Kristian arrived home, she made reservations at Tarantino's for seven o'clock. It was only because she and her firm had done some outstanding work for the owner that she was able to secure the promise of a table at such a late hour. Then she checked her machine.

"Hello, Kristian, it's Alex. I just wanted to make sure everything was all right and to remind you of the conference we have scheduled with the Robinsons for Monday at eleven. Call if you need anything, dear." Alexander Wheaton was the founding partner of the firm.

"Hi, Kristian. It's Nathan. I thought we might get together sometime this weekend. Give me a call if anything works. Take care. Bye."

"Kristian, it's Maureen. I cleared my calendar. I'd really like to get back together with you and hear more of your story. Call me if tomorrow works."

"Hey, Kris. Give me a call as soon as you get in. Something's come up. Talk to you later." It was Jane. Kristian dialed the number.

"Hi, Jane. It's me. What's up?"

"Kris, guess what? We're going to Acapulco!"

"Terrific. When are you leaving?"

"Tonight. You're going too."

"What are you talking about?"

"My company wants me to go down to cover a show down there. I told them three months ago that they should send me, and they told me it couldn't possibly fit into the budget. Now they call and tell me I just *have* to go and that they'll spring for whatever it takes. Of course the show starts tomorrow morning. I told them they would have to pay all expenses, first class, for my husband and a personal secretary. How's your shorthand?"

"You've got to be kidding. Christ, Jane, this is outrageous, even for you."

"Hey kiddo, how often do you get to grab your boss by the balls?"

Knowing Jane, it was probably more often than not.

"I only squeezed a little."

Kristian thought about the proposition. Then she thought about the film.

"It sounds great, Jane, but I can't. I have work to do and an important meeting on Monday."

"Yeah, yeah. That's what you said when you left this morning. Just where the hell did you go after you left here? I called your office three times."

"I went over to Berkeley. There was something I had to do."

"I'll just bet. So whaddaya say? You need to get the hell out of San Francisco for a while, and the sun will do you good."

"I can't, Jane, really. But thanks for thinking of me."

"Screw it. Then we won't go either. What time are our reservations for?"

"Don't be ridiculous. I'm okay. I don't need you to hold my hand tonight."

"Are you sure? I know what a wimp you are."

Kristian smiled. Jane was the only person who knew her who would ever call her a wimp. "I'm sure. Have a great time."

"You can count on it. We'll be staying at the Mayan Palace. Don't hesitate to call if you need to talk."

"I won't. Have fun. And Jane... thanks for everything."

"Forget it. I'll get it back in baby-sitting."

"Deal." They hung up.

It was probably all for the best. She really did have to get some work done. Now she would have no excuses or distractions. It was getting rather late to go into the office, but she could work on the drawings in her townhouse studio and go into the office tomorrow if need be.

Kristian surprised herself when she looked up at the clock. She was pleased to realize that she had actually worked for more than two hours. The plans were coming along nicely. She was surprised again when her doorbell rang.

"Yes?" she inquired over the intercom.

"Kris, it's Nathan Goodman."

Kristian hesitated a moment. It would be okay, she thought. And after all, she still hadn't canceled the reservations at Tarantino's.

"Come on in, Nathan."

Chapter Thirty-five

Twelve inches of new snow had fallen in Lincoln County over the last twenty-four hours, and it was still coming down. But twelve inches in February was not unusual for northern Wisconsin. The plows were working. Power was on in most places, and the Blazer Pub was just the ticket to relieve cabin fever on a Saturday night.

The bar was crowded, noisy and smoke filled. The film was scheduled to be shown at eight o'clock. Jonathan VanStavern arrived at 7:56, having checked things at the Travis homestead once again.

"Any word, Jon?"

"Not yet. Do you have any hot coffee, Pat?"

"Sure thing."

"What's it now, three nights?" Lloyd Hendricks asked.

"This is the third night."

"Christ, that's a long time."

"What are ya talkin' about? Hell, he was gone for a week when he was on that one up in the Boundary Waters."

"Jesus, Ed, that was different. Hell, for starters, it was summer. He had DNR people with him from the U.S. and Canada. And they had radios with them to call in a chopper."

"I'm just sayin' Joshua knows how to take care of himself. Don't he?"

Nobody answered.

"Lookee here, I got fifty bucks says we ain't seen the last of ol' Josh Travis. Any takers?"

There were plenty of would be takers. But the people of Lincoln County loved Joshua Travis. Hell, hadn't they forgiven him for not taking that full ride to the U of W and going on to star for the Green Bay Packers? Nope, he was their hometown hero. No one would bet against him that night because it was a bet nobody wanted to win.

"Show the damn game film, Patrick!"

There was no relief from cabin fever for the people at Jay Peak, Vermont. People were getting edgy. Patience was wearing thin. Even Sam Hanson was unable to keep up much of a front.

"I don't want Mr. or Mrs. Martin left alone. Understand? Not for a minute."

Johnson and Beard nodded.

"George, how's Nancy holding up?"

"Pam says she's hanging in there, but that she sometimes goes into a vacant stare."

"Make sure Pam stays with her. Have somebody relieve her if need be."

"You going to go looking for the bodies when the storm lets up, Sam?" It was Bill Peterson.

"I don't want to hear that kind of talk," the sheriff replied. *Besides,* he thought to himself, *I wouldn't know where to begin.*

"Maybe we can get Leah back here once it clears," Johnson offered. It was probably the worst thing he could have said.

"I guess," Hanson groaned.

Then, at 8:59 P.M., something happened that lifted spirits for the first time since Joshua Travis had arrived and gone into the storm. The phones came back on. Ma Bell had come through even if Citizens Power had not.

Joshua and Kelly lay in the tent. He knew there was nothing to be done but stick to his routine, conserve energy, and pray. *God, isn't this storm ever going to end?*

When the child is awake he tells her stories, some made up but mostly true, about his travels and adventures, or about his dogs and their misadventures like big King, the pure bred German shepherd, who would always carry a rock for you to toss and for him to fetch. Or the time Buck stole a little boy's ice cream cone right out of his hand, and Joshua was just glad Buck was at least considerate enough to leave the boy his hand.

"That little stunt cost me a buck, didn't it, Buck?"

"What does cost a Buck mean?"

"It means it cost me a dollar."

"That's a lot of money."

"It sure is, honey." Joshua was happy it hadn't cost him a lawsuit.

He plays French-Canadian jigs on a small mouth-harp, to keep their spirits up, and he sings her soft Quebecois lullabies to help her fall asleep so that the time will pass more easily, at least for her.

Periodically, he checks Kelly to make sure she is not overheated, to give the antibiotics, and to check her feet. The left foot is swollen and stinks to high heaven, but Kelly still shows no evidence of wet gangrene so they stay put.

Periodically, he leaves the tent to check the shelter and its passages and to chuck a toilet bag while trying to gauge the storm.

After forty-eight hours, he sets aside the empty Thermoses and reserves the rest of the granola for Kelly. He shares a slice from the fourth summer sausage with the dogs, who have been cut back to one slice each, every twelve hours. The Hershey bars are gone. He has read of terrible blizzards in the plains and mountain states that went on for over a week, but he is not worried about making it as long as the wickiup holds. What he is worried about is the price he may have to pay in order to make it, and he wonders if this is one deal with God he is willing to cut.

Joshua knew he had to be careful. He had a lot of time on his hands. His mind could start working overtime. He did not really think that the storm would last for a week, but he had to wonder what he would do if it did. He had packed plenty of food for a couple of days, but two people and two large dogs can use up a lot of calories when they're out in the cold, and there were limits to how much he could carry. Joshua kept telling himself that if worse comes to worse, you just have to remember that a dog is just a dog. But he did not know if he could make himself believe it, and that night Joshua prayed like he'd never prayed before. Joshua prayed in English and in Latin, as best he could. He even threw in some prayers in French just in case that happened to be the language that pleased the good Lord that night...

But his prayers did not stave off the nightmare.

At Tarantino's, on Fisherman's Wharf, Kristian and Nathan sat at the bar. Even with reservations, there was a twenty-minute wait for their table. That was just fine with Kristian. She was in no hurry.

"You're a difficult woman to get a hold of."

"I was visiting a friend in Marin. She's going to have a baby."

"Congratulations. When is she due?"

"Early September, I think. She just told her husband yesterday. She's a real maniac, but I love her. She and her husband were the ones I was supposed to have dinner with tonight, but she's going to Acapulco instead. She conned her company into picking up the tab for the two of them."

"Good for her." His hand lightly covered hers.

Basketball was on the barroom television, the traditional rivalry between UCLA and U.C. Berkeley. Kristian and Nathan desperately rooted for Berkeley. UCLA won handily. Then the news came on, delayed an hour by the game.

The storm in the east continued to be the lead story, especially on a Saturday night. This time there was something different.

"We have a special report from Jay Peak, Vermont, courtesy of WVTV in Burlington. Go ahead, Helen."

"Thank you, Dan. As you know, six-year-old Kelly Martin has been missing since Thursday. A rescue worker, Joshua Paul Travis, from Wisconsin, is also missing. Since Thursday night we have been cut off from the Jay Peak Ski Resort. But just a few minutes ago, phone service was restored, and we have Barry Steiner, of the Burlington Free Press, on the line."

Two file pictures, one of the ski lodge, the other of Barry Steiner, appeared on the screen.

"Barry, what is the situation at the lodge?"

"We've been snowed in for three days, Helen. We're on emergency power, but we're relatively warm, and there's plenty of food."

"Any word on the missing child or the man who went after her?"

"Nothing definite but it doesn't look good. I was talking to Jim Beard, the head of the ski patrol up here, and he said it was the worst storm he's ever seen. Even Sam Hanson, the local sheriff, wasn't very optimistic. I don't think anybody here really believes they could have survived."

"What a tragedy. How is everyone else making out?"

"People are getting tired of being cooped up. Then we think of the alternative and we don't complain."

"I understand. Well, there you have it, Dan. Grim news on a cold Saturday night."

Nathan looked at Kristian. She was pale.

"I'm sorry, Nathan, I can't do this. Please take me home."

Nathan slipped the Maitre d' a twenty with his apologies as he escorted the visibly shaken woman to his car.

Chapter Thirty-six

For Joshua Paul Travis, the nightmare always begins with the endless droning of the engines. The endless droning of the engines and the reddish-orange glow.

Joshua is flying through the air, racing to another rescue. He is not moving. The plane is not moving. Only the hands of the instrument panel clock move, driving home his helplessness. The knot in his gut is tight. He thinks he may vomit. He chokes it down. The crew is relaxed, business like. They point to the glow in the distance. Why aren't they getting any closer? It must be the sunset on the horizon. Then he remembers it is not. Damn!

Suddenly he is on the ground. He has two dogs with him. One dog is Jenny. Who is the other? It's not Buck. Which one is it? Maybe Ellie. The dogs shake their heads and sneeze. Joshua is having difficulty breathing. He is perspiring, but he is cold.

"Mr. Travis, I'm Deputy Macauley..."

"I'm sorry we didn't do better, Deputy..."

Joshua is airborne again. It is a bumpy ride. Bumpy and noisy. Who is that next to him? His friend? Jonathan VanStavern? Some comrade-in-arms? What does that Indian woman want from him? He calls her grandmother.

On the ground again, racing through the night. Running, riding, running, breathing, coughing, choking. KEEP CALM!

"You'd best stay here, ma'am," he tells the woman as he heads off into the forest. Into the night.

He is optimistic. His dogs have found a trail. The wind is fierce, swirling. The fire is moving, jumping. The trees are old and dry and brittle. Burning limbs fall all around him. He can not breathe. His friend helps him. They find the little girl. He does his best to save her. It is no use. She is dead. He kisses her cold, dead lips. "God bless you..... I'm sorry we didn't do better."

He is running again. He is carrying someone across his shoulders, running alongside someone. The deputy? An Indian? Is the deputy an Indian?

"You must emerge from this world into the next," he is told.

"You forgot your hat," he replies. "I'm sorry. Oh God, I'm so sorry."

Joshua is shivering, freezing cold. He is holding on for dear life, but he does not want to live. He wants to let go. He passes into oblivion. Then he hears the droning of the engines.

And it all begins again.

"I'm sorry we didn't do better..."

It was Buck who first detected the change. His alert whining woke Jenny-Dog. Now she knew too. Both dogs whined. Jenny-Dog barked. Joshua awoke with a start, drained and frightened.

He shook himself and swore softly when he realized he had overslept. He checked his watch and was struck with fear when he saw it was 3:59. He had missed the scheduled 2 A.M. airway clearing.

Damn, he thought. *Okay, no need to panic. We're all breathing. No need to panic.*

"Good guys," he told the dogs. That didn't settle them down.

The tent was unusually stuffy. It stank from panting dogs and Kelly's foot.

"Easy does it guys. I'm up. I'll take care of the air holes. Now settle down." Jenny-Dog stopped barking, but the whining continued.

As Joshua sat up and slipped on his moccasins, the two agitated dogs crowded in excitedly whining and nuzzling him. Their behavior was not normal.

"What's the problem, guys? You really have to go out that bad?" Given the rations they had been on the past twelve hours, Joshua was surprised. Maybe they were thirsty. Then he realized what was going on.

The tent was not moving and breathing as it had been for two days and three nights.

"Hush up!" The dogs briefly settled. It was quiet. That was it! It was quiet! The wind wasn't howling and raging as it had been. Without going outside, Joshua could not know if it had stopped snowing. Nor did he know if the storm was truly over. But he did know this was the break they had been praying for. He took off his moccasins and pulled on his mukluks and his overalls.

"Kelly, wake up, sweetheart."

The little girl stirred. The excited dogs made it difficult to sleep.

"Wake up, sleepyhead. We're going home."

"When?" Kelly asked. Still alert, a good sign.

"Just as soon as we can. I'm going outside to see what we're dealing with. Do you have to go potty?"

Kelly indicated she did. Joshua helped her, then placed her back in the sleeping bag.

"Eat some granola. I'll be back in a jiffy. Then we'll go home."

Joshua was surprised by Kelly's calm acceptance of the news. Probably still half asleep, he hoped.

To Joshua's relief, the air holes were still clear. The dogs were still agitated.

"Yes, guys, I know. You guys want to go home too. Just let me dig out and we'll see what the situation is."

Even before the passage was cleared, Joshua knew he was right. Outside, the absence of wind made the below zero temperature feel downright balmy. There were even stars visible between the breaking clouds. The tree crowns swayed gently.

Joshua dug out the area near the shelter entrance. He would need space to get the child-carrying backpack out and up onto his back. As he worked, the dogs barked and spun. It was the first time both dogs had been out together since they found Kelly. They were excited, he guessed, at the change in their situation and their prospects.

"Take it easy, guys. We'll be heading out soon. Just let me take care of business." Joshua maintained his rock solid control. There were things to be done, and he had to do them. He wasn't about to screw up now, after having come so far. But he couldn't blame the dogs for being excited. And excited they were.

Still, there was something not right. Joshua wasn't certain what it was, but he could hear it in Jenny's incessant bark and whine. Buck barked and howled too, but Joshua didn't know him as well. The noise Jenny made worried him.

Maybe she was worried about tackling the deep snow. If it looked too hard for her, Joshua would leave her in the tent and return for her later. Maybe she knew this and did not want to be left behind. Sometimes it seemed as if Jenny-Dog could read his mind. Maybe this break in the weather was just temporary and the dogs were trying to tell him to get a move on. There was a real possibility of that. Joshua looked up to check the night sky. He caught his breath as he saw what the dogs had been warning him about.

Thirty feet high, a major vertical branch of the great old maple tree that had saved them was broken directly above the shelter. The branch hung grotesquely perpendicular to the tree. Its crown was supported by some brittle red cedars, its twelve-inch base attached by no more than bark and cambium. It would not take much wind to bring it down. There was no telling how it might land, but Joshua knew they didn't want to be under it when it did. From all the time he had spent cutting firewood, Joshua knew the limb had to weigh one thousand pounds or more. He forced himself to stay cool.

"You guys stay out here. Watch out for that branch," he told the dogs as he scrambled back into the shelter. This time he didn't bother taking off his mukluks when he entered the tent. He took off his parka but kept it near by.

"Time to go," he told Kelly. He tried to keep the fear from rising to his voice.

"Now just trust me and do exactly as I say, sweetheart. I want you to snuggle all the way down to the foot of the sleeping bag." As she did, Joshua unzipped the bag zipper to just above her head.

"Okay, Kel, now just stay still. I have to cut the bag and I don't want to get you." He took his lock-back knife and methodically sliced away the top four feet. He placed the excess out of the way and removed the loose down from the top of the remaining segment.

"Still got your head? Good. Now turn on your side while I roll the bag." The child rolled to her right.

"Not that way, Kel. Roll over on your other side." Kelly complied. Joshua rolled the bag so that the zipper was on top when Kelly lay on her back.

"Okay, sweetheart. Here comes the tricky part. I'm going to slide you into the back pack and tie you in. You try to scrunch down however you have to to fit, okay? Okay, here goes."

Joshua carefully worked and stuffed the sleeping bag containing the child into the modified backpack. He tried not to over stress the zippers or the seams, but he really didn't have much choice. He knew he had to get the child out of there, and this was the only safe way.

"Okay, now I'm going to stand the pack up and you try to snuggle down into it. Okay?" Kelly nodded. Joshua stood the pack on its end. He worked the bag and the child into the pack. It would have been easier if the little girl's arms were outside the pack but Joshua could not permit that. Too much of the child would have been exposed.

Joshua bounced the pack and stuffed the bag in from the back.

Kelly was in as far as she would go. There was no more space. Only her head was above the top of the pack. Her foot throbbed and hurt, but Kelly did not complain. She was too scared. She sensed something was different by the way the man moved and the tone of his voice.

Joshua rigged his snowshoes to the back of the pack once again. "Okay, Kelly, this is what we're going to do. I'm going to lay you back down and slide you out of the tent and out of the shelter..."

Even before he heard it, Joshua knew intuitively what was happening. He barely had time to lay the pack down and cover the child with his own body. The branch crashed down on them with a crackling *whommp!* The last thing he heard was a yelp from Jenny-Dog.

Kristian felt she owed Nathan an explanation. After they had abruptly left the restaurant, Kristian had asked Nathan to drive around in the night. She told him the story as they drove, struck by the irony of the situation.

Nathan was dumbfounded. He alternately looked over to her, then back to the road. Kristian looked straight ahead. Nathan did not know what to say. There was nothing to say. He brought her home.

"Kris, do you want some company tonight? I'll stay on the couch, if you like."

"I can't, Nathan. Not tonight. I'm sorry. Thank you for putting up with me and for being so understanding." She reached over and kissed him on his cheek. Then she exited the car.

Now she was alone in her townhouse again. *Damn,* she thought, *another long night.*

Jenny-Dog jumped clear. Buck was already in the open. Both dogs barked. *Where is He? In there,* she knew. Jenny-Dog started to dig through two tons of snow and trees. The snow was compressed.

The vines were tight knit. She couldn't get through. *Try another place. Dig, whine. Try another place.* Buck looked on, puzzled. Then he left.

In San Francisco, Kristian threw back another scotch. She put the Dylan album on the turntable.

Gogyeng Sowuhti knows the conclusion is near.

"*Help me, Taiowa. Show your face. Help me, Huruing Wuhti. Taknokwunu must be calmed. Help me, Great Spirit. Save the one you sent.*"

"*Remember your grandfathers when they hid from the Tavasuh,*" *she is told.*

The old woman recalls the legend of her people: How a band of young Hopi kalatakam led an approaching Tavasuh raiding party across the desert, away from the main body of the Hopi village. To evade capture, the Hopi warriors buried themselves in the sides of a muddy arroyo near Pakabva, breathing through the hollow reeds they found along the bank.

"*There are no reeds here,*" *observes Gogyeng Sowuhti.*

"*You must imagine them.*"

Beneath the crushed snow and fallen trees, enveloped in rip-stop nylon and urethane coated taffeta, lay the man and the little girl. All was darkness. The candle drowned in its own wax. The only sounds were from the terrified child, sobbing. Joshua lay still. He was afraid to move in what little space was afforded them. His impulse was to dig madly for air. He fought the impulse with all the control he could summon. Digging wildly was no guarantee of air. He would have to dig in the right direction. Where would he put the snow? Would his arm be long enough? Most importantly, how stable was their situation. Right now they were trapped but not pinned down or crushed. Joshua had to secure an air flow without collapsing whatever was above them.

"Are you okay," he asked Kelly.

"Are we dead?"

"No, sweetheart. We're not dead."

"Are we going to be dead?"

"Not if I can help it," he assured her. "Now, I need for you to lie very still and be very quiet. Can you do that?" He could not see Kelly nod.

"You might even want to go to sleep. I'll wake you as soon as we're ready to go." He wanted the child using as little air as possible. He would try to do the same. There was no way to gauge how long the air would hold out. The very things that had kept them alive for three nights, the tree, the snow, the tent and the fly, were now working to kill them.

Joshua felt around for a light. He found none. He cautiously felt around with his hand. They were surrounded by collapsed tent, but there was a little room to maneuver. Joshua carefully rolled to his left side and then shifted to his back. So far, so good, but it was getting stuffy. Goose down choked the air.

Joshua examined the interior of the crushed tent with his hands. Most of the material was taut with snow, but there were pockets of space. He felt for his knife and cut away as much nylon and taffeta as he dared. If any air was getting into the pile of snow and brush, he wanted it in the tent, but he knew he couldn't count on it. Somehow, they had to get access to the outside. They had to get it quickly.

Jenny-Dog tried another spot, then another. It was no use. The compacted snow shelter was now too tightly woven for her to penetrate. The only other possibility was to burrow underneath. That would take time. Jenny knew it would be hard, dangerous work. She began digging at once.

Buck struggled and bounded and fought his way through the deep snow, farther and farther from Jenny-Dog and the two buried humans.

Joshua believed he and the child had just one chance. He surveyed the tent material with his hands and found what he was looking for, the lateral support pole for the geodesic dome tent. Joshua shifted to his right side and tested the pole to see if it was supporting any weight. It did not appear to be. He deftly sliced through the tent and the pole support sleeve to gain access to the Easton aluminum tent pole.

It was awkward, working in the cramped space. Great strength was required to free the pole from its securing posts. Then it was difficult breaking down the pole into individual sections. The section fits were tight, but that might come in handy.

Joshua cut the shock-cord linking the pole sections, withdrew the elastic cord and stuffed it in his pocket. He cut a twelve-inch square from the tent-fly material. The tent pole sections were two feet long. They had a hollow inside diameter of one-quarter inch. If he could work them through to the outside, he and the child would be able to breathe through them. But he had to do it without plugging them in the process.

Joshua covered the end of the pole with the square from the fly. He secured it with the shock-cord by wrapping around a slip knot and looping through an improvised trucker's hitch. Lying on his back, Joshua guessed a good angle and cut a small square in the material above him and the girl. Some snow fell on his face. He prayed that the shelter would not implode as he twisted and worked the tent pole through the snow. When the tent pole neared its end, Joshua coupled a second section of pole to the first. The tight Easton fit served them well. He was able to work it through another six inches. Then it struck something hard and would bore no farther. *Damn*, Joshua thought. *Don't panic. Try again.*

Jenny-Dog dug. Buck struggled. It was difficult for the great winter dog to make any headway. He had to rest every ten yards. It was difficult to know which way to go. The ground scent was buried. He could see only when he bounded above the deep snow. Maybe he should have stayed with Jenny-Dog. But there was something in the air. It wasn't constant. The wind had changed. But when he caught it, Buck caught images of warmth and food and humans. The big dog fought on.

Sam Hanson stood outside on the chalet porch, alone and quiet, marveling at the break in the weather. As the sheriff lit his pipe, Steiner came out on the porch also. Steiner was a card, Hanson thought as he watched the reporter, all bundled up in a goose down parka, trying to manage a cup of coffee in mittened hands. Sheriff Hanson was surprised to see anyone else up and about at that time. For some reason, he resented the intrusion on his privacy.

"Don't look like you'll get much of a story, Mr. Steiner." The two men stood together on the timbered porch of the lodge in the Vermont pre-dawn. In most places the snow was up to the porch.

"You'll be going out in the morning, Sheriff?" Steiner asked.

"We'll go if the weather holds. News says we're going to get walloped again, this time from the west."

"Not much hope, huh?"

Sam Hanson paused from his pipe and looked at him. "No Mr. Steiner, not much hope. Chances are we won't find anything at all before spring. And even if we do, what the hell can you expect after three days of this goddamn weather? Maybe the tip of a snowshoe sticking out somewhere, if we're lucky."

Three damn days – hell, a goddamn lifetime. Steiner looked down and then turned to go back inside the warm, cozy lodge.

"What was that?" Hanson heard him ask suddenly.

"What was what?" the sheriff growled.

"I thought I saw something move out there." Steiner pointed off to the south.

Sheriff Hanson looked long and hard. He didn't see a damn thing. "Probably just a shadow, or a reflection on the snow."

"There! A little to the left! There it is again!"

Sam Hanson looked again into the dark countryside, but he still didn't see a godblessed... but then!... naw, he thought, just a reflection... and then!... there it was again!... kind of like a bounce, just a flicker of movement and hard to tell if he was really seeing something or just wishing. Maybe a deer, was what he told himself.

"There it is again!" Steiner cried. "What th... Holy shit! It's a dog!... Look! A dog!"

There was no way... not after three days. But there it was, by God. A dark mass struggling and bounding through the deep powder, persistently working its way towards the lodge. "Jesus Christ!"

They looked at one another and then back towards the dog.

"Is it one of his dogs?" Steiner asked.

"It has to be. Where else would it come from? But how the...?"

Both men were so wrapped up in watching the struggling dog that neither noticed the ominous sky to the west. There was no question now. It was definitely one of his dogs. That big gray-brown monster wolf-like dog working his way in a desperate and irregular path towards the chalet, resting every few yards, then struggling some more.

"Can you see him? Can you see the man?"

"No. All I can see is the dog!"

"Jesus fucking Christ, I don't believe it! It can't be!" Steiner was really getting excited. "Do you think he's out there, Sheriff? Is it possible that he's actually still alive?"

"Damned if I know. All I see is one dog."

The sheriff was getting pretty worked up himself but *I'll be a sonofabitch...* was about all he could manage as he raced inside.

"Andy, Andy, get up." Hanson shook his deputy who was sleeping on the couch near the fire.

"Huh? What's up, Sam?"

"We've got a dog outside, coming from the woods, heading in."

"A dog...? One of Travis's dogs?"

"Yeah, now listen up. Get Jim Beard and the patrol people and some gear. Make it snappy. I don't know how much time we got before the next storm hits. I'm going out to meet the dog. Maybe he'll take me to Travis, or maybe I can follow his tracks."

"You think he's still alive?"

"I don't know, but one of his dogs sure as hell is. This may be the only shot we get before spring."

"What about the little girl?"

"Who the hell knows? Right now, all we got is one dog."

Steiner couldn't contain himself and kept shouting at the bewildered assistant manager who happened to be on duty at the time.

"There's a dog outside! One of his dogs! He's coming in!"

Sam Hanson was under a bit more control and started putting on his terrapin parka and grabbing his mitts. This time he took snowshoes, not skis.

"Better find the doctor," Hanson told the man behind the desk, who by this time was beginning to sort out at least some of all the noise Steiner had thrown at him.

"What about the little girl's parents?" the night clerk asked. "Should I get them up also?"

Sheriff Hanson thought for a moment, then told him, "No, not just yet... No tellin' what's what." Then he remembered they were sleeping by the radio in the office. "I'll tell you what. They're bound to wake up sooner or later. When they do, keep 'em here manning the radio. Tell 'em you're out of snowshoes, or some damn thing. There's no telling what we may find, if anything. I don't want nobody but professionals out there. That goes for the rest of the guests too."

Now Steiner was busy on the phone, talking to the night editor of the Free Press. Trying hard to explain, in spite of himself, what was going on.

"Yes, yes, that's what I'm trying to tell you...! We got a dog! Yes, a dog! He's almost back here. What?... No, no, I don't know whether he's alive or not, or if he ever found the kid. They're going out to look for them now... Christ, the very fact that anything survived out in that storm is a miracle in itself!"

The sheriff stepped out of the lodge, put on his snowshoes and mittens, and pushed off to look for a man he'd thought sure to be dead for at least two days.

The assistant manager first rings up Doctor Whitman and then calls the manager of the resort. The manager himself, disregarding the sheriff's warning, goes to the office where the missing child's parents sleep by the radio. He wakes them and explains the situation to them as best he understands it.

On a small farm outside Merrill, Wisconsin, Jonathan VanStavern lies awake in his bed, next to his wife of thirty years. He has not been able to sleep since returning home from the Blazer Pub, well past midnight... He damns himself for what he has done, thinking, hell, what other choice was there?

In San Francisco, on the balcony of the stylish Mansard townhouse, Kristian Fisk-Travis looks out at the empty lights of the city and the bay. She puts out another cigarette in a small china ashtray and wonders.... She turns and goes inside, takes another pill, and hopes that this time she will be able to sleep.

High on the Tusayan Plateau, in the ancient Shongopovi pueblo, the old Indian medicine-woman is having trouble breathing through her vision. She must awaken soon or she will die.

Joshua withdrew the tent pole from the hole he had bored above him. He had to break it down when he got to the joint. He still had hold of the shock-cord but the fly-material cap was lost in the snow.

Joshua cut another. His arms and neck and shoulders were getting stiff from working in the cramped quarters. He was getting a headache. That worried him. Deep within, he had an impulse to go for broke. It told him to summon every last ounce of his strength and use it to crash through the frozen mound of snow and wood, just as he used to crash through three defenders to score the winning touchdown. He spit goose down from his mouth and fought the impulse with all the courage he could muster. Patiently, he worked the tent pole through the snow at a different angle.

Joshua could not tell if the pole was through or not. When he thought it might be, he pulled the length of shock-cord that released the trucker's hitch. With the cord free, Joshua placed the end of the hollow tent pole in his mouth and blew with all his might to clear the covered end. Nothing happened. The pole was not through.

Damn!

Jenny-Dog dug. Buck struggled. Sheriff Hanson lumbered through the deep powder snow. It was hard work, even with snowshoes. Hell, he hadn't used the damn things since he was a kid on the family farm outside of Burlington.

Hanson carried little gear, a knapsack with some food, a Thermos of hot cocoa, and a radio to keep in touch with the lodge. He would break trail. Beard and the ski patrol would bring shovels and rescue equipment on the special snow-rescue litters they would drag behind them. The sheriff looked up and to the west. He didn't like the sky.

Early as it was, things were waking up at the lodge. The sounds and lights from snow plows firing up and working were so welcome that many guests hastened to get dressed without even checking their clocks. Downstairs, the minor commotion of Jim Beard readying the ski patrol to depart had awakened desperate hope within the Martins.

"I'm going with you," John Martin insisted.

"I can't allow that Mr. Martin. We don't have enough snowshoes. Besides, you need to be here to take care of your wife. You can man the radio for us if you want. That would help out," Beard told the anguished father.

"I'm going out there with you!" Martin insisted.

"We're wasting time, Mr. Martin! I'm sorry, but you need to do as I say. Either you cooperate or I'll have to ask Deputy Johnson to confine you, and I don't want to do that. I need him with us. What do you say?"

John Martin looked outside. Even in the dark, the prospect looked frightful. "I'll be on the radio," he told them.

"Good man," Beard replied. "Hang in there."

The ski patrol and the deputy stepped off the chalet porch. They dragged two rescue litters carrying shovels, blankets, first-aid kits, and food. Hanson's trail was easy to follow.

The sheriff was wary as he approached the struggling dog. He wondered when the animal last ate, and Hanson wasn't wearing his service revolver. Buck was resting on top of the snow. By distributing his mass, he could avoid sinking more than twelve inches into the powder. He barked as Hanson approached.

"Easy does it, big boy. I'm coming to help. Where's your master, big guy? Where's Mr. Travis?"

Buck did not move. He continued to bark. It was impossible for Hanson to read the dog in the early morning dark. Better not take any chances, he thought as he maintained a prudent distance from the large dog.

"Where's Travis, big guy? Can you take me to him?" *What had Travis called him,* Hanson tried to remember. *One was Jenny-Dog, what had he called this one?* The sheriff thought back to the little girl's room when the dogs were on the bed. *Buck!*

"Buck! Where's Travis? This way?"

The dog continued to bark but he did not get up. Buck was totally exhausted. It didn't matter. Hanson followed the dog's tracks. He picked up his pace when he realized it was starting to snow again.

Like his dog, Joshua Travis was exhausted. He did not think the air in their limited space could hold out much longer. One more time, he withdrew the Easton pole. One more time, he cut and secured a taffeta cap to the end of the pole. One more time, he worked the pole through the snow and the branches that had them buried alive.

Hanson held up when he got to the woods. Like Travis before him, he took off his snowshoes. He stood them in the snow on the leeward side of a large white pine. The snow in the woods came up to his hips, higher in some places.

Sam Hanson huffed and puffed as he worked his way through the woods. He needed to lose thirty pounds and give up the pipe. He rested momentarily, then he moved on. Ten minutes later the dog's tracks ended.

Hanson shined his light around. He did not see any sign of life.

"Mr. Travis! Travis! Kelly Martin! Mr. Travis!" the sheriff shouted. At first he heard nothing. Then he heard a slight rustling sound followed by a whine and a bark! Travis' other dog was on the other side of the mound in front of him. Hanson got excited. He worked his way around to her and surveyed the situation with his light. He found the burrow excavated by the dog.

"Where are they, girl? Where's Mr. Travis and Kelly? Are they in there?" Jenny barked. The sheriff's heart sank. The mound before him looked pretty damn solid. He tried to be optimistic. Perhaps the dogs had become separated from the man. Maybe they had holed up here while Travis and the girl were somewhere else. Hanson shined the light around the mound and into the woods.

"Travis!" he called. "Joshua Travis!" The sheriff was out of options. He began carefully dismantling the mound of snow and wood, while he waited for Beard and the others, afraid of what he might find. He used a small limb to scrape away snow. He tried to lightly test each branch before he moved it. Each action brought fear. Inaction was worse. Sam Hanson didn't know if he was more afraid of finding nothing or of finding something.

There were no signs of life as the sheriff dug through the snow. *What was that?* A sudden slight flutter was caught by his peripheral vision. *Ah shit, just some fallin' snow.* Sam Hanson continued to dig. Jenny-Dog panted nearby, exhausted. *There! There's another one! What the hell...?* The sheriff backed off the mound and shined the light along the surface. *There it is, a little to the right!* Sam Hanson couldn't believe what he saw.

A .370 inch O.D. metal tube extended four inches beyond the snow. His heart leapt when he saw the tube move!

Beard and the ski patrol had difficulty negotiating the toboggan-like litters through the trees and brush. By the time they arrived, Hanson had made contact and dawn was coming on.

"Mr. Travis! Are you in there? Hold on! Are you okay?" Sam Hanson was truly excited.

"We're in here," came the muffled reply.

Hanson was stunned by implication of Travis's words. He swallowed hard and then dared the question, "The little girl? Is she in there too?"

"Darn tootin'. I couldn't have made it without her. Be careful digging us out. I don't know how stable this mess is. Sure would hate to have it all come down on us now."

"My God, I don't believe it. I just don't believe it...." Hanson repeated.

"What have we got, Sam?" Jim Beard asked as the rescue team arrived.

"They're alive, by God! They're underneath this pile. We'll have to watch it digging them out, but by God if they're not alive! If that's not a blessed miracle, I don't know what is."

"Well I'll be damned," Beard replied.

"Dang," was all Andy Johnson could manage. He was grinning from ear to ear. The other members of the rescue party were smiling too, congratulating each other. Jenny-Dog barked. Buck brought up the rear and crouched down in the snow. He was too winded to bark.

The team cautiously moved limbs and branches and dug through the snow. The work was a giant game of pick-up sticks. When they finally made it through to the tent and fly, Andy Johnson nearly lost it as he flashed back to the body bags he had seen in 'Nam.

Joshua sliced through the tent from the inside. Kelly Martin lay motionless, still in the sleeping bag stuffed into the backpack. She continued to breathe through the aluminum tent pole in her mouth. The second tent pole, used by Joshua, stood near by.

Once extricated from the confining space of the collapsed tent, Joshua removed the hollow pole from the child's mouth. "We're going home, Kelly," he told her. We're going home right now."

Kelly Martin had been through too much to say anything. Now, with all the people and commotion surrounding her, she was happy but scared. She didn't know whether to smile or to cry.

Beard and Hanson helped Travis up out of the pile of snow and vines and branches. Together, they extricated the little girl. Joshua detached his snowshoes that were still hooked to the back of the pack. They lay Kelly on one of the litter sleds, taking her out of the backpack but keeping her in the sleeping bag. Beard and Kathy secured the child with a blanket and straps.

"Get her back to the lodge quickly," Travis told Jim Beard quietly. "She may have gangrene." That reminded the sheriff to do something he had forgotten in all the excitement. He dug out the walkie-talkie from his knapsack and radioed back to the lodge.

"This is Hanson to Jay. Anybody read me?"

"Sheriff! This is John Martin. Have you found anything?"

"We've found them, Mr. Martin! They're okay! Kelly's got a hurt foot is all. We're on our way back. Put Dr. Whitman on, will you?"

"Diane, Kelly's okay! Kelly's okay!" Martin told his wife, his voice breaking.

Diane Martin was too stunned to move, much less speak. She crumpled to the floor near her husband and wept.

"Sheriff, can I talk to her?"

Hanson held the walkie-talkie near the child's face.

"It's your daddy, honey. He wants to talk to you. Go ahead, Mr. Martin. Give it a try."

"Kelly! Kelly, honey, are you all right? How are you, sweetheart?"

Kelly smiled when she heard her father's voice. At first she was mike shy and just nodded her replies.

"Go ahead, honey. Say something to your daddy," Hanson coaxed.

"Snug as a bug inna rug," Kelly finally replied.

Everyone at the rescue site had moist eyes. John Martin wept.

"Put Dr. Whitman on, Mr. Martin."

Hanson explained the situation to the doctor. Whitman called the hospital in Burlington for a med-evac chopper. They all hoped the snow would hold off.

"How about you, Mr. Travis? We got another sled." Beard told him.

"I'm okay. My snowshoes are still in one piece." He had gone into the rescue with over one thousand dollars worth of equipment. Now, only the snowshoes were still intact. It was a good bargain.

"I would be obliged if you could leave that other sled. My friends here might need some help in this deep snow." Joshua indicated the dogs.

"We don't mind sledding your dogs out, Mr. Travis." Kathy told him.

"Hell, no," the others put in.

Travis knew it was foolish, but he felt guilty. He had been willing to sacrifice his dogs in order to survive. They hadn't been willing to sacrifice him. "That's my place," he told the woman rescuer. "You guys get Kelly back safely."

"That's your place too, Mr. Travis. We don't want to be first back and get the credit." Beard told him. The others agreed.

"This isn't about credit," Travis told them. "Now get Kelly back quickly and safely." The team understood.

Before they departed, Travis went up to the little girl in the litter.

"You take it easy now, partner. I'll see you back at the ranch."

"It's not a ranch. It's a ski place," Kelly corrected.

"See you back at the ski place. Don't forget those French songs I taught you. And I expect a Christmas card at Christmas."

Kelly nodded. As she looked up at him, she noticed something.

"Look, Joshua, the Indians were right!"

Joshua looked up and noticed the quarter moon hiding behind the closing clouds. He smiled and nodded. "The Indians were right."

The ski patrol departed, carrying the litter to the edge of the woods. Joshua, Hanson, and Andy Johnson handled the litter with the two dogs.

"You know," Travis told them, "I was surprised that the air held out long enough for us to get the poles through."

No one had noticed that the tunnel Jenny-Dog had burrowed went all the way through.

Chapter Thirty-seven

The snow was falling again, but that's all it was doing, just falling. What wind there was, was behind them. The lightening sky was gray and white in the early dawn. Once in a while the remnants of the moon peeked through. Joshua Travis trudged through the soft, deep snow, harnessed to the rescue litter, sledding the two dogs. It was small atonement for what he had been prepared to do.

Hanson worked the rear guy lines, making sure the sled did not spill. He was tickled pink.

The phone at Kristian's townhouse started ringing at six A.M. The architect let her machine pick up.

"Hello, Kristian, it's Maureen. I just got a call from Bill. Your husband is all right! So is the little girl! I hope I didn't wake you. I thought you would want to know."

At ten, she got a call from Jane.

"Hey, have you seen the news. Christ, it's all over the the radio and TV down here. They're calling it the Miracle of the Snow Dogs. Of course down here they think anything that can stay alive in the snow for more than twenty minutes is a miracle. Anyway, I'm happy for you. So what are you going to do now, hot shot?"

Minutes later, Nathan Goodman called.

"Kris, I just wanted to make sure you heard the good news. Your husband is okay. I just heard it on the news. They say that he's a real hero. Let me know if there is anything you need, or anything I can do. Bye."

Kristian played the messages over and over. She was too drained to cry.

Sheriff Hanson and Jonathan VanStavern arranged the logistics home. Sam Hanson was good enough to take time away from the family he had not seen for three days to come back up to the lodge and drive Travis and his dogs to the Air Force base at Plattsburg.

Hitching a ride back took some doing, especially on a Sunday night. They lucked out and managed to catch a lift on a C-130 that was only making one stop in Rome and then going on in to Madison. Jon VanStavern said he would arrange transport from Madison to Wausau.

This crew was straight as an arrow, and the major in command was a real book man. He didn't think much of having a civilian and two dogs on board, and Joshua was glad that the crew that had flown him in had been different. But he was also glad to be thumbing a ride instead of having to go commercial, which would have taken all night and been a heck of a lot rougher on Jenny-Dog and Buck. As it was, they didn't get into Madison until almost midnight.

Jon was waiting for them at the gate. He hadn't been able to wing anything with the Guard, it not being an emergency anymore, and he hadn't wanted to press it. But he didn't want Joshua to have to fly up commercial either, even if there had been a flight up before 7 A.M., which there wasn't, so he drove down to fetch them himself. Joshua was sorry to put his friend out, but he wasn't surprised.

"We all saw you on TV, Josh. All those news people fawning all over you... Hell, a few hours earlier, they had given you up for dead. They all had to eat plenty of crow. It was great!"

"We were lucky, Jon. It could have gone the other way."

VanStavern looked at him. "Pretty rough, huh?"

"The worst part was the wind bringing down trees and such and not knowing when one was going to hit you. That and worrying about Kelly developing gangrene."

"How's she doing?"

"She's doing great. The doctor at the lodge called the hospital. They said I had been right about her just having cellulitis and not wet gangrene."

"I'll bet her parents were happy."

Joshua did not answer. When he and Hanson and the dogs got back to the chalet, he had tried to go about his business unnoticed. It was not to be. People at the lodge went to clapping and shaking his hand and patting him on the back. Flashbulbs were popping off, mostly from that darn reporter. Joshua nodded and looked to scout out the kitchen so that he could rustle up some real food for himself and his dogs. Before he spotted it, Kelly's parents left their daughter and came over to him.

John Martin took Joshua's right hand in both of his and said, "Thank you, Mr. Travis. Thank you for my daughter and my family and my life." Tears welled up in the father's eyes as he added, "If there is ever anything at all that I can do to repay you..."

Joshua knew that he meant it.

Then Kelly's mom had started to take his hand. She looked up at him and decided differently. Diane Martin threw both arms around the man from Wisconsin and laid her head on his chest. She went to pieces, crying softly, and Joshua thought he had heard her say, "Thank you."

Joshua smiled as he thought about what had happened next. Kelly's mom looked around for the dogs. Joshua told her that he had left them outside on the porch. George Hoffman had let him know that they were welcome inside, but Joshua told him that he preferred it the way it was. Diane Martin went out on the porch and gave each dog a hug and a big kiss on the top of the head. Joshua was surprised that Buck was so tolerant as to let her do that. Jenny-Dog was no surprise at all. She loved every second of it and made that low pitched sort of croon, something between an ecstatic moan and a soft howl that she makes whenever she has done a good job and she knows it. *One helluva good job*, Joshua knew.

"Who took care of the animals?"

"The Nelsons, mostly. Rod Kielor kept the place plowed out and kept an eye on things."

Joshua nodded.

The last hour or so, both men were quiet. Joshua was glad that Jon was driving because he was dead tired, and route 51 was just too dang straight and too darned empty. He would have nodded off.

They drove through Merrill about 2 A.M., and the town seemed lonely at that hour. Less than thirty minutes later they arrived at his home.

"You want to come in for some coffee, Jon, or maybe a shot?"

"No thanks, Josh. I got to be at work in the morning."

"Yeah, me too." But Travis wasn't so sure he'd make it just then.

"Thanks Jon… for everything," Joshua let his friend know.

Jon VanStavern shook Joshua's hand and clasped his shoulder and said, "No Joshua, thank you," in a way that, for the first time in five years, almost made everything worthwhile once again.

The sheriff turned around and drove off as Travis was sending Buck and Jenny out into the yard. Joshua grabbed his duffel and made his way into the house.

Once inside the house, he decided to let everything go until morning and just hit the hay. That was unusual for him, but he didn't have much gear left in his duffel, and, the fact is, he was bushed. He had one shot of Canadian whiskey and was leaning against the door jamb in the den, about to turn in, when damn, if the phone doesn't ring. And you could have knocked him over with a feather as he picked up the receiver and knew somehow, almost before he even heard her voice, that it was Kristian at the other end.

High on the Tusayan Plateau, in the ancient Shongopovi pueblo, the old Hopi called Blue Corn Woman has recovered from her three day ordeal.

"Grandmother! Grandmother! We thought you were going to die," explain her grandchildren, happy they were wrong.

The grandmother smiles at the children and answers, looking out across the mesa.

"It was not time. It is not finished."

CPSIA information can be obtained at www.ICGtesting.com
Printed in the USA
BVOW032143070713

325228BV00001B/4/P